Curses of Scale

S.D. Reeves

RIVERSONG
BOOKS

An Imprint of Sulis International
Los Angeles | London
www.sulisinternational.com

CURSES OF SCALE

Riversong Books
An Imprint of Sulis International
Los Angeles | London

www.sulisinternational.com

Cover art by Kiri Østergaard Leonard, 2017.
Cover and book design by Sulis International.

Library of Congress Control Number: 2017949580
Paperback ISBN: 978-1-946849-12-0
eBook ISBN: 978-1-946849-13-7

Acknowledgements

This is all your fault. All of you are to blame. Oh sure, my parents, who have always supported my creative atrocities, can claim an inability to have a direct intervention on account of me moving to Switzerland. And my loving wife Alessandra will, naturally, downplay her pivotal insight and emotional support as a necessary evil in order to keep me away from her coffee, library, and shiny breakable things (in this order). But there is no excusing my editors John Rickards and Mark McFaddyn, the cover artist Kiri Leonard, or the fine folks at Sulis International for their outstanding work. This is on you. May whatever restless nights, adventures, or silly daydreams this book inspires, be on all of your heads.

Table of Contents

Chapter 1
Pinched

Night spilled o'er all
Inking the canvas of cities, of forests, mountains, in a
shade of gloom
And here in the pale he came again

A sliver of light skirts past root and trunk, occasionally peering skyward through the canopy of leaves that gives the Grey Forest its name. The light shakes and freezes. Two fingers trail along the face of a boulder.

Snow? Calem mouths silently. Autumn clashes with summer, rumbles through the rock and his hand. "Chords," he reluctantly admits. "I'm going to be deep in it."

Over a log. Under a branch. Metal scrapes against glass while the lantern swings and exposes more than just the fire-thinned brush. Calem hesitates at the edge of a small field. The squeaking of the lantern's chain becomes quieter with every lost moment, winding down like a badly-oiled clock.

Were they in the trees on his left? Closer than that, he realises. As the shadows of leaves fly around him, something glints just off to his right.

There's no time. Calem slides into the dirt and swings his lantern in an arc. The dagger glances off the glass, but still shatters the silence.

So, that's the right. Light reveals her; small, no more than ten hands high. One long dagger shifts between hands while she circles in step with the flicker of the lantern. *And the left...*

"Four, six." The woodsman's eyes narrow. "Eight."

The second hunter's shocked expression as the lantern hits him sprays the forest, reflected in shards of glass. The lantern's metal frame, now bloodied from the crash, clatters to the ground, and Calem has only a second to turn and find the first attacker lunging. Her dagger slices into his leather jerkin, but a quick right-hand strike against the small huntress's arm drops her blade into his palm. He exhales.

"Nine," Calem growls into her hood. She tries to scream. Tries. But as her body falls to the ground, a different sort of count rattles him.

"Galen sais." The words of power extinguish the fire from the spilt oil. "Two lives, Oberon. All this for a piece of bark. You'd better keep your end of the bargain."

Calem's face cringes as the trickster's answer rattles the inside of his head. *You think that's bad; you should watch your dance number. Terrible choreography!*

Flaw number one in his plan, Calem now realises, was never considering where the fairy might wait until the ritual was complete. Flaw two was faith in Oberon's sanity. Squatters are generally an annoying lot. Even more so when they are disembodied lunatics who lounge around the inside of your head. Only completing the ritual and bringing the fairy into the world would evict him.

"Calis en graten." The click and clatter of insects fill the air at the utterance of Calem's spell, and his left hand comes alive with twinkling lights. "Your magic didn't work, Fey! Their dog's noses smelled right through the illusion, and now, now I have to slum through town as a murderer."

Pickles, the fairy's voice whinges, making it nearly impossible for Calem to think straight. *Hmm? You want pickles. P-i-c-k-l-e-s.*

Calem rubs the joints of his right hand. Unless he can beat the Lord Duke's agents there, he's in trouble. His wife was right; this is getting costly.

But Oberon's voice tramples all over his thoughts. *Didn't you once say that any price would be too cheap?*

"Niena," Calem whispers. "Yes. Yes, I did." His gaze moves past the smoke, turns from the bodies, and slips out to the wild. The rest of him follows.

The stars are the first to join, and they help lead him through the old forest and to a craggy field that clings to the edge of a cliff. Calem kneels and drinks from a patch of moss that caught the yesterday's rain. A feeling of doubt squeezes his stomach. It had been with him for nearly two weeks now, since he left Niena behind to raid the Lord Duke's castle. If only she could see things as clearly as him; now was the time to be bold. The water is cool and crisp. It helps to ease his fear.

Dull light forces him to squint. Near the moss is a fallen marker, a way-stone. Calem searches his memory. There must have been a road here once. He reaches out to touch the surface of the ancient rock with something akin to reverence and runs his fingers gently over the crumbling runes and arrows chiseled into its face. He can feel the old songs here; they dance to the music of the approaching spring. But it is still winter. The presence of the wind pushing and filling his hair hushes him.

"Going to have to climb down," Calem says nervously at the edge. Below him rise the pointed ends of pines, arrayed like spears over the hills. There is a steep drop whose end is hidden below the forest canopy. His hand feels into a waxed tube, withdraws from it a crinkled piece of parchment. Fireflies from his earlier summon smack and cling to the paper as he holds it aloft, causing obscene shadows to flit between markers of old roads, buildings, and the river drawn on the map. A cautious smile crosses his lips; it won't exactly be the easiest time, but there is a way to the town from here.

Laughter. Oberon is back. *Don't tell me you fear heights?*

Calem snarls. "You wanna help? Shut the chords up!"

How would that be funny? And on another matter, you'd better be nicer to me. Your wife is Wyrmspun, Calem. You need me way more than I need you.

"Like an arr—"

Arrow!

The elf-shot slices across the leather on his shoulder, and Calem drops to the ground instinctively. More arrows fly just overhead, raining down from the forest behind him.

"Damn this all!" he screams and clutches his head. The fireflies from his spell crawl on the grass and wildflowers that lay upon the cliff, shining through the petals of a rare mountain flower.

They really, really don't like you, do they?

His hand trembles as he reaches over the edge. Calem doesn't want to admit it, but he hates heights. Being shot at doesn't make it any better. "Wonder why—can't have anything to do with the being robbed part?"

Harumph! Are you sure there isn't a better way down? But Calem's attention is elsewhere.

Dirt and shale crumble between his fingertips, throwing dust into the air and filling his nose with an earthy scent. He clings to the cliff's edge, relying on cracks in the rock to wedge his feet while his other hand seeks a hold further down. The fireflies hinder more than help, illuminating the rock face but also at times blinding his eyes.

Sweat drips from his forehead and wells up in his moustache and beard. Calem licks his lips, eyeing a deep fissure below. It's at an angle. *If I can just...* His feet find purchase in the crumbling shale. *There, just a little more.*

The cold stone presses so firmly against his face that he can hear his own terrified heart echo. With his soft soles meshed against the sheer mountainside, Calem takes one quick breath and starts to drop down the crevice in steady bursts.

Those hunters aren't following, so you know. Oberon's words slowly filling his head.

"Thank the chor—"

They're going around. For a former druid, you aren't very observant, aren't you? How old did you think that way-stone was? Older than the mountain? They are taking the path down that you missed.

"Shit." He wanted a stronger curse. "Why didn't you mention that?"

You're the one with the map!

Calem groans and presses his head against a weed. "This cliff runs a long way along the east rift. That will take them time; I just need to find my way around this. Oberon, give me something I can use!"

You know what helps me think? Pickles. Did you know that pickles have been around a long time? Not just cucumbers; people have made pickles out of all sorts of things since near the beginning. Of course, I am being facetious; I doubt the gods created pickles before they created the folk. Or did they? Hurumph. I bet they did, that would explain how amazing they are!

Bits of roots dug up in frustration fall into the darkness. Pleading with the fey would serve no purpose. *Focus.* Calem's thoughts press inward. Slowly the buzz of the old fairy's voice disappears until it is little more than a ringing. His smile returns with the respite.

Clouds flail above as a firefly slips into the cliff face, its light fading into the earth. Before long the stars will fall before the cover of an approaching storm. Calem knew this was coming, as he felt the air shift earlier; the warm southern thundercloud had hit the wall of cold nestled in this vale. It will make for a rough night, one which he cannot afford to pass pinched above the forest veil. Luckily he has already cleared more than a hundred feet of the cliff.

Calem's boots slip. Icy rain that has seemed so distant before now begins to find its way down to him. The cold stings. Needles. His grip weakens.

"Be careful," the memory of Niena's last words to him repeat in his head.

"I've done dumber things," Calem muses, straining to keep his back up. The stone is now very slick and the stars recede fast. A shake of his head admits the plain truth. "No, no I haven't."

The wind sweeps by. Cloud speaks to cloud through cracks of lightning. It is during one of these brief flashes that he sees his goal: a lone cleft, jutting out from the mountain below. Thirty, maybe forty feet straight down there is a landing.

Calem bends for a hold, and immediately he knows something is wrong. Shale breaks underneath his foot, throwing his left leg away from the cliff face. The force shakes him from his perch and sends him tumbling down and away. Terrible cold air whips around him in the black.

It is his back, already cut and torn by the crevice edge, that meets the cleft first. The shock of hitting the landing steals the air from his lungs. He paws at the slick slate crevice, his fingers peel against the grooves as he pulls himself up and onto the ledge.

"Niena." His hand reaches up towards nothing. "It will snow…"

Chapter 2
Everything Changes

"Those are either torches or big fireflies down there. Duke's men, my guess," Calem mumbles. Somewhere in the back of his mind, Oberon's voice buzzes angrily. He ignores it and lights his pipe. "Only place they probably aren't looking for me is the castle."

Snowflakes twirl around his head like ballerinas on a forgotten stage. Gracefully they flirt before his eyes and the cliff face above. *Kill me*, he thinks as his eyes climb. *I am not going back up that.*

He shivers. A blue curl of smoke lifts from his pipe, and he leans back. The drawstring of his undershirt went into the crude stitches patching his side, leaving the tails of it to flutter in the night's breeze. But it's more than just the cold that has him shaking. His wife's name trails off his lips. And whether it is the chill, his hunger, or trauma from the fall, a recollection of their last conversation summons something visceral, almost a vision.

"Do you know where you are?" His wife's voice steps out of the memory and into the waking world. "This bridge leads over the river Lilven, and beyond into the shadow of the Grey Forest."

"Then I have another week at least."

"At least," she says. "Calem, can we—"

He swats away the argument he knew was coming. "How can I—"

Niena raises her hand just as he was about to interrupt her. "No! You're going to listen this time!"

"Niena."

"This plan of yours is reckless! It's — I can count at least five ways it can fail, even before we finish the fairy's ritual." A look of frustration builds on her face, but he stares right through it. "What are we doing, Calem? Where are we? "

He can feel his lips pull back as if something nasty wants to pass, but he thinks better of it. "Between the Weld and the Grey Forest."

"That's not what—never mind," Niena sighs. "You just don't get it. If everything doesn't go perfectly now, without my family, without the chant of the Drel'nu, our world will change. I will become the wyrm, and the wyrm will become your everything."

"That fey is bound to the deal. He will end the curse, but I must go to Ebonmuire, that damn duke has the last ingredient!"

"A fairy bargain can live no deeper than your lips, it always dies before reaching the heart," she says sadly.

"Poetry now?"

Niena sighs. "Yes, and a tragic verse…I will lose it all playing Oberon's game. And when I lose this, this." Her hands outstretched towards him. "Everything will change, but I will still have you.

"But now you are going to gamble with that aren't you?" She continues over his protest. "You could die! And if you die running after this dream of yours, I will have nothing left. Not even my family to welcome me home."

His arms unfold while her tears fall.

"Not anymore."

The embers from his pipe fall through the smoke like meteors through the night sky. "Galen Sais," he whispers, and the smoke dies on the wind.

Stars peek. Clouds move. Calem will have to do so as well, only down into the forest below. And while the sky doesn't hint at how far he may have descended, the scent of pine needles meets him as he leans over the edge. What once was a bed of nails now marches across his vision like spearmen. The view is both breathtaking, and unnerving, but there is little time to enjoy the moment. Calem steadies his hand against the rock wall.

Fingernails scape on shale. *I am a druid,* he reassures himself as he gingerly tests his hold. *A druid of the second order.* The healing spells working through his body still need more time, and the pain tears at his side. The plummeting temperature also graces stretches of stone with sheets of ice. Cold bites deep into his unprotected hands. And there is worse. Pieces of the ice break off with every move, threatening to send him tumbling again. Calem's eyes betray him, and briefly, the thinks of climbing back up and waiting on the ledge until morning strikes. And then he remembers his pride.

Am I going to be just another fool in a fairy-tale? Calem asks himself, feeling around for the satchel. The bag pulls free. Beneath worn leather bands, and wrapped double in silver silk, is a piece of rose bark. With this, and the rest of the contents of his satchel, back at the Inn, he will be able to summon the fairy halfway into this world. And out of his head. Calem takes the strap and throws it around his neck. A tense glance down shows him a debris field of shale swept against the thin forest, no more than a hundred feet below. Wind whips around him. His fingers are bleeding, torn. But this time he holds on and continues down. The smell of frost-bitten leaves and grass welcome him at each handhold.

Every inch is gained against the protest of the wind. Sixty feet. Fifty. He counts the passing minutes by the panicked beat of his own heart. At thirty feet Calem descends into a huge indentation gouged from the rock that probably fathered the scree below. Here the wind cannot reach him. What waits instead is exactly what he feared: silence.

Here's to grand entrances and exits, he thinks, mimicking Oberon's dour commentary. He knows if the Lord Duke's men are in the forest, they are likely hunting anything that moves. For the spectacle he is about to make, he might as well jump up and scream "kill me."

Only twenty feet remain. At the point where the cliff breaks and slopes into the rocky field, Calem turns, and leaps. Debris crumbles and slides under him as he hits the ground, rolling past scraggy trees and the wiry grass that lives on the edge.

"Dul Mac T're," he says with his hand resting on shale from an older avalanche. The words of power wrap around him in the still of the forest and ring his body in a glow that shines against the black and grey.

One step. The shale tears at his hands and feet. Somewhere a bird trills a greeting and Calem pauses, his ears twitching in the wind. The faint smell of fresh water, of grasses touched by frost overwhelms him. But there are other things making his new tail quiver.

Another step. Calem shakes off his tunic. He does not need the clothing; coarse fur thickens on his body with each breath. Two more steps, slinking around the rough bark of an old trunk. Calem stretches his paws on the snow. The slender frames of pine trees roll downward along the sloping hill. With any luck, he can reach the water before being noticed. The smell of the Lord Duke's hunters surrounds him.

He takes off. Winter flurries around him while he runs into the heart of the forest where the snow barely reaches. On the edge of the scree the wind shifts and sprints past him, bringing a faint croaking to his ears. Calem, in the guise of a wolf, continues, pausing here and there whenever the wind turns. Soon the noises grow clearer, the deep throated cacophony of the frogs leading him to the river.

Twigs snap. Calem's tail bristles in response, and in a moment of panic he leaps forward, banking off the high edge of a root to gain level ground. In the air above him a sharp whistle cuts the falling snow. Calem jumps back and forward in confusion, then over and under a large log.

The toads quiet. He is close, but so are his pursuers. Calem's ears go flat as he crouches down, unsure of what to do next. He waits. Nothing. Pushing back the instinct to stick his head out and growl, he sniffs again. The air underneath the log is fouled by mushrooms and peat. Calem licks his teeth and bites down on the strap of his satchel.

Bursting from underneath the log like a murder of crows, he speeds around and under the boughs and trunks of trees and runs towards the sound of the river. His eyes widen as another shot bounces off a rock ahead of him and he turns against it. It is a mistake. The bag goes tumbling from his mouth and into the brush, leaving him sprawled in front of a small cave. The moments afterward beat like the tattoo of a soldier's drum. Calem lunges at the dangling strap. He misses. Behind him in the forest, limbs crack and bend. He whinges .

So much of his future depends on him completing the ritual. Because if he doesn't? Thorns bite. Underneath all that bravado, doubt builds. And Niena's words feed that. *Murder. Theft.* Calem shakes his head and pushes back the memory of her tears to lunge at the bag again. This time a sharp crack of the branches heralds the satchel ripping free. He pulls himself up and shakes. The river is no more than a hundred yards away—he can hear it even over the approach of the guards.

More twigs and branches snap in the forest behind. *I'm going to have to fight.* Calem pauses. *The cave!* He can turn this ambush around. As the footsteps of his hunters close in, he drags the satchel through a dusting of snow and into the mouth of the cavern.

But not as a wolf. A lifetime's experience of living in the wilderness parades a list of creatures through his mind. Calem settles on the largest he can recall in any detail: the brown bear, though this beast may be too big for the cave. Either way, it is too late to change his mind. The spell acclimates to his mindset. Calem was the wolf. He is becoming the bear, and a world of sound and smell reshapes around him. Breeze from the entrance spirals into the slowly shrinking chamber, bringing voices. Two hunters. Both men. One of them hesitates at the threshold of the cavern. A torch makes him look pale against the grey rock.

Another breeze. Mountain heather, spiced with fear. Calem shakes, brushing against the stone roof in the process. He finds their smell intoxicating. Infuriating. *Yellow.* That's the name he's given to the man at the cavern opening. Yellow and Red.

Swords ring when drawn, nearly drowning out their whispers. Red places his hand upon the ground and stares into the darkness. "S'blood here," Calem hears him say.

Charge them.

Calem snarls. The *thump* of the hunters' footsteps stops abruptly.

Charge them now! Don't hesitate!

Oberon, Calem bites back in response. The presence of the fairy sits just behind his temple, as if coaxing up a migraine. The transformations must have weakened him, letting Oberon come back.

Why are you letting them drag that in here, that fear? Drive it out!

Don't need your help, he answers. *Go back to whatever hole you crawled out of.*

You mean where you push all your worries...

Oberon's whine fades. Fades. Then erupts, crashing through Calem's defences and efforts to push him back down.

And doubts, Oberon continues. *Your own fears.*

I fear nothing!

You fear everything.

Nervous jingling from a sword belt steals Calem's attention. His head is swimming; the efforts to both control the transformation and fight the fey are too much.

"If it's blood, we must've got him." That is Yellow.

Pluck too many strings, druid? Oberon's taunting melts into the smells and sights, until the cavern is awash in a tide of random feelings. *Breaking from the melody is always a dangerous thing to do.*

"Maybe," Red says cautiously.

The fairy's words string together into one long hiss inside Calem's head. *Magic is not something for the weak-minded. Or the careless.*

Calem paces with anger and...desire. Emotions, some new, some old, fog his mind.

But you were never one to listen. Not to your mentor, before you summoned me.

Rage drips from Calem's fangs. A growl rumbles in his head.

Nor your wife after.

All manner of senses writhe within Calem as the discordant magic wracks him, until he is blind to everything but the desire to-

Drive it out, Oberon and Calem say in unison.

Gnarly muscles groan, and he stumbles forward. The guards' swords strike through the black, flashing steel, and then red in the darkness. But the cavern is too small, and Calem's anger drives them back to the mouth. There the fight pivots. Red, armed with his sword and torch. Yellow by sword and shield.

Beads of sweat appear on the latter's brow, reflected in the meagre light. Yellow retreats further from the cave. And Calem follows. Drool drips from a grizzled fang, slavering over his black lips as his head lolls from side to side. Red takes advantage and lunges, but Calem swats the torch into Yellow's shield, sending sparks to glance off the metal rim and fly up into Red's face. Calem charges. Five hundred pounds crash into Yellow, the impact hurling him into a pocket of mud. And as he falls, Calem the bear rises to his full height.

Yellow rattles out a broken cry while holding the shattered remnants of his shield against another blow. When it comes, splinters spray and the smell of blood fills Calem's mind. Again. His roar steals away the sound of bone breaking. Again. Metal from the shield's rim twists, biting down into Yellow's arm. Again. The man no longer moves. Calem pries his claws from the indentation in the hunter's chest.

And if you die running after this dream of yours, a woman's voice echoes, unrecognised, and ignored in his head, *I will have nothing left.*

A helmet clatters against the rocks. Calem's head swings. The empty sockets of the iron cap stare back up at him, but another heavy thud sets him into motion. Out of pure instinct, Calem rushes towards the river, chasing his new prey; Red is gone, but the sound of his armour and weapons being discarded trails him.

It's enough. Brush breaks as the man flees towards the water. He's losing ground with every passing moment, with every breath. Until Calem is so close that he can smell the stale mix of urine and sweat, and when, barely twenty feet from the water's edge, thorns seize Yellow's gambeson. The sudden jerk pulls the hunter right into Calem's face, and with one large paw he immediately swats the man down.

And if you die running after this dream of yours, I will have nothing left.

Rage. Calem's girth crashes down onto the hunter.

Die running after this dream of yours, I will have nothing left.

Red for blood. In his eyes, in his maw. Calem's grizzled head rocks side to side as roars at the prone man.

This dream of yours, I will have nothing left.

Black for murder. In his fangs, upon his breath.

This dream…I will have nothing left.

Grey. As the adrenaline fades.

Nothing left.

Niena? Faded greens stretch just beyond the briar patches, branching with flashes of brown and yellow. Even purple, sticking out from the snow. The guard's gorget slides out, off of a long, curved tooth. But the taste of blood remains. Everything else, the anger, the rage, slips from his mind to fade into the cold earth. Calem's thoughts, once scattered, slowly come together as his conscious bottles them like fireflies in the dark.

Niena. Pain answers, from his wounds, his joints; whereas the night has firmly wrapped the evening in black, so has his body been saturated with a growing ache. Calem trudges forward while frogs, birds, and the river replace his wife's voice. Fifty feet. Forty. A thin line of water crosses his blurred vision, emerging from the thicket. Thirty. Calem begins to shake. Twenty.

Before the shoreline is swept into blue, the forest first tumbles into patches of straw-coloured reeds and grass. Ahead of this, white water leaps over the rocks and boulders that poke out from the shallows. Each step is agony, and the strength Calem needs to hold onto his transformation wanes.

And if you die running after this dream of yours, I will have nothing left.

He stumbles. Four fingers slide into a deep groove, swallowed by the bear prints that he has left behind. Calem's growl twists into a low, quivering moan, and he collapses into the musky peat near the water's edge.

"I am," he gasps, dragging himself into the water. Mud mingles with blood, both his and another's. Then cool water. And more. Brown muck swirls, lapping the edge, and the rocks that form a small basin on the shore. Calem stares into the pool, and two green eyes look back up at him—sparkling, like emeralds cast from a thief's purse. He runs his fingers over the bump on the bridge of his nose, his bushy eyebrows, and into a tangled black beard. He peers hard at the man in that reflection, with his pointed features and rough face—as if he needs to reacquaint himself.

"Dream," he says to his reflection. "Nothing left."

Calem clutches at the wounds left by the guard's sword. At his leg. His whispers break into a hoarse cough. The healing spell dies on his lips.

"Oberon?" As he binds his wounds with mud and reed. "Where are you?"

No answer. Calem slides on the smooth rock of the riverbed. Then staggers weakly into the current beyond the basin. There he rests against a small boulder on the edge, and follows the course of the river with his eyes.

The silhouette of piers and ships mark the horizons, deep, deep into the widening girth of the water's path. Spice, or Spice's Landing — the main port of the shire of Ebonmuire and the castle that bears the same name. Yet the locals still call the town Mirepoint, after an older name. Calem sighs. The night for him is not quite over, but in this one image he finds a little bit of strength. The flow of water pushes against his back, urging him onward.

Chapter 3
Inn and Out

The alleyway see-saws between light and shadow as the lanterns of an approaching carriage sway. Calem leans against a gate. Meltwater flows around the iron bolts and the smell of rust trickles.

There goes a dealer with his strays, like always…

He sighs weakly; there's little Calem can do to mute the fairy.

The same old mix of drugs to sell!

Two horses stumble along, pulling a coach better suited for the country road. He shrinks into the door and the glow from the carriage lazily passes over. There's a fresh sheen of red on Calem's hand from where he's been holding a thigh.

Every morning it's a game, full of violence and shame-

"Gram, you take two to the Third and Second cross-road, and meet up with the men there."

Night Watch, and they're close, very close. The cold iron of the door is like lightning against his bare back. How many are out tonight?

"Haran," the gruff voice commands again. "Take Poiroy down this old temple row. I don't want to hear any…"

A sigh of relief escapes from Calem's lips. His wounds are not healing. The raid on the Duke's castle was botched. And the fairy is singing. Despite all of this Calem feels relieved. *Not us.*

His eyes open. The *clack* of the carriage disappears, falling into the steady march of the patrol and the noise filling the background of the city. Calem sucks in a quick breath and steps away from the alcove. There is little to see; morning may be teasing, but it's the cold wind that finds its way here. Garbage rustles. Filth is pushed up and into a freezing mist. The stench, the needles of frost, and a decaying town of wood and stone meet him.

Calem stretches around a cobbler's sign—just enough to see the guardsmen disappear. *The inn.* Are they even looking for him? *Us.* He needs to get to the inn; there they might be safe.

Us? Oberon asks. You mean like we? As in a royal we? Or a wee-wee? Or as the French say, oui oui! Either way, it's rude to do that in public.

Above, open windows and crooked roofs leer. On the ground below are fouler things than trash. Calem steps carefully, avoiding the pottery shards and excrement.

Remember, hang a left.

"I know where I'm going," Calem says.

The main road into Mirepoint curves around the bastion walls that face away from the cliff, and the castle at its apex. It dips in the west and follows the edge of the river as it spills into the sea.

"Nearth na i'mpróidh," Calem whispers.

How is this spell going to help you?

Once past the main gate, like many other roads, it splits into several different streets. These wind and roll around the various districts. Some follow a forgotten route, encircling the remains of a long-buried fort. Others slide alongside the river and into the centre with seemingly little rhyme or reason.

"Nearth na i'mpróidh," he says again. "Spirad." The magic seeps into his muscles, filling him with a queer energy.

You need healing, and you are using your last bit of strength for this?

But one divides the town into two halves like a massive scar. This is Wayroot Crossing, and it follows the foundation of the eastern wall of the old city. This street is always busy, and Calem hears the bustle long before he sees it. A thin fog hangs in the air.

"I just need to make it to the inn." Pressing his throbbing head against cool stone, a cough slips out of him like a stream from a busted pipe. "But I'm not fancy, and neither are you. So long as everything is still in my room, we only need a fireplace to complete the ritual; you'll still be bound to the bargain, even if I die after."

Fingers of wind sweep past, coaxing his chin up to the sky, where clouds wane before tired eyes. Occasionally pockets of light pop up between the swirling storm, revealing a secret: dawn has already arrived. Calem braces for some snide remark to this, or his earlier comment. Instead, he is left in silence between the jumble of buildings.

Ahead, his road crosses the Wayroot. Calem crawls along the edge of a building bordering both streets. He moves to peek around the corner, but then stops abruptly. The thump of cargo being unloaded rumbles the stonework while he presses against the building's side.

Could he have taken a wrong turn? His eyes skip past the men milling about, the shadows of legs and arms bobbing in the mist. Then along the rooftops, where fog clings heavily to the red tiles, and in some places is so thick and full that the clouds take on the form of pale hands and bloodied nails in his exhausted mind. *This spell won't last much longer, and...*

There! The chimney of the Lucky Elf Inn rises out of the miserable marriage of grey. The stones of the rim, pinched like a classic seaman's pipe, are black — remnants of an old smuggler's mark - and its breath a cheery white. The curls of smoke bend over a conspicuous set of copper tiles, around the heads of other buildings and under rain gutters before blending with the mist.

"One," Calem says. The temporary strength from the spell is passing quicker than the warmth from his feet, and the rhythmic plod of hobnails nearby signals a possible oncoming patrol. *Two,* this time in silence. *Or might be a carriage?* The odour of fish sinks into the dirt and grime. Calem bites his lips. *Three.*

Cries from the left. Men laughing at his nakedness. Jeering as he sprints into the street. Shouts from the right. Calem's feet plunge into cold water pooled around the road's middle, sending chills through his wounded leg. Rats scurry as he spins around a lamp pole.

"Stop!"

Calem's shoulder crashes into a pipe as he careens into the entrance to the alley. Shouts continue, bouncing along the stonework behind him. He reels, further in. Shapes, sounds, and lights spin in the grey, and then a large cloud passes in front of the sun, severing the little light as scissors to a ribbon. In that moment, only a hundred feet beyond Wayroot, he hesitates. There are two paths that could take him to the inn.

"Chords," he curses, feeling that noose. A shrill whistle climbs up the hairs of Calem's neck, and he twists just in time to feel the nails of a guard's fingers slide against his shoulder, and then see the man skid and tumble onto the cobble. Calem spirits past the first entrance for the second a little ways ahead. One door. Two doors. Another narrow way and a long bend of street fall into recent history before he realises the mistake.

Clop. He stops, a frown cracking his pale face. That was a shoe; a hobnail on the right foot, he guesses. *Clack-Click-Clack.* Almost all at once. He hasn't lost them, and the twists and turns beg them to investigate. This gives him time. Calem swallows and continues slowly, trying to regain his sense of direction. The road this narrow way spills into curves around the foundations of a ruined watchtower, which he can see rising to his right. Tepidly he follows, even as he counts the echo of steps behind him. Until he is halted by a box of outbuildings and warehouses. Calem swallows. He's freezing, wounded, and confused. And he made a wrong turn.

You are wise to be afraid of the dark.

Calem can feel the old songs; the five chords still play nearby. But his mouth is dry, and he can't seem to touch the magic. No more spells today.

The end. Oberon answers the dread swelling inside of the young man. *Tell me, do you know what happens to oath-breakers?*

This isn't over. Calem's bark ricochets in his head. The inn is on the far side of a day worker's house. He runs his tongue along the edge of his front teeth. A trio of voices call at his back. One man trumpets over the other two like a lone horn between hunting dogs, "Steady now boys."

As he limps towards the house, Calem can't shake the feeling of being trailed. He looks up and quickly scans the timberwork. A second storey of wood sits upon an older bottom of river stone. Yet its roof, like most of the ones in the old town, is slanted, with hooks to stop snow from falling into the streets. He might be able to use those as holds.

"No way out here, just keep your eyes peeled, don't let him slip." They're on his heels.

Desperate, Calem climbs the house hand over hand, and the beams around the window groan with his weight. Snapping, popping. Breaking. Splintering wood bites his knees. Still, it holds, and he manages to pull himself up and onto the ledge. Whatever glass or tin had once been there was long ago stolen, letting Calem reach for the roof.

Metal pings on stone, over the whispered curse from his lips, as one of the two hooks he dangles from breaks under the strain. Calem immediately grabs at a third and pulls, even as the first rings to a prolonged halt on the cobble. The patter of boots answers, but around him the town rises in pockmarked darkness; the sun has begun to cut into the clouds' skin, leaving some areas lighter than others. And like clockwork, the patches grow more numerous while he crawls over the roof.

"The Lucky Elf," he mumbles. Tile upon rough tile marks his rump as he slides into a gutter on the opposite side. Calem follows a retreating shadow with his eyes, circling past brickwork that sinks deep into the street. Seemingly half-buried in the cobblestone is an open door. As the distinct smell of horses disappears around the corner, he drops, crashing more than landing.

Broken jugs and other debris force him to take extra care. Between the stairs leading down into the cellar and the street, the air turns again. Calem listens. Distant laughter dances through the clanking of carts and the yowl of an alley cat, but nothing distinguishable emerges from the basement. Only the smell from the tavern is strong enough to greet him at the door. Shadows stretch around barrels in the deep pockets of the cellar, and the fumes from the casks fight with the odour from the alleyway.

At least I won't have to climb the walls. His thoughts wandering. Flickering torchlight frames the doorway as he nears. He stops and then listens more intently. Someone is coming.

"Same damn shit every day." A young boy's voice emerges through the roars of the tavern above. "Too good to take a piss."

Sliding inside and behind the basement's staircase Calem cups a dirty rag firmly against his face and waits. The cellar is freezing, and the cold walls raise goosebumps on his unprotected arms. But it is the smell — the strange brew of alcohol and sludge — that keeps him preoccupied even as the thick stomp of someone carrying something heavy stumbles down the stairs above him.

He jerks backward as foul fluid splatters on the open steps. Moments later a boy carrying a pan hobbles down the stairs and then disappears through the open door Calem came through. The distinct *slop* of the contents of the chamber pot turns his stomach.

Just think, you walked through that.

He opens his mouth to shoot back a retort, but the boy's return forces Calem back into the shadows. The empty pot rattles the railing and clangs against the brick wall, punctuating a trail of curses.

Calem lets out the breath he had been holding. "Don't you laugh, Oberon." Gasping, heaving. His face is white as he leans over the stair's railing. "You say anything about this to Niena and I'll gild your pants with iron."

Promises, promises.

The nausea falls off quickly while climbing the stairs. But Calem seeks a different sort of relief, one he finds just before reaching the tavern common room.

I still think it was a bad idea leaving everything in your room like that.

"Nobody cares about this pit," as strings of bawdy tavern songs grow in clamour. It is morning in the Mirepoint, and this place is packed. Calem tenses when the warm light from the inn crawls around him.

"The Lucky Elf," he says at the entrance to the common room. "Where sweat loosed from the backs of patrons mingles with sawdust. Where bits of food and blood stir. Where the morning sun simmers. Where an open door dashes the spice of the street. Here, one can find themselves in a stew."

Taking up poetry now?

"Niena is a bad influence." He smirks, taking one last glance at the tavern patrons before mounting the second stairwell.

I think it's the other way around. Your reasons, your desires…

"If she were here, we'd already have a backstory for all this." Calem scrapes his toes on the steps, removing bits of sawdust mixed with the filth of the alleyway. "That fireplace, not sure you remember it. She'd say something about how the stones might've been pulled from the river by the town's founder, and belong to the blackened remains of an old temple. And the wood from the bar? War trophy, made of enemies' shields. Pine, like the thick forest of the Forweld. She's good at pulling little stories together.

"But for the stories…" His words trail. A row of four ruddy wood doors stretch down the hall. Calem's fingers twine around the iron key and he walks up to the third on the right. "Time to turn this one into a fairytale, Oberon. What I am about to do will make you very happy."

Yes! A thousand times yes, but aren't you already married?

A shake of his head emphasises Calem's frustration. "You know what I am talking about: the ritual. I am going to complete my end of our bargain." The stairwell is now very cold.

The key rattles the lock. Then clicks. Calem weakly pushes the door open, and is soon swallowed by the stillness of the room. He slides his hand over the corner of a dresser, his lips mouthing, "chords protect me." In the centre of the room is a single straw bed with a thick lump in the middle, covered by sheets. Calem moves toward this and with a flick of his wrist throws back the covers to reveal a stashed backpack. A relieved sigh eases from his lips. Remembering his earlier run-in with the guards, he rummages through the pack with more urgency, tossing clothing to the floor before gently setting aside the other ingredients for the ritual. Powdered silver elk horn, winter moss, a lock of elf hair, then finally the rose bark.

"And now the fire," while rubbing dust from his fingers. He sends the door behind him creaking closed with a push from his foot, leaving the last bit of torchlight alone in the hall. He fumbles around in the darkness and hesitates between the fireplace and the window, then turns and locks the door.

Every phrase. The fairy says, reverently labouring over the phrasing. *Every sentence uttered. Every word.* Oberon's tone drops, just as the first coal in the fireplace is lit. *Has meaning. A place in the greater story.*

The flame bites into the wood, and Calem closes his eyes.

Yours, the fairy continues.

Downstairs a song passes from person to person like the plague.

Mine.

One by one Calem lays the components neatly before him. He pours the vial of elk horn diagonally over the moss, pressing the contents firmly into the peat, before tossing them into the fire.

And more.

Calem breathes in deeply as he kneels.

"I hear the tales my grandfather's father told me. In the time of the great hunt." Taking care to pronounce each word precisely. Despite Oberon's warning, he knows the power of stories and the importance of telling them properly. "When the two brothers chased not each other."

Pieces of the tavern song stumble against a breath of fairy wind. The song fights hard, but as time wears on it slowly loses rhythm. Ghosts of trees slip in while the room dozes. But it is more—the two realities fight for the same space. He can feel his legs wet with rain. Calem tosses in the elf lock. With a pop and a crackle the hair is committed to the fire.

He rises, eyes cloudy with some deep, unnamed emotion. "I see the grace of the great stag. Cloven in the silver of nameless stars and shifting in the wind like mist on the mountain."

The vapour dances around several phantasmal stones that awake in the music. A faint melody of crickets begins to tease. Calem forces himself to relax. The furniture of the room drifts in and out of the dreamscape.

"I smell the blood and the grime of a hunt ending." Stealing brief glances in the ghostly light. From all directions, there erupts a high-pitched discord that reminds him of children babbling. Leaves dip and shake. The memory of the forest slips further and further into his reality.

In the back of his mind, he hears a faint knocking. Calem blinks, almost losing focus. No, it is not in his head.

Someone is there, in the hall, though the echo is too faint to be his own door. He reaches over his left leg and picks up the rose bark. There, as the last of the moss curls into smoke, he scrawls one name into the red wood with his own fingernail: Oberon.

"I remember the taste of flesh shared."

Smoke from his offering begins to curl, carrying a faint scent of the old wood. The knocking returns, closer this time, and louder. It's clear from the violence of the pounding that it is some matter of urgency. He takes a short breath and continues.

"Long has it been since we have sought prey together. The sorrow of the two brothers, no longer united in the sky, has split their faithful hounds."

All the chattering stops. But he is not alone. He feels their eyes around him, even as the forest grows still. "My bow is unstrung, but I yearn to hunt again," he whispers.

The smoke grows fuller, thicker. It weaves its way into his dream mind and lays a spell upon his heart. Calem struggles to keep his eyes open, waiting. Finally, whatever it is fogging his mind subsides. But it leaves something; he hears a voice. Distant, ethereal. As if lost on the wind it drifts away, until he can no longer perceive anything but the fire in his room.

Calem shivers. Again the knocking comes, this time accompanied by the crash of breaking wood. The bed, the chairs, and the rest of the room slowly settle back into focus. There is no forest, no stones. Calem rises, eyes on the door.

"It's done," his lips miming the fears that scream inside his head: *and so am I.* Calem hastily throws on spare trousers as the murmurs of men out in the hallway pool around the door adjacent to his own. His eyes dart from the bed where his shirt lays, and around the room. *The window? No*, he thinks to himself. If there were any archers, he'd be terribly exposed.

The bed's shadow grows and reaches towards the fire.

But wood creaks, and then the wall between his room and the next shudders under the impact of something heavy. The murmurs roll into cries. Calem pulls the shirt over his head, while simultaneously fumbling around in his pack. And as the voices clear from unintelligible clamour into authoritative commands, he nervously readies his hunting knife. Silence.

"Oberon!" He tries to sound confident in his whimper. "Where are you?" A scream from the other room steals the wind from his lungs.

Thin lines of darkness stroke the edge of the cabinet nearest the window. But Calem barely notices; his world centres upon that door. The boots migrate, they mill about the hall. He sucks in a strained breath.

Thump.

"That's not the door," he whispers to himself.

Thump.

His attention briefly skips to the cabinet. The flickering light from the fireplace dies at the edge. The cabinet is covered in an inky black.

Thump. Calem retreats against the bed as the sickly noise repeats. *Thump.* The sound is becoming distant. *Thump.* As if something heavy is being dragged down the stairs. *Thump.* He forces air evenly into his lungs, steeling himself. *Thump.*

A lumpy caricature folds around the corner nearest the bed. Calem squints, swearing silently to himself that he can see a figure laughing, as if he is watching a shadow puppet play. The fire dims.

"I'll come out," Calem says before the knock. "Just let me get dressed."

"Fat chance!" Even through the thick oak door, he can hear the derisive snort. "Come out! If I have to break the door in, we are bringing a lot of pain with us!"

Coals and faggots one by one fall into darkness. Except two. Two remain fixed in a canvas of vapour.

"Oberon," with a raspy breath. "Ever punctual."

Calem slides further from the fire. The banner of smoke writhes between him and the bed until the glowing embers can no longer cling to the fabric. There, two fireflies emerge from the cover of smoke, buzzing around the flame in a strange dance. Back and forth, to and fro, blinking and pulsing.

"The deal, Oberon!" he cries. "Remember our bargain!"

Blackness seeps into all corners of the room. Only the light from the fireflies remains. No longer dancing, they now burn in place just above the bed. There, they rhythmically grow in intensity until they look like piercing red eyes in the darkness.

Cracking, snapping; a sudden crash against his own door lures Calem back. And that moment is when the shutters at the window are thrown open. Sunlight pours into the void, blinding him, and then revealing the truth. Sitting comfortably on his bed is a peculiar figure: a stooped old man bound in simple clothing. Only his embroidered red shirt stands out from the tartan bed cover.

"Hey, good looking," the old man chimes, leaning heavily on his skinny hands.

It takes a moment for him to pair the hook-nosed fey with the voice that has been tormenting him for the past month. Calem sputters, trying to pull everything together; his quest, his struggle, it all has become personified in one instant in the face of a wizened and gnarly old creature. Even the buckling of his chamber door can't wipe the look of stupor from his face.

"What the chords are you jabbing about?" Calem finally manages to say.

"You're right, you're right," Oberon cackles. "Should save that for the honeymoon! Now what's cooking?"

"Cooking? I am not cooking anything. We are about to be cooked, though!"

The pounding stops.

A vision of confused incredulity creeps across the old man's face. "You're going to make a terrible wife! We aren't even married yet, and you're already starving me!"

"I am not marrying you," he snaps.

Oberon circles him, tapping here and there. "If you aren't my missus, then you must be dinner. Hmm, a bit big. But what type of silly sot offers herself?" His eyes narrow with a look of fear. "Unless you are a poisoner! That's it, that's the ruse! You were hoping I would eat you and get sick!"

Facing the fey. "We must get out of this city. We—"

It isn't a noise that interrupts Calem, but the realisation that the air around the old fairy seems to swallow all other sounds. He looks to Oberon, then the door, which bends inward, split in the middle. Nothing stirs beyond. Calem's gaze jerks back to the fireplace. The last sparks have not died, they are frozen!

"Then start walking! What do I look like, a taxi service?" Oberon pauses, and nods before continuing. "But what would be a good way to make a little…No, no, that's daft, boy. Do you see anybody else out here? What am I supposed to do, carry squirrels around on my back? That's plain nuts, boy, plain nuts…

"Squirrels and nuts!" The fairy pulls at his hair, nearly knocking the glasses off of his long nose. "Now look at what you made me go and say!"

Calem steps back, alternating between staring at the frozen men visible through the crack in his door, and the fairy. This isn't madness. This is a distraction, he notes, as the fey blathers on about the prices of nuts, and giving change for roots.

Not just a distraction. Somewhere between the topic of tax rates on fig leaves and licensing for rucksacks, it dawns on Calem. This is his game. *Remember where you are, remember what you've done to get to this point. Focus!* he tells himself.

The two fireflies from earlier return in Oberon's eyes. Fear creeps up Calem's spine. The fairy's voice is cold and sharp. "Where are we now? We watch your kind in the darkness, dangling on the spider's thread. What makes you think this old spinner has dined enough yet?"

The last shade of power from his earlier spell is slipping, but still, Calem replies with steel in his tone. "You cannot harm me. You are still mist underneath nameless stars."

"Ah, but dreams can still kill; ideas can kill."

"And oaths are more than just words," Calem says in a quick whisper. "The ritual may be complete, but you will not be free to walk this world again until you end Niena's curse. That was the agreement, or have you not forgotten our pact at Del Am Rin?"

Oberon's eyes simmer. "I have not forgotten. But as you have mentioned before, your survival was never a part of that."

"Listen." Calem licks his lips. The wound. The exhaustion. They all vie for his attention. Mortality presents itself in hues of red, and growing black. "Am I not more useful alive?"

"So there it is," the old fey cackles mirthlessly. "You children! You speak the words, but do not respect them. Why should I help you run from this as well?"

"Run? What are you talking about?" He coughs. "I don't understand—"

"No you don't, even now. But…" The fey's long fingers tap together. "You've made a fine career out of tucking tail lately."

"Never!"

"The castle?"

Calem's back straightens ever so slightly. "I did not run."

"Screamed like a little girl even!"

"I did not!"

"Most certainly did." The old man throws his hat in the air in mock horror. "Like this I think: 'Aaaahhhhh-heeeehhhhhhaaaaa!'"

"But—"

"Or maybe more like an 'Aeeege-aaaaggghhrrraawaaaa,'" Oberon yells in his high, nasal voice. "That I think makes more sense. Very woody in all. You druid types like that."

"Please—"

"Or was it, 'Ooooeeeoooo?'"

"I will be in your debt," Calem says softly. "Take me to Niena, heal me, and you can name your price!"

Pleading eyes peer at the fairy through locks of wet hair. Oberon regards Calem, scratching at his long nose. Finally, he speaks again. "Is that all you can offer?" Then icily. "First place both of your hands over your eyes."

Calem does as told. Somewhere above his head, he hears the faint sound of knuckles cracking, and the swoosh of a cane waving.

"Now repeat after me, ahem." Oberon clears his throat. "Nooooaaah!"

The old fairy waits. Calem's voice trembles but gains strength as he drags the vowels. "Nooooaah."

The night seems to hiss with the power of the arcane. The whirl of Oberon's cane stirs the air around him. Is it just Calem's imagination? The smell of ripening berries, of the apples, the orchards of the little vale he left Niena in flood the room. Something is happening, he knows it. The desire now to open his eyes eats at him, and it is all he can do to keep them closed as the old conjurer continues with the spell.

Oberon with his cane raised high, "Freebeees."

Calem squints; that does not sound like any sort of spell he's heard before. "Freebeees."

The *thwack* of the cane echoes over the reawakened and chittering fire in the background. The voices from earlier have returned, circling around the two. Calem drops to the floor, shaking with pain and shock.

"You hit me! Why did you hit me?" Between moans.

"Because!" Oberon sputters. "Because! No freebies!"

Calem grits his teeth, doing his best to hide his anger. "What is your price?"

"Give me something real. What is your life worth? Your firstborn son?" Oberon's voice is suddenly soft and gentle, breaking from the heightened energy he had a second prior. "No, wait, wait. That's a terrible idea. I'd have to pay for college and…Oh gods, what about when he needs to learn to drive? And the sex talk!?"

"I don't have children." Watching the fey cower behind his hat. Then, with exhaustion, "I don't know what you want. Pickles? I'll stuff you with them till you puke."

Oberon sniffs and wipes his glasses on his cuff. "Agreed."

"Pardon?"

"It always worries me how easily your kind are ruled by emotions. Do you have any idea how many pickles I can eat? Probably at least twenty," he remarks sadly. The old creature then rolls up his sleeves and begins to stretch. "Well, well, all is well, and a pond. We begin then!"

Wind twirls around him like hearing a bard on a stage. The depth of the room peels away, and they are once again in a forest. Of dreams, and nightmares. Leaves and twigs are swept up in the dance, spinning, twisting, and falling around the two silently. And then Oberon raises his hands up to the sky, waving his cane in wild arcs.

"What are you doing?" Calem asks with one hand reflexively holding his head.

"No, my boy, I won't lay a hand on you, just stay put." With a smile, Oberon dances now, circling the druid. His movements are quick and supple, like the fingers of a fiddler. His high voice flutters with the leaves in the air as he sings. It is silly, and scratchy. Like boots crushing dead leaves in autumn.

> *Fold the shoes, and shine the shirt*
> *Hippy Trippy Colourful Squirt*
> *Feed the flu, but starve the cat*
> *Picky Wicky Filipus Rack*
> *Dance all day and into the night*
> *Cause your lover a horrible fright*
> *That's what we do today*
> *To send this boy along his way*

Time seems to lose its grip on reality. Oberon's song dashes forward and retreats just as quickly. It reminds Calem of an odd foreign toy he once saw, little balls attached to a paddle with string. That is what the old man is doing with his eyes, bouncing forward, lingering, then shooting back in perfect reverse. It is mesmerising.

Break the mirror, but mend the leg
Steppy Peppy Calamitous Peg
Steal an ear, and mime your manners
Whippy Flippy Pompous Banner
Sing the song tis what we do
We must go no time to stew
He wishes to flee the attack
So lets send him packing with a good ole…

Chapter 4
A Bard's Tale

Time will sunder all binds
Of heart, spirit, and mind
Leaving only dreams
Nightmares

It begins with the clear sound of birds and the wonderful smell of breakfast on the stove. Old or young, knight or damsel, all share the same moment. Poppies and snapdragons saunter with the smell of fresh bacon through an open window. And in a nearby oak, a little tanager cries *perky-tuck tuck-tucky*. Smell and sound, touch and sight swirl together to set the stage for a quiet afternoon in Maidenhill.

A wisp of wind slides down from the mountain, wandering past flax that kisses the cheeks of the town. A month has passed since the crop was touched with dashes of purple flowers. Farmers and day labourers now toil there, preparing the harvest. Soon their wagons will be laden with stalks for the fair.

But farmers are not the only people who are busy in the hill lands. Soldiers — militiamen — or Bluecoats, as the locals call them, are present too. They linger primarily around one centre tower. For beyond the hills, and bordered by the marshland and forest, there is a river. It ties up the countryside between Kimbesh and little Maidenhill like a blue ribbon on a green bonnet. This tower stands at the last craggy summit of rock, overlooking the closest ford. Silently watching. And here, in the shadow of the spire, two people banter. Marny and Squirrel. Grandfather and granddaughter. One is an old soldier, the other something else entirely.

"Not bloody well happening."

A bead of sweat slides down Squirrel's clay-streaked face. She licks her lips, ignoring Marny's comments. Twenty yards ahead a scarecrow with a crudely-drawn target on its breast leans against a sack of hay. The string of her bow is taut and ready.

"Are you ever going to take your shot?" Marny growls. "Or should I go shit?"

"This isn't a race." Three arrows are lodged in the dummy, but only one came close enough to tease the target. That shot is Marny's. Squirrel's are geography.

Her grandfather rocks back and forth. The string of his bow goes loose and tight against the rhythm of his movement. "Let it go."

The muscles in Squirrel's shoulder are beginning to ache. "Are we talking about the college or this shot?"

"Yes."

The light snap of a loosed bowstring answers. In a lingering instant the arrow arcs through the field, tips a feather to the scarecrow, and then disappears deep into the wood behind.

"Spit," he hisses.

"It's a bardic college." Flicking back a lock of hair. "And Taledric's is the best in the Empire." The gesture earns a frown from Marny, but Squirrel ignores it and violently unstrings her bow. "The last thing I will need is to know how to shoot."

"It's not for the bloody college," Marny says. His lips move like the knots of a gnarled stick as it's being bent.

A stick you might use to beat someone with. "The roads aren't safe now."

Squirrel sighs. "Deliah says they've *never* been safe."

"Your *nan*," Marny snaps. "Don't call your grandma by her first name."

"I'm not twelve!"

"And if you were half as able as some of the twelve-year-olds here, I might let you go. But I'd be chords-cursed to send you out there now. You've learned all the wrong lessons from your father's tavern crawls."

"I'm not stupid," Squirrel says, stepping up to him. "I'm not the one wasting time teaching their grand-daughter how to shoot a bow. What am I supposed to do, ask a bandit nicely to wait while I string it?"

Marny's knuckles turn white on the stave. "Stupid? No. Lazy? Inattentive? A silly little brat with her head up in the clouds? Yes, yes, and chords yes. But not stupid."

The old man sounds as if he is trying to gargle rocks — and this extra frustration makes the words stick in his throat. "I'm trying to find something that you can do," he continues. "Anything. Everything! Because odds are, girly, you're going to have to knife someone if you travel anywhere in this chords-forsaken empire now. You might have to knife more than one someone."

Knife someone? There is something to be said about having a grandfather who is captain of the Bluecoats, she notes. *But knife someone?* As Squirrel stares at the tall, silver-haired soldier, Marny's face cracks like an egg-shell as his temple furrows.

"You heard me right," he says. "There's a lot of in-fighting amongst the Lords. Hardly anyone can spare a bugger for regular patrols. It's too dangerous if you can't handle yourself."

"That's…So tell me." Tossing her bow to him. "Tell me why can't I just go with a caravan? It's not like I have to crawl through the woods."

Marny sighs. "You're not listening. Did I not just say that the *roads* aren't safe? And you wouldn't know who to talk to, or where to go."

Someone coughs loudly. Squirrel spins around to look at the tower. The men, the soldiers on the stairs and rampart leading to the great oaken door are now all too quiet. *Could they be listening?* Marny doesn't budge. Yet when she turns back, his cold blue eyes march down that crooked nose of his, looking forward.

"I'd almost rather have you try to crawl through the woods," he says quietly. "There are nastier things than wolves on the old roads, and you'll find them all out there — ready to steal more than the twinkle from the eye of some runaway."

Squirrel finds herself looking back towards the tower. They *are* listening. Embarrassment pinches her, but doesn't prevent Squirrel from absently saying, "I can take care of myself."

"Like bloody chords you can," Marny crows, neck arching like a rooster ready to peck.

"I can play in taverns…"

"Complete that sentence, and I'll take back what I said about you not being stupid."

She digs in. "Plenty of aspiring students have paid their way to Taledric's by playing in taverns," Squirrel says, over Marny's howl of protest. She reaches over and tries to pry the old captain's hand from his temple, but he instead grabs her by the wrist.

"This isn't fantasy, girl," he growls, shoving her back. "This isn't one of your silly books."

"Those books were written by some of the most respected—"

"Liars and thieves ever born," finishing her sentence. The tattered edges of his long blue coat sweep over weeds as he paces. "I've spoilt you; I should have taken you out on the road with me more. Play in taverns, for what, bedding? Oh, you'll find bedding."

"Now you are just being ridiculous."

"And you aren't taking this seriously!" Squirrel's face goes pale under a lock of raven hair. "You haven't taken anything a lick seriously yet." Marny flinches as if the conversation hurts his head. He quiets then, but is no less harsh, even as her tears begin to flow. "How am I supposed to trust you'll suddenly start doing it when you're out of my house? On the road? You won't pay attention, and will just get hurt." His eyes add: *or worse.*

"You don't trust me?"

"No," with a resigned shake of his head. "No, and I believe we are done here." The old captain is now looking past his granddaughter. He's rigid, ready to march off towards his troops. Yet more. There is a change in his inflection as if he's tallied up the score from this debate, made a decision, and *he* is letting go. Squirrel catches it.

Squirrel reaches again for his arm. "I'll die if I can't go!"

"Don't go saying nonsense like that," her grandfather snaps. "You make it sound like I'm beating you."

"Marny! Listen to me!"

The first man to laugh is the sergeant, his feet dangling off the wood stairs behind them. The second and third follow almost in unison. The laughter grows into a small chorus and ripples around the base of the tower, eventually dying when it meets Marny's frown.

The old captain brushes her arm off. "You aren't ready. Let it go, Squirrel. Go home to your nan."

"I can't!" Crying. "What am I supposed to do?"

Squirrel steps aside as he walks past. That pinch of embarrassment escalates to a punch in the gut, knocking out whatever breath still remains in those lungs. Still, that's not the worst to come. Before she can say anything, her worst fears are realised in the form of five words from Marny: "Learn to live with disappointment."

Sun-touched red. Leathery brown. The faces of the soldiers lose their colour when Marny's gaze meets theirs. Squirrel's doesn't. "Why don't you just lock me up in a tower," she says to his back.

"Ritter." Marny's command startles a young wagon driver, forcing a salute that makes the man look like he just received the business end of a flagpole. The soldier's red hat poking out of a ho-hum mesh of brown leather doesn't help the image. "Ale run? Take my granddaughter with you."

An awkward salute meets the creak of the wagon wheel. Squirrel watches her grandfather storm the stairs, up, up past the decaying first battlement. Until he disappears into the shadow of a set of oaken doors, and the wagon rider—this man called Ritter—beckons Squirrel over. She fumbles with the latch of her lyre's case, staring up at the doors when they finally close and shut out a last chance at reconciliation. Without so much as a glance in that direction again, she shoulders the case, along with another bag, and climbs into the bed of the cart.

From the tower's grounds, a long trail leads towards the ford, or back to Maidenhill. The path itself is dry, cracked. It spirits over and around several hills, secreting the city from sight between one curve to another. These hills, marked with blue, red, and dashes of yellow, patrol along the line, to be lost amongst the rigid formations of flax crop. But for now, they are here, welcome company for the ride.

"So, how long to Breach Point?" she asks, not really interested in an answer, but more to hear the sound of her own voice. The soldier smiles at her, waving his one free hand back and forth in exaggerated motions. The cart lurches to the right, and Ritter grabs at the reins with both hands. The bed of the wagon Squirrel is sitting on heaves up and crashes down as he rights it. It takes him a few moments to bring the cart back into the ruts. She leans back, bored with trying to get him to talk. A lone cloud above breaks rank and warm rays of sunshine walk alongside the cart, but Squirrel's mind floats above it all.

What if I were to stay on? The images snowball. From a light dusting: picturing those first moments trying to convince the silent Ritter to take her to Humdel. To the deep drift: dreams of smoky taverns, and late nights playing for the coin to take her to Ravendown, home of Taledric's Bardic College. *No, it can't be that easy.*

A slow, melodic dirge begins to fill the back of Squirrel's head, as the memories of those late night stories her grandmother impressed on her come to life. The cart fades, and on the horizon, the dream of a college rises. White columns lift a gold leaf-adorned roof where stylised friezes of musicians parade, time-worn, but still merry. She can see herself, walking up to those massive wooden doors, and getting lost in the hall behind them, where the pillars spread out into the roofed night of the ancient canopy.

Bumps in the road break up Squirrel's daydream like staccato in a lullaby. She looks at the pudgy soldier in the driver's seat at her back. He has pulled on an oddly chequered overcoat that not only clashes with the pot-boiled jerkin but makes him look entirely ridiculous.

She sniffs, and an idea wiggles its way up into her noggin, flashing silver into those two blue eyes. Her heart begins to race. "So I was wondering…" Ritter's bushy moustache bristles with a twitch of his nose. "What are we doing in Breach Point? Since Marny wanted me to come with you."

No answer. She squirms in her seat, looking for any reaction from the young man. Again, nothing. After a few moments, her attention slips back to the road, the hills, and to the town slowly coming closer and closer.

Feh. Fifteen is two years too old to join the college anyways, she tells herself. *Whatever was I thinking; it would involve lying.* A herd of clouds have moved between the sun and her, making the sunbeams poke holes. *Not lie, but tell a story. A bard's tale.* That little taste of irony amuses her.

Nearly an hour passes, and with it, her anxiety, replaced by the returning dreams of a fifteen-year-old girl. To the east, the midday sun stirs in the field alone. That's farmer Bracket's field, and he's been sick for the past week. His land is pockmarked with old stone grain huts and other rubble. These slowly flow into the towers of Squirrel's imagination. West, the more traditional flax crop ripples in hazy gold. There are farmers in the fields even now, but from where Squirrel is riding, they are hard to see.

Waves of gold are spilling over the land, reaching for the spires on the coast. The wagon hugs the road to the right, and Squirrel pretends it is the edge of the beach and the water. The town opens up to her daydream. Trees and buildings shift into idyllic foreign counterparts, harkening to the gently curving roofs of the western island provinces — descriptions of which she has only read. The side of the hill is shorn in this imagining, creating a steep drop off to the flaxen sea below.

She looks again to her silent companion, tilting her head as she watches him wave. Several times he opens his mouth to say something, but all that comes out are little gasps, sometimes mixed with an odd cry. It is then she realises that Ritter wasn't being rude, he is mute.

By now the crowds of townsfolk make it hard for Squirrel to hold onto the little dream. White walled buildings. Dark green roofs. Men and women in long robes. Slowly, surely, they flutter away. The curved roofs are replaced by short and regular angles. Uniformity amongst the people disappears; overalls and sundresses reappear. White walls melt into the red brick of her country town. And then the cliff is just a hill. The sea is only a field of flax. Squirrel sighs.

But those fantasies are not the only things vanishing. With each plod and pop of the wheels in and out of the cobble grooves, with every *clop* of hoofed feet through the crowd, the town fades. Fades, passes, disappears just as any imagined thing. Squirrel looks to the man behind her, who makes no motion of stopping as he pushes them through a shepherd's flock, and around the weathered stones of the city's fountain.

"How much longer till Breach Point?" she asks, but only to calm herself. Ritter clenches the reins, and waves off an elderly couple coming from the opposite direction in their ox cart. Squirrel's nails dig into the wood railing as they round her grandparent's house. And inch by inch, foot by foot, a little tinge of excitement sinks in. The feeling grips her. Grasps. It doesn't let go until the last house at the edge of the town dwindles into a blur. Up ahead a sign reads: Breach Point, Coppercreek.

Chapter 5
Before a Fall

A soft melody flowers between bough and limb, haunting the dead forest with…

Squirrel moans and drops the pen. They have been on the road for three hours, leaving the fields behind and embracing the woods. On both sides. Tapestries woven in her mind tatter and shred as the canopy promises to tighten with each turn of the wheel.

"We're never going to get there, are we?" Tired words slur back into thought. *Really, if it wasn't for Ritter, I'd wonder if I was—*

"Alive," Squirrel gasps. The sound of scribble joins the trot of the horses and the crush of hard dirt.

A soft melody flowers between bough and limb, haunting the dead forest with…

Its liveliness, she writes with a flick.

Jolts in the carriage signal a change in direction. Squirrel hugs the parchment to her dress. The road dips again, and curves due north. After another turn, the moonlight and their lanterns cross.

This music does not belong here. The bare tops of several old pines stand out from the snow like spears from a forgotten battle.

"Ow!" Another hard jolt sends an ink bottle to the cart bed, Squirrel's head to the back of the driver's bench. Three and a half hours have passed in silence. The last of them hand in hand with the setting sun. It is almost time to put away her journal, but the oak trees leaning over the road whisper encouragement between their leaves. "You're in a good spot for it," they say. "Don't waste that ink on your pen!" they chide.

The sadness waiting in the wood did not touch Michael. He plays, and skips, and makes his own way.

"Lingering sounds better than waiting," muttering while she scratches away a line on the parchment. The monotony nearly made her doze, and the writing is barely legible. Squirrel stretches against the pine wood. Clouds swirl around a dull bulb in the sky. There moonlight crackles soundlessly. And Squirrel peers deep, deep into that maelstrom. Lights all around her fall, muddle, into a mesh of grey. Finally, after several minutes the edges of her lips curl into another smile.

Silver fingers of light tease the length of the waterfall…

Squirrel's head lurches forward, just before a dropped pen can stain her dress. "Waterfall, what the chords does that have to do with, wait, what did I write?" She holds the parchment up to the lantern.

"Remember the three chords, boy," she reads. "Your home is here, not with the men under the barrows."

The story flutters. "I must have fallen asleep." She yawns, folding the parchment and tucking it under her shirt. "Only a dream. I wonder how long we have been out here. I didn't think Breach Point was so far away."

You'd think it was in the Weld. *Or out on the frontier.* The rhythmic roll of the cart wheels is grinding her thoughts into dust. The effort not to talk to herself is failing, and she speaks out loud again while rubbing sleep from drooped eyelids. "Breach Point."

The horses whinny excitedly, stirred by something on the wind. A sudden jerk of the reins only makes Squirrel's head loll slightly. Between the cart and the forest, a strange tension hangs, which she ignores and passes off as just another sign she needs to fight to stay awake. *Why would they name a logging camp that?*

Ritter's frantic movement and the swerving of the cart should stir her from sleep. But they don't. Instead, she wearily peers into the forest dream. From every direction, there erupts a high-pitched discord. Squirrel leans back against the seat. It isn't comfortable, but she still finds her eyelids closing.

"Should have named it Beech Point," she says. One gentle stretch of road then ends the struggle, and Squirrel only utters four more words: "but Marny does…say…"

Silver fingers of light tease the length of the waterfall as the moon peeks over a rise of grey clouds. It is now half past the hallowed hour here in the lands of Near Earth, and the gales sing far off in the distance under their roofed night. Together they join with the gentle rush of the water and the quick whisk of an autumn breeze, turning the pages of the world song so that the music of the forest will unfold.

From their dens and clutches all manners of birds and creatures come in the passing hours to drink from the pool. Among the visiting beasts is a beauty. Below the grin of the waning moon, and twixt two white-washed stones, a lady bathes. She stands tall in the failing light—proud and fair. A glimmer of red touches her skin lightly, splitting her image from the whiteness of the rocks.

She pulls at tufts of the wild grass and slides herself onto the bank, nearly slipping back into a crop of mud. Brushing raven hair from a thin face, the girl lays her head back and yawns. Far overhead thunderclouds clash and break against each other in waves. And though the main line still lays off to the northwest, the storm's heralds, with their swirling banners and great steeds, have already bounded past the mountain and beyond. Cold tears run down her unclothed body as the fore-guard of a storm marches onwards.

"And the skies flow grey—as the sea, and the night till morn." She closes her eyes and drifts off to the soft splish of the rain and the smell of wet grass. Around her a haze of fey luminescence dances on the ground as each droplet seals a part of the retreating starlight. "Light carries the days—like leaves, lost in the wind."

The drizzle slackens momentarily and then turns into a steady downpour. "Fair way, come again." Thunder rolls over her song, shaking her out of the dream and nearly back into the pool. Blue eyes flutter open, looking for their match in the sky above, but they do so only in time to see the last of the Traveller's Stars drown in a sea of grey.

"And the waves crash—against shores, heaven bred." The young woman stretches, rings the length of her hair and then lays back down, letting the cool rain wash over. "Where time is born—and remains, a rare guest."

"Fair way, come again." Long furls of dark rip and fold in the sky above. Growling, she pulls her clothes from a nearby branch, donning them hastily. "And I wish that it would remain a rare guest."

Lightning splits overhead as the girl kneels to pick up the dagger. In the brief light Squirrel catches her own image. "This time everything will be different."

"They always say that."

Squirrel jerks awake. Whipping her head around, searching for the source. She finds one lantern, two horses, and the back of Ritter's head. Nothing else between them, but just beyond the stretch of their lanterns light is a long rectangular building.

"Waterfalls? Chords, it felt so real. And that voice, it sounded like, no, I must have dreamt that too." Above her head, a tavern sign rocks in the wind. Squirrel groggily squints at it, mouthing the letters as she reads: The Beech Point.

"Can I take tha' sir?" the squeak of a stable boy pokes the evening air.

Squirrel scoots off, clutching the lyre and satchel to her chest while the wagon jerks forward. The two, Ritter and the boy, have already exchanged the reins between strokes of the horses's muzzles. She watches them. An annoyed whinny fills the background of her thoughts and plays as some sort of prelude for her climb towards the tavern's entrance.

What now? Even as her hands wrap around the iron latch on the main door, a little dose of reality begins to settle. She swallows. *I guess I have to hide in the tavern, or slip away and find another carriage.* Ritter will be leaving again soon. *Will he look for me here?* Another whinny. The driver and the boy disappear into the stable, leaving Squirrel alone and standing on the porch of the Beech Point. Her mind puzzles again over the name briefly, before she finds other thoughts to wander into. Like the building itself. The oak posts and red windows of the plain structure are an outlier. A remnant. She is already beginning to make up a backstory for the old building and has to force herself to stop before she falls into another fantasy.

One deep breath. Again she grasps the cold iron latch. This time, the *click* of the lock pulls the atmosphere from the tavern out. Smoke tickles her eyes and the smell of sausage her nose. And she can see all of the small rectangular room here at the threshold. At the far right, a chimney of jumbled stones and earthy colours waits. And the smell? It hangs from the ceiling in lines of dried meat, stopping only at the counter of the innkeeper in the left corner. There are a few tables. Fewer customers.

Even so, the air is warm, and the light warmer still. A faint song wanders among the tables. Hummed by the one barmaid.

Two steps in. Few look up from their drinks at Squirrel, but the barkeep, a portly man of middle-years, leans over the table. *This brings me back.* A twinge of nervous excitement spins in her stomach. *Got to work this right. I don't know if I can do the things Dad did. I don't want to survive like that.*

Three feet from the counter the bartender turns towards her, sets down a glass he was cleaning, and smiles. Squirrel slips onto the stool opposite, eyes wandering from his bald head to the not quite as shiny mug in front of him. And then sticky breath clings to the back of her throat when recognition slaps her.

"Wha'll ya have, Miss Squirrel?"

Her stomach sinks. Sinks! The bartender leans, and all three fat folds on his neck quiver with laughter. "Ho! Ho! So what brings you so far from your Da, eh? Don't tell me you finally gone and runs way, eh?"

"Nothing of the sort," unable to avoid sulking into the bar. "My granddad asked Ritter to bring me here, and so I am, on my way to Taledric's, that is." Squirrel fixates on the stains in the man's blue shirt, before meeting his cheerfully moustached smile with a glare of her own. "And my name's not Squirrel."

"Grandad? One's good sass another," he says with another chuckle. Squirrel couldn't tell if his slow draw was due to him being a northerner or the drink. "Squirrel's your name, ain't it?" Apparently ignorant of her glower. "Always used to call yourself Squirrel. Say, you don't remember me?"

It's the drink, she thinks. His breath smells like garlic and stale beer, an odious mix she would have never thought possible until today. "Ten years ago. And I was trying to say 'girl.'"

He slaps the counter. "So you do remember!"

"Yes," talking to the floor, until something sparks inside of her head, and Squirrel's face lights up. *He can only really guess why I am here; no one passed us on the road.* "Cortny? Do you…do you know of most of the caravans around here. Have you heard of any making a trip tonight?"

"Perhaps I have," he says, after a moment. The bartender rubs his ruddy cheeks as if trying to massage feeling back into them. He clears his throat several times as Squirrel leans closer, his voice slowly retreating back from the nasal pitch it had just a second earlier.

Squirrel abides, expecting Cortny to continue. But when the "and" doesn't come, she pushes. "Can you help me find one that will take me?"

"May…be…" He squints. "But I think…I think it might be best you get goin' back home inna morning."

"Don't give me that. I need to get to Taledric's." Heart thumping so loud she can barely hear herself. "Do you know any caravans going up to Ravenwood or not? Or at least Coppercreek? Come on, you have to know at least one that I might catch a ride on."

Cortny scratches his chin. "Yes. No…prolly not a good idea I sass anything. I have a business to run, without them Bluecoats getting up innit."

"My granddad is the captain of the Bluecoats." Squirrel leans back. "If he has to take a day out to meet up here to set things straight, how mad do think he's going to be?"

She can see his gears working. Working—then grind to a complete halt. "Less mad than if'n I'd helped you run's way," with a heavy laugh. And then his eyes bulge as he tries to talk and think at the same time, and does neither well. "Ach, I remember too! He says to me, 'Cortny,' he says. 'Don't you be taking my daughter nowheres. Don't you be letting her run's way if you see her. And you will see her!'"

"I don't…I don't think he'd say that."

"No," Cortny considers. "No, he had a lot more curses in there if'n I recall. But you must forgive me, miss; I am not goin' to be repeating them."

His meaty hand then waves at someone behind them. Quickly followed by a yell, right in Squirrel's ears. "Tab! Take some of those dishes inna back, will you?" Then he rounds back. "Why don't you go sit next to the waterfall?"

"What?" Squirrel says.

Chatter swirls around her, and the staccato of mugs slamming down in succession separates Squirrel from the bartender. Confused, she presses between him and another patron as Cortny begins to fill a queue of empties.

"Cortny!" she yells, squishing between the barmaid and an elderly gentleman's stool.

"What cha want now, miss?

"What did you just say to me?"

"What, about our waterfall?" Running his fingers over the gold buttons on his bright red shirt. "I was just saying that if you are tired, you can go sit next to it on the grass behind you."

"Are you drunk?" But she follows his nod across the floor anyway. And stops, grasped as if by a phantom force. For there the snap of the fire gives way to the patter of water upon rocks. There too, she sees the fire in the pit lengthen, chill to a silver blue, and fold under and over itself until the flames bend like water from a mountain stream, taking her breath along.

An unintelligible murmur finally escapes her lips. She spins to ask Cortny something to the tune of "what the chords is going on." But only the still of a forest greets her vision. Squirrel slowly pans around, trying to find the walls of the tavern. Once. Twice. Until dizziness and nausea take hold and set her down upon the cool earth.

Light tickles the full stride of the fall and silver fire writhes over rock, bough, and limb. This strange water pours into a pool below, glittering with a soft light. And Squirrel stares into the shimmer, mouth agape, while a gentle song weaves its way alongside the growl of the forest fall.

"Where the bleeding chords am I?" she says, channelling her grandfather.

The clatter of shutters beats against walls that aren't there. Squirrel rises to her knees. A dull metallic noise rings from the water, and as she stands the speed of the pulse undulates.

From the pool itself comes an answer. "Where are you? Where, indeed, Wyrmspun."

Squirrel swallows. Even with the falls roaring just beyond, she can hear the voice, its high-pitched call supported by a low, rumbling echo and seasoned by the music. With each word a bubble of light roils to the surface, so that even with the twilight settling in around her, she can see it too.

"Why is your kind so focussed on the where, and the when? You are here," the disembodied voice continues. "You are then. Ah. No, no, child, I know you didn't ask 'when' yet. That question is for another."

Grass and flowers bloom in splashes of phosphorescence around her. They seem to be herding Squirrel closer to the pool. And whether or not she wants to do so, her feet keep moving. "I'm dreaming," she whispers. The water near glows an eerie silver and is ringed in flowers and grass whose colours drain into the pool. "I fell asleep on the cart."

Happiness. Anger. Anxiety. Enchantment. And, *sadness?* A cacophony of emotions twist into words inside Squirrel's head as it speaks again. "You are not dreaming. Not entirely. But that does not matter. You should have asked me 'why' you are here. Now that question could be very important. Very important indeed. For instance, step closer, and tell me. Would you like to know why you will never study at Taledric's?"

The air near the pool sucks the warmth out of her breath, leaving it to dwindle on the wind in frosty huffs. Tentatively, she stops at the edge. Pieces of grass and soil from her boots fall off into the water. The surface ripples. Roils. And then begins to reform.

"No! Wait, what am I doing?" she says. "No, don't answer. I know why." The cold causes Squirrel's hands to ache. She stretches them, marvelling at the vividness of the scene. "Because it's a dream, and that's the thing to do, isn't it? It's not like listening to a weird invisible man ever turned out to be a bad idea. Right?"

Patterns of stars burn through the water below, and a city slowly emerges, with lights awaking on the periphery. One. Two. Then more, many more burst into view. Torches in the streets, even the candles of peasants slowly push away the curtain of night.

"What the—? Oh no, no, no, no. I'm not playing this game." Though she is unable to tear herself away.

These fires coalesce, gather, and throng along the streets. Slithering into a long procession. Writhing like a great serpent. Through the gates. The countryside. And up, up the side of a lone mountain.

As the little tongues of flame snake towards the summit, the voice returns. "I told you. You aren't asking the right questions."

"What then?"

"No! Wrong again!"

And at the end, a pyre burns. She swallows, watching the crest become nothing more than tinder to the ravenous hunger of the flames. Charring. Singing. "W...Wh...Why?"

The ground where she stands shakes, swaying side to side as if a giant hand grips the land, to toss against a game table. Feet slip. Squirrel's hands thrust forward in a vain attempt to catch her. But in that last moment before she falls, and the rush from her tumble into the silvery pool hits her ears, an awful shape rises from the mountaintop. Wings of ash unfold in the catastrophic light, pinned in an arch around the shade of a monster. And, just before the plunge, the water's growl becomes the roar of something terrible.

Chapter 6
Cast Off

"It's freezing. Hear me? Freezing out here."

There is a hiss and a sudden flame. The old captain stretches across the battlement as sparks fly from his lit pipe. "What? Forgot your bleeding gloves again?"

"Damn near. Should be warmer than this."

Twin pinpricks of light blur into the marsh. Marny rubs his tired eyes; the fog always makes it hard to see anything. Though after ten years up in this tower, he doesn't need the long glass to recognise a carriage from Kimbesh.

"Look at my hands, Cap, I can barely move em. S'like they're covered in syrup."

Ten years. Hardly how the old man thought he'd be spending his retirement: captain of the poorest militia in what was once the Empire, stuck in a crumbling tower listening to a new-horn whine.

"So damn cold my mug is steaming, see that?"

"Not the only thing steaming up here, you pile of shit," Marny growls.

The trim of his blue coat dusts the stone where he spins. But there isn't much room up on this side of the tower to pace. Two other soldiers huddle around the beacon light in the centre. Marny scowls at them before turning back towards the countryside with a sigh. Gnarled hands work at the cold that needles his joints.

"Worthless bunch of cast-offs," he mumbles, and someone coughs behind him. This day has been a long one, born in the morning, and still not put to bed. And there is a creeping feeling of unease that has been with him almost all night.

Marny scratches his nose. Only the moon is out, its ample body half-hidden by a porridge of clouds. The other lights have fully retreated—and everything else too. As if the stars might be children, caught red-handed past their bedtime. All of the toys, all of the games have been snatched away, leaving only that one forgotten lamp and the sheet they hid under.

The *clop* of boots from a heavy-set man tells him all he needs to know about who is approaching. "Gab," he says.

"Don't tell me you're up here complaining again like an old woman?" Gabin says from the top of a ladder. Of the men here the quartermaster is the finest and most warmly dressed. His blue coat has been neatly ironed, and there are no stains on the grey wool shirt. His girth, emerging out of the trapdoor to the main room below, doesn't flatter, though.

"I've been stuck up in this mud hole for a week shitting in my helmet," the old man answers, head cocked. "You can bugger off."

"Captain," he chastises. "Why don't you let someone else command the watch this night? Come down and have some nice hot ale by the fire."

"Well."

Gabin's hand grasps him around the shoulder, trying to move him towards the ladder. "And we can spend the rest of the evening talking about wool swatches, and the latest handbag fashions in Everwatch." Marny laughs, pushing off. "You really take me for some ninny?"

Gabin's glasses slide down his nose. "Of course not," he says, with Marny at his side. "I think you are a bleeding ninny. Now let's get out of this cold."

"You go on."

Gabin hesitates. The ends of Marny's tattered coat flutter in a breeze as the quartermaster watches him lean back against the parapet.

"You know Deliah wants to move, Gab? Seems Reef's wife has been putting things into her head again."

"Ahh, yes. Well, we are the dregs of polite society here," answering with a shake of his head. "It never was a place for your wife, and you know that."

Marny follows the quartermaster's meaty fingers as they jab over his right shoulder, pointing towards the marsh beyond.

"Not much to look at, I know," Marny spits. "Nor is there anything but cows in town. But I didn't drag my arse here for the tea parties. I did it because I like *eating*. That hasn't changed."

"That's all well and good. But you promised her it would be only temporary. She's been patient."

His answer squeezes through clenched teeth. "I also promised to take care of her. One comes before the other."

Both men are chilled by a sudden strong wind from the south, from Kimbesh. Yet the sky remains overcast. And the fog still. A fact that is not lost on either of them. Marny answers the look of bewilderment in Gabin's eye. "You should be on watch with me more often, Gab. It's a strange place."

"I prefer to keep my visits to the tower brief," he whispers back. "Though I know the stories. I think the only real export Kimbesh has now is madness, from those who have the terrible fortune to live outside its walls."

"Saying I'm crazy then? Because I've seen my fair share of queer things lately," as Gabin joins him. "In the fog." He gestures towards the road where the carriage meanders.

Gabin nods his head. "No, I would never say that. But between the marsh lights and everything else, even the most focused mind can be tricked. Thankfully the tower is always lit."

Marny's eyes drill into the quartermaster. "I've been here long enough, Gab, I'm no homesick new-horn. I can tell a curl of fog from…" The captain's back arches, and the pipe that was so rigidly clenched between his worn teeth loosens in his hand. "How the chords did we get on this subject?"

"By gossiping like women, or about women. I don't remember. Either way, this is not exactly the place to be doing so. Downstairs?"

"Yeah," he answers, looking at the men next to the beacon.

His friend pats him on the back, and they both leave to climb down and into the main room below, passing off a few commands to the remaining soldiers on the battlements. Warm air from the fire meets them, and their intrusion causes paperwork to fly off of the solitary desk. Notes and forms scatter close to the hearth, under a bookcase, and even down the stairwell leading to the lower portions of the tower.

A murmur passes between the men above. Marny sneers as he looks over his shoulder. "I am not sure I should leave Sebastian in charge. Before you got here I was ready to toss him over the edge."

"And I'm not sure why you care," Gabin says as the captain lands. "I wouldn't trust all of these men together to be able to hold off one pack of raiders."

"Raiders aren't interested in mud."

The quartermaster makes his way towards the fireplace, where mulled ale steams in a pot. "But southern armies will be interested in the livestock, and the crops." Then quietly. "And perhaps slaves."

"Lot to happen before then," Marny says. The stem of his pipe clatters as he raises his voice. "There isn't any place safe from this sort of nonsense, you know? Deliah's good here as anywhere, in case that's your angle."

"Think better of me, Captain. This is just speculation, is it not?" Regarding his friend with a tilt of his head. "We are talking about war, not women. Though I admit, the two things are not entirely separate."

Red sits with grey, fire and stone in the old chimney. Both are welcome totems to drive away the chill and wind from above. Marny's feet steal him away from the open trap door and into the waiting maw of a plush chair. It devours him.

"You think there will be trouble soon?"

"Hard to say." The quartermaster's chest jostles a shelf as he reaches for the mugs. "If one of the southern dukes manages to coalesce power, things could change real quickly. And if the war does spill over, you can forget about the March forts. The canton is not going to raise taxes for a better army. We are here as an illusion of security, nothing more."

"On about that again. Well, maybe you aren't wrong. But don't tell Deliah that. She doesn't need the worry, and I am not fit for another argument today." Marny rubs his chin. "I swear though, if they keep sending me farmer's boys, I am just going to start having them plant potatoes, and put the scarecrows on the walls. Bugger this job."

"That's the first thing you've said that I can really agree with," Gabin says.

"But I still got family here." Watching Gabin ladle mulled ale into a jug. Slowly Marny begins to relax, and idly to count the changes his friend has made to the former tower barracks over the last few months. All manner of personal items from the quartermaster's clan decorate the room. Marny chuckles softly to himself. As little time as his friend spends up here, he has it arranged like a second home.

"I'd send them north, or east," Gabin says. "Shipped my wife off when I first heard of the Emperor's death."

The Iron-Fisted Brewer. That's the sigil that emboldens all of the tapestries that hang in this office. His quartermaster's house. Marny rubs his eyes. A motto swirls underneath a stylised tankard clutched by a gauntleted fist. *Strong hands, stronger ale,* he thinks to himself, surprised at his memory of the old tongue. Still, the whole picture doesn't fit with the painting of Gabin's brother that rests crookedly behind his desk, wearing a ridiculous hat that looks like a distressed teapot buried in dollies. *Nobles.*

Squinting. "Not all of us are lordling's sons."

"Surely you have some money saved from your campaigning days," Gabin sighs, looking back towards his work scattered on the floor. "Or your inheritance?"

"Not as much as I'd like," Marny admits. "Besides, I'm only worried about the war as far as my granddaughter faffing about in it. If something from the south does come, we will just have everyone run to the hills. And that'd be that. Personally, I'm keener to watch the noise coming from the old capital. And don't you go on about me being superstitious. You've never been there."

Gabin shot a glance over his shoulder. There is a commotion amongst the soldiers above, yelling and screaming profanities. "I'd rather talk about something else, if you don't mind."

Marny frowns. Shadows from the fireplace reach around him and through the bars of another chair, making a mock prison for him against the stone walls of the windowless room. "Still take the Emperor's death personal, eh? Are you aware of yesterday's sterling report?"

Calm falls over the quartermaster. "Only too aware. I think, though, it's not worth mentioning. What took that tower was nothing more than recklessness." Gabin sets down the jug of ale upon a nearby table; it begins to shake — but not from his hands.

"Now," spreading his fingers. "What's this I hear about your granddaughter?"

Marny squirms at the change of subject. "She's got it in her head to be a bard, just like Graham."

"Her father?" Gabin says. The wooden chair creaks when he sits, and his form fills in the bars of the shadow prison. "That won't end well."

"Not at all," he sighs. "All that trouble, Gab, it was a miracle he got back here with the whelp before…" His fingers rub the bell of the pipe nervously. Marny squints with one eye and points at Gabin with the stem. "He always knew better. Wouldn't, couldn't listen."

"And the girl?"

"She's just like him. I was hoping she'd get some sense in that fool head of hers." The more he talks, the further into the chair Marny sinks. "Buggered that. I thought all that training would open her eyes to it. Change her mind. But it didn't. It won't. She's pig-headed, starry-eyed, and lost in those books. Just as he was. I should have tossed them things a long time ago."

Gabin stares at the jug of ale, and huffs. "I don't know what I was expecting to us to do. Drink it from our hands I suppose."

The quartermaster stands, making his way slowly back to the shelf near the fireplace where he left the mugs. "In regards to your granddaughter. You are overthinking it a bit. There's little wrong with being a dreamer," he says over his shoulder. "Or reading."

"Until it gets you killed," Marny says. The quartermaster seems to shift uncomfortably under his gaze and stiffens when the captain speaks. "About reading though, don't be so quick to dismiss that report. You and I both know of what sleeps out in the capital wasteland."

"Nonsense," he huffs again. "Utter gobble-minded nonsense."

The mugs ring where the quartermaster near slams them on the table. Marny smiles to himself and taps the side of one as Gabin stretches for the jug. "No normal fire I know of can melt stone. This had-" He stops mid-sentence. "Is that wind?"

"Most assuredly." Gabin clenches his coat against the chill. "But why haven't the men said anything?" Both listen to the chatter above, but only the quartermaster moves to get a better look. "Should we bother involving ourselves? Or do you think they can handle securing the beacon alone?"

"That one, Sebastian, we're lucky he hasn't stabbed himself with his sword yet," Marny fires back, but he hesitates to get up. He is all too aware of the dangerous weather that can come down from the mountain, but with the fog, a sudden storm just doesn't make any sense to him. The details of that report play upon his nerves.

"Sebastian!" Gabin yells with his foot on the first rung of the ladder. "Have you secured the lantern against the rain?"

Dusk outlines the former farmhand kneeling at the top of the ladder. "S'not rain, sir!"

A guttural groan at the quartermaster's back has nothing to do with any storm. Marny launches from the chair and pushes Gabin out of the way while simultaneously thrusting his finger upwards at the soldier like a lance. "You bleeding *halfwit*! 'S'not rain sir,'" mockingly. "I don't care if it's unicorn farts, secure the damn lantern!"

The soldier's head jerks back and words are shared between him and the others. Marny's eyes narrow at the excited chatter.

"The fire's gotten to the keep?" Sebastian says to another, before turning back to address his captain. "You need to come see this, sir. Kimb—"

The crack of Sebastian's head against the wall shatters the conversation as the tower itself shudders violently. Both Gabin and Marny catch all two hundred pounds of the former shepherd, and the captain is driven to the ground. Paper and dust that collected between the wall and the bookcase scatter.

Gabin clings to the ladder. Marny struggles with the unconscious soldier, squirming out from under the man's armour. Curses mount, boldly charging in ordered lines of vulgarity. He looks up to the still-standing quartermaster. "Are you alright?"

Gabin brushes flakes of stone and wood from his hair. Even in profile, the quartermaster's face paints a perfect stroke of surprise and alarm. "Did…did something just hit the tower?" his lips barely moving.

Again the walls heave, sending wood and debris down upon the three men below. Gabin falls to his knees. Marny's shout of: "What the bleeding—" is cut off by the cries of men adding to the clamour of the shattered tower.

The wall opposite, along with part of the roof, falls away, and two men tumble down, and down. Marny, still prone, looks on in horror as the screams are lost in the thunder of trees snapping. Crashing. Sweeping. Gusts push into the room, stealing breath and light with their foul reek. One by one sparks from the fireplace trail off into darkness like lit arrows. The air is filled with smoke.

And flame, Marny's lips mime a line from the report. "We must get him down from here." He grabs the prone soldier by the arms and rolls him over to the side, while the quartermaster's attention is fixed on the gaping wound in the tower. "Gabin?"

His friend's limbs move in slow motion. "Lords bless and unite us," he whispers.

Unfazed, Marny pulls himself up, using the cracks in the old stonework even as the floor below him sways. "Put your head right, Gab!"

Banners to the right ripple and a last barrage of embers from the fire are sent against the black. The quartermaster steps back. "By the three chords," he says weakly before his words begin to drift into prayer.

He wasn't the only one to see the canvas of wings in that brief flash of light. Marny recoils and covers his mouth with the edge of the cloak. But that is not enough to keep out this stench. The smell of sulfur bites. He looks to the fallen soldier. To his friend. All around them the tower resounds to the grate of something both hard and slick.

Dark shapes shatter the roof above the fireplace, and a pit opens into the floors below. There is little between them and whatever it is that assails the tower. White flashes. Once. Twice. A row of spears at the edge where a wall had once been. Ash floods what is left of the room. Pushing, pulsing. Marny coughs. His hand wraps around a length of Gabin's cloak and pulls, trying to direct his friend towards the stairs down. "You're a soldier, damn it! Save your last rites!"

"They who taught us the three chords." The quartermaster clutches his chest. Light begins to creep back into their ruin. But it is queer and evil; flames spread over the great sprawl of Kimbesh in the distance, rolling across the rooftops of the urban menagerie and setting upon them as fast as sunlight in the quiet of the dawn. "They who gave us music to keep back the silence of the night."

Marny rushes to his friend as he collapses onto the cold floor. "Gabin!"

The outside world is cut off by the body of the beast, and Marny's face twists in a sneer as he kneels. In the centre of the gash, the stone seems to breathe. *Not stone,* Marny corrects himself. *Scale.* The smell of his blue wool coat smouldering mixes with the creature's breath. Throbbing. Breathing smoke and fire into where the wall had been. He leans over his friend.

Out of a cloud of fire and ash realisation spills into Marny, and his eyes bulge in pain and awareness. From the spark, a terror emerges. Thunder crashes in the half-roofed night, and a wyrm that had been hidden below the tower rises to its full height.

"Demons take it," Marny snarls into the reek. Even while the pit in his stomach hollows. The floor creaks and rumbles around him with the shifting of the dragon.

The moon, which had dominated the night sky even against the flames of the burning city of Kimbesh, is replaced. Marny watches one pale orb become two. Glowing. Mocking. The eyes of the beast are crescents of yellow surrounding twin pits of black. He looks to his fallen friend. To the soldier at his side. To the open stairs below. The dragon rears, almost as if it senses his fear.

Its long neck arches. Scales glisten. He feels for his sword, watching the creature's eyes retreat. "You son of a—"

Air above and behind him scalds with dragon fire. One, two seconds. Marny's blue coat sprouts flames while he is in mid-dive, towards the stairs. Three, four seconds. Fire chases him as he plummets down the open gap to the stairwell. Smoke mixes with fine dust to choke the air. Five seconds. The roar of the blaze. The feel of old wood splintering. The pain of tumbling down six, seven, eight steps and crashing into a wall. His arms shake with the strain to get off the landing. Stair after stair, Marny's body endures every jagged edge as he crawls and rolls down the remaining flights.

And the roar of the beast follows him. It reaches deep down into his guts and pulls out those terrible memories from the wasteland. He staggers. Heat rushes down, pushes him through the door at the bottom and out of the tower, into the open air, where desperation forces a face-first meeting with the grass of the embankment below. But he is not left there in peace. The collapse of the south wall is preceded by the sound of thousand bat-wings threshing in unison. Flames surge out of the ruined building, threatening to overtake him and the stables beyond. In this moment, Marny's eyes are beguiled up, up into a vision that sinks his stomach.

Wings like a terrible canvas. He struggles to a knee. Wings, painted by the light of the burning tower. He swallows, and the insufferable heat beats down upon him as the monster rises into the air. Here emptiness finds him, and his gaze rakes back to the falling remnants—now the pyre of his best friend. He shakes his head in disbelief.

"Deliah..." His thoughts circle with the dragon. Maidenhill is in danger. His family is in danger, but there is no way to fight this thing. The smoke, the smell of burning wood, mixes with the blood in his mouth. Distorts his vision. Closes his eyes.

The pain, the helplessness, press on him. His eyes open to the night sky—into that former blank canvas, now bubbling away with the ire of the dragon's flame. But from somewhere deep within him, that feeling dredges up the memory of the day they left to come to Maidenhill. Marny fights to stand. What did he tell his granddaughter then? Somewhere in the back of his head, he can hear Squirrel setting her bowl down, flipping the rim with her finger. It rattles for a few seconds before coming to rest. Empty.

"Niena." He remembers now. The laughter. The sweet way she mispronounced "girl." Most importantly, what he promised. Marny spits, grimacing at the acrid taste, but finding in that moment another way to keep his oath. He lurches stiffly but quickly towards the stable.

Wood crackles in the distance and wind peels past the exposed timbers of the old and long ruined building. Yet the structure is untouched by fire for now. Marny hurries to saddle his horse, worried that every second may be one too late. The whinnies of the other stabled mounts here don't seem to fit in, all free life having long fled the devastation. Unfortunately, he knows, they may have to end here. With luck, the fire will remain upwind.

"Traveller," he says smoothly. The beast's mane stretches against the reflection trapped in a broken window and the firelight beyond. "Once again I need everything."

Without a bit, Marny spurs the horse from an amble to a gallop. And out, into the night. And out, into the wind. Patterns of stars peek through the clouds above, but the city ahead still sleeps. The old captain presses on, knowing that the rumble is no storm, and the wind at his back carries fouler things than rain.

Chapter 7
Thread of Lies

Grey.

Calem's tattered coat slumps to the ground. Sweat soaks every inch of his clothes, and the pain of the moon's glow forces his eyes shut.

Black.

He grabs a sapling to try to stand. Wherever he is, the world swings like a pendulum. "Oh chords, I think I am going to be—"

Black again.

Calem wipes his mouth. Deep and incessant *thombs* echo in his skull. Covering his ears only makes his heart beat louder.

Grey.

"I'm alive; I get it. Chords, I get it!"

Dust drifts through a moonbeam and settles on his coat. His eyes are raw, aching from the intrusion of light. Slowly the brown, grey and green tinged blur below his knees separates into distinct surfaces—brown, giving way to dirt, green to grass, and grey into the stone foundation of a ruined house. He struggles to stand again and fails.

Fired red bricks, softly illuminated, sprout from the weeds nearby. *Softly illuminated?* Past a forest canopy, a sky steeped in black mixes with the white of the clouds and the yellowish-brown face of the moon. Canopy, cover, and clouds all work in tandem to hide the stars. *I haven't lost much time.*

Pools of water lie all around him on the muddy ground. Calem crawls towards one. Over the red brick. Over the rain-slicked grass. As crickets string in the background, he dips his fingers into the murky water, then dangles that hand above his face. Chin-up. Cold water trickles down his lips and cheek, streaking both with dirty lines.

There is a low rumble. Quiet, and close, like the slow buzz of a bumblebee. A drunk bumblebee. One elbow slides in the mud as he meets the hazel eyes of the scraggly creature. *A tabby cat?* Then with a frown. "Oberon!"

Purring. Oberon purrs at him.

Calem cups more of the water to his lips. Cool, dirty. Also foreign. Droplets fly from his flicking hands, pelting the surface with ripples. "So where the chords did you send me? This doesn't taste like Ebonmuire water." Angrily he dashes a reflection of the moon with another flick. "Or Miniel. What game are you playing?"

The cat blinks.

Sore hands rub at tender arms and legs. They find pain. They find stiffness. What they do not find are any of his wounds from the fight. Relief holds his trembling arms and whispers at least this one answer to his worries. Yet Niena could not have traveled far from Miniel in the short time he has been gone.

"I know where this is going." He spits, watching the cat's tail skim the surface of the water. "You took me to Niena. You just played with the 'to' part of it. So how far is she from us? One crow, twenty?"

They are now eye to eye. Cat to human. Mouse catcher to druid. Calem slips in the mud again, trying to shake his finger at the feline. "I fulfilled my part of our main bargain," as the cat's eyes follow his hand. "You haven't even—actually, I don't know why I am arguing with you."

Knees wobble. Calem makes drifts of mud as he stands, pushing, sometimes flailing on the ground. Anger and excitement power him more than strength of limb. "If you think I'm going to make any more deals, you are insane!" he says with a careless gesture that almost sends him back to the ground

"Where am I?" he snarls, palms outstretched. One swish of the cat's tail. Two. Calem hovers over the feline, who seems more interested in the strings dangling from his shirt. "This is some nasty shit, but I tell you, I am going to find Niena. And when I do, two things are going to end: the curse and our partnership."

The tabby sneezes on his feet.

Calem squints, finally able to see the trees for the forest. "And I'll be the happier for it."

Every joint, tendon and muscle groans at him for mercy as he straightens. Walking is worse. But all around him the last shadows of his awakening sickness retreat: flowers dip from long-neglected planters, trees bloom solid greens and browns. All into focus, and Calem realises he is closer to civilisation than he previously thought. The outline of a cart, lanterns still lit, graces what could be a road.

Several moments stretch between the groans and grunts. Moments that would have otherwise been spent in silence. "Care to clue me on what's going on over there?"

Though he doubts the seriousness of anything that sounds like a hairball being coughed up, Calem is still somewhat happy for an answer. And that brings him back to the wagon. His brow rumples as he peers at the road. "I suppose you want me to go explore it? I think that's a bad idea. A real bad idea. Which is why I am

going to do it. But just so you know, fairy: I hate sur-
prises."

Soggy leaves crinkle beneath his feet, and the smell of
decay drenches the air. But a different sense than sight,
sound or smell affects him on approach. It's the music,
the thread of old magic that, while not uncommon in
wild places, should not be as strong as it is here. He pon-
ders the sensation from under an oak, his feet shifting
on thick roots that stretch almost to the road itself. To
his right, a flash of orange fur means the cat is following.
Calem's glare tracks the tabby until it rejoins him at the
tree.

His eyes glint while sizing up the contents of the cart
bed and bench. A sliver of the rascal, the old thief that
dwells in Calem's heart, jumps. Because of this, his gait,
as he steps towards the road and into clearer view of the
possible treasures, is jerkier and more anxious with each
step. Even while worry gnaws at him.

Where are the horses? Two lanterns hang from the posts
of the otherwise unremarkable cart. Could bandits have
done this? *I was right; this is a bad idea…why am I still walking?* These and other questions bubble to the surface, but
immediately pop as his feet touch the dirt of the road.

Calem jumps back to the safety of the forest. Back to
silence. Stunned. Shocked. Uneasy. Fingers twine
through his wet beard. *Oh, oh ho ho ho. There we go. That
road is soaked in it. Soaked in fairy magic.* What is Oberon
up to? *Briefly twisting left and finding the cat again at his
feet. And what does this wagon have to do with Niena?*

He doesn't expect any answer. Realising this, he
knows there is only one way forward, all the while hoping that memories are the worst thing the magic will
summon. Sighing, Calem again steps onto the road and
again is treated to the same shock as before. The sharp
shot of memories forces his eyes briefly closed, and the

same word he wanted to shout before thunders in his head.

"Wyrmspun."

The pitched voice of his former teacher runs down his spine, into his hands, and numbs his fingers. Vivid. Deep. Calem wheezes softly as he reaches the bed of the wagon. And is once more overcome.

"Curses exist," the priestess continues. "They wait on the lips of every man, woman, and child. Your breath gives them life."

Back out of the memory. The magic is more personal than any summoning spell. This is specific. And his wife is the centre. Calem grits his teeth, concluding that the disappearance of the cart's occupant must have something to do with her and Oberon.

There are two bags in the wagon. One a rucksack of the standard variety. The other an instrument case. He swallows, letting his fingers slide down the waxed leather. Silently he braces himself.

"Even those that have passed into everyday talk." The strength of the taproot exaggerates her mannerisms. She twitches at the crackle of the flame, drags the end of every sentence. "Don't fall into the trap and think they have no meaning because this isn't so. Many people who lived before you did believe in them. Do believe in them."

Torn away again. "The curse of the Wyrmspun," his soft voice is emphasised by the pop of the instrument case's lock. "Niena's curse." The moment doesn't last, and her voice returns.

"Finally, there are those ancient ones, born of older magics." Powder sifts from her hand and into the fire.

Acrid smoke from the cart's two sconces finds its way to Calem. He spits, but that taste will linger there for weeks. This plus the constant see-saw between waking life and dream is tugging at his already strained stomach. He carefully opens the case, knowing that doing so will trigger another-

"They are greater. And truly wicked. Filled with power and a terrible need only desperation can create."

If he had anything in his stomach, it would now all be on his feet. Instead, Calem's head rests against the cart while he dry-heaves. To his right, the patter of four little feet echo like drums on the wooden bed. He lifts his head from its position, nestled between his arms, to stare once more into the thin face of his new friend.

"You…you really are just a cat, aren't you?"

The tabby's swishing tale confirms only one thing: it wants to be petted, and he isn't petting it.

He sighs, lifting himself up. "I'm the damn fool in every tale."

Underneath his fingers, a pale velvet shines. There the lines of an ancient harp that once hugged the interior. Calem'a fingers trace where the strings would have been. The slick imaginary whine of the note rips into his head, and he buckles.

She smiles sadly. A long, slender line of flame coils in the air, and then strikes the evening in a flash of red. Wings of fire. A serpentine tongue of ember. "Curses of scale."

"Wyrmspun." The whisper drifts between memory and the waking world.
"You don't understand what this is—this thing you meddle with. Your Niena carries a terrible doom."

Calem shakes his head vigorously, desperately trying to keep from slipping back. As to the portent though, every child knows part of the tale, of how the last dragon cursed the elves that slew it. "By this hand, I die," he recites. "To live in restless hate, and winter lie."

"You are fooled," the priestess warned. "This fairy, this Oberon has you now, for there are only two ways to deal with the curse, and one is a deceit: the winter chant of the Drel'nu, to make it slumber within the vessel. The other…"

"Is to slay the dragon," he sighs, speaking directly to his memory. "And become the new vessel for the curse."

"Yes. It is the story your new wife does not want to tell you about. How did a girl of her age ever destroy such a beast? How did the Drel'nu find her? You know nothing! Yet you look to steal her from them, without a thought to the girl if you fail? You have little time to sew together a blanket of truth from a thread of lies."

A quick breeze from the west gives him some release. "I think, I think that's it. Chords. Look out there, there's something strange here, and I don't like it. You look at the sky, and tell me I'm wrong." Stars are revealed. By lay, and light, what he sees is fitting only to the Midlands: a country too far from where they were to make any sort of sense. His smile finally disappears. "Have both me and Niena been dragged half a world away? But why?"

A sharp chill seeps into his arm, and Calem's fingers spread across the face of the moon. "No," dropping his hand. "That spell's not going to work. I am going to go about this a different way."

Hazel eyes. Maybe that would make a good name for the cat. For a new familiar. "Looks like you've lived outside for too long." *Maybe lived too long, period.* "I'd prefer a wolf or a hawk. Or…well, let's be honest, anything else."

He leans close. "A Éineacht lim." The chords strum in his head, as they always do when practicing magic. The rhythm slows. Flips order. Changes. The music that made up the harmony of the cat's fate begins to merge into Calem's own greater melody. Until they entwine.

"I'n fiach d'ais, agne a intn, spirad spirad."

The cat's eyes flare red-orange, then simmer into two darts of light pinned on a black mat. Calem reaches out and strokes his familiar's chin. "We need to find the owner of this," he says, holding the harp case. "Let's hunt."

Chapter 8
Curses of Scale

Squirrel's arms shiver. From cold, shock.

Fear. Confusion. Feelings and thoughts collide in a perfect jumble at the entrance to the doorway that is her subconscious. *Is this a dream?* Guilt. *Marny, I'm so sorry for running away.* Doubt. *I can't do it, he was right. He's always right about me.* Sadness. *Grandma.*

Now the hush of a forest. She peeks through the gaps in her fingers. It is night in the Black Weld. *Where is Ritter?* The cart and road are nowhere to be seen.

A twig snaps. Smells of wet leaves reach from the right and left. Squirrel rubs her neck as fear shoves a half moment between breaths. *Did something move?* There is only black. Empty—until she notices that ahead, a moonbeam swings on tired branches. The light, while it gives some purchase to the forest, really serves only as a tool for her imagination to fill the void. A mist drifts past leafless branches, straining through the light, which makes the trees look ghoulish and the mist like the— *whispers of unloved dreams.* She shivers, lips mouthing this thought as she walks slowly backward. Another twig snaps. This time, Squirrel stays in place. The touch of the grass is twisted by her fear. Into hairs, hairs that bristle upon slender legs, legs inking over roots.

Spiders. She shivers again. *Why does it always have to be spiders?* The images move soundlessly in the under-growth, closing the distance. Squirrel recoils slightly. Barely a twitch.

There is the rustle of feet through grass, breath hitting the air. Nothing else. Her toes dig into the mud and roll over both ends of a broken stick. A sigh slips into a nerv-ous laugh. *I am such a ninny.*

"Ritter?" she yells. "Are you there?"

A burst of activity, things scurrying away in all direc-tions. She fidgets, her eyes darting from the grass and back to the forest black. Then they stop.

In the trees, a collage of features reflect: her own. A thin face. Long fingers. The jerk of Squirrel's hand dis-torts and curves in mirror over fist-sized spheroids. Orbs…no, eyes, black, faceted eyes. Her visage of terror emerges from the darkness to the left and right. Both profiles. All angles. She can even see the quiver on her own lips. *Spiders,* disbelief colouring the thought.

This time she runs. Into the forest. Deeper into the night. Branches and leaves whip, vines and roots cling. They leave marks everywhere: red on unprotected cheeks, arms, green on the white of the dress. Squirrel stumbles and, breathless, collapses forward into a tree trunk. Her feet feel around in the darkness, finding the roots, and inching down. These few seconds pound in-side her head.

Behind there is nothing. Ahead—*wait, is that?* A glow breaks through the sombre forest, far, far in the distance. Squirrel takes one step away from the tree and plunges face-first into the undergrowth. Thorns bite, bracken is crushed. And she swallows, fear clenching her fists tightly together. There was no sound accompanying her fall, only the pain and the spring of foliage underneath.

From every side, the quiet closes in, and Squirrel lets out a ragged gasp. She rises slowly, and terrified, lets her feet slide into position to bolt again. A lone drop of sweat slides down her nose, which twitches reflexively. *Now? No.* Scents of crushed grass mix with the wet bands of hair that fall across her face. Still nothing.

Squirrel rushes on, towards the beacon. Flashes of insight churn up the darkness around her, allowing glimpses of bulbous shapes herding her from the periphery. Stabs of fright twist her own footsteps into those of the attackers. And this continues, pushing her further, and further. The gleam on the horizon grows from a sliver to a stain, from a stain to a mark. Then clear sight stops Squirrel right in her tracks.

Now once more, the hush of a forest. She falls to one knee, then the other. It is night in the Black Weld. It is always night here. The dusk rests her sight upon the same trees and breaking moonbeam from before.

"Terrible!"

Wet hair slips from her quivering hands. Squirrel peeks between her fingers, searching for the source. His voice — *that voice*—the same from the dream. "This can't be real."

A reply comes in a slick whisper. "Reality and belief are an old married couple. You have one; the other won't be too far away." She cringes as it touches a nerve. But the voice continues. "You are not dreaming, Niena. Though take care, else you will haunt this forest with your nightmares."

"Where are you? How do you know my name?" Her shoulders tense. "Those spiders are —"

"Nowhere near as awful as this prose!"

Squirrel, Niena, blinks. This wasn't the whisper of before, no, this strikes the silence. She spins around, rising from her knees and into the face of a strange, stooped old man. He wears a red, perhaps too red, velvet vest, and it is a wonder for his long nose that he could hold a book as he does now.

"Those spiders aren't the worst things to come out of that head of yours." The book is brown, worn. The type of ledger a clerk might use to keep stock. Or a captain his daily log.

"That's my—"

"Hmm!" with a theatrical page flip. "Deep within the arms of the Weld Mountains the white hag still slept. When the grey waters of the Dwem'aimá seethe, and a red sun breathes…Dwem'aimá, sounds like what a demented man puts on his pancakes."

"Hey! Don't be nasty!"

The old man ducks again behind the worn cover, his beard twitching like a horrible thing from the deep. "Nasty? I'm not nasty," he growls. "Nor am I cantankerous, cranky, spiteful, or plain mean. You sour wad of moose shaving."

With a pause. "Why are you calling me names?"

He taps his nose and adjusts his glasses as if deeply considering the question. Then his eyes narrow. "Because I'm nasty."

His long beard. His crooked nose. His clothes, which follow a list of oddness capped by a conical hat. She sizes up the old codger, tying a ribbon around this picture of ridiculousness with a nervous smile. "Who are you?"

"Asking a dream its name? Do you ask the sea its depth? Or sky its end?" He pulls his hat over his ears. "What name shall you give me? What name shall I give you? But if you don't trust? Then I suppose, give something, we must! Before you stands the ostentatious, the bombastically egomaniacal…"

His movements jar against a frantic mess of branches and leaves teased by a new wind—a wind that began with "dream," and has grown into "ears."

"Riotously objectionable, curiously pedantic! The, uh…" He spins and spins. Leaves whip around him, caught in a tornado of movement. Round, and round again. His arms flail wildly, and his face lolls back and forward like he is getting ready to—

The hat and the glasses go one way, and the rest of the old man crumples to the ground at Niena's feet in a heap. Eventually, his eyes catch up with the rest of him, and they meet her stare.

"Are you mad, or just daft?" she says.

"Magic is neither," he says, as she helps him up. "And what I was doing was important, terribly so. The whole fabric of reality could have been upended if I did it wrong."

"Well, you were about to upend something all over your fabric." Niena laughs as he snorts. "And what the bloody chords were you trying to do anyways?"

He looks at her cross-eyed. "Tell you my true name, girl. But I can't now; I can't!"

"Why not?"

His pale face wriggles in the moonlight, and there is a twinkle in his eyes that flirts between mirth and menace. "Because I've plum forgot that it's Oberon."

Niena stares, dumbstruck, while the old man waves away her arm. His face is a painting of concern and worry, white-washing any menace she may have caught. "Wyrmspun. Do you know what I am?"

Niena shakes her head. "I know I must have drunk something back at that inn that will make my grandpa really, really mad at me. That's what I know."

"Humph. Want to hear what I know?" He presses closer. "You are Niena, daughter of Graham. You are here in my Black Weld. The Fairhome." His eyes smile, and he taps on the gold buttons that march down his chest. "A guest."

"A guest?" she says. "So what does that mean? Are you the reason I am here in this awful place?"

The hiss returns with the pop of toadstools from the black near her feet, phosphorescent and blooming white. One. Two. Not a circle, but a trail, spreading with Niena's stare. Into the forest. Into the night, and beyond her sight.

"Awful?" He regards the change with a satisfied nod. "Maybe a moment before, but look: it only took one smile for this to brighten."

"You were there, weren't you? At the pool in my dream?" Niena's attention is slowly drawn back to the bowing man from the bubbles of light that arc out of the toadstools.

"But that was not a dream. Or no more of a dream than our memories tend to become." The old man's movements are surprisingly lithe as he slinks around the tree. "As to why I brought you here? Because of our bargain."

"Bargain?" Niena says cautiously.

"Yes." Not a blade of grass moves. "*Our*... bargain was a gift born on the warm lips of a lover, and carried by dancing stones under a cold druid's moon."

With one movement he pulls up to stand within arm's reach. His head lowers, and he looks up with upturned eyes. "And sealed dearly, by tears, and blood."

Pages flip inside of Niena's mind, and then an imaginary finger jabs into the middle of an equally imaginary book. "You're a fairy," in a voice she thinks is confident.

"Correct!" Oberon says cheerily. "And I am here to complete our deal, Wyrmspun, signed, sealed, and delivered!"

"Why do you keep calling me 'worm spun'?"

His smile is soft and gentle. Like a leaf drifting on the wind. "Wyrmspun is what you are, were, or may yet become. Depending on when, if, or how I succeed in my task. I have come here to keep what happened from…happening." The wrinkles on his face scrunch and his gaze slips to the forest behind Niena. "What may befall you is a curse, that much you should know. Yet, I am not sure how much I can tell you here as your imagination is powerful. I will say more in time, once I know it is safe. That's fair. I am always fair."

The fair folk. Niena bites her lip and swallows whatever she was about to say. Her nan told stories, made them seem nice. She wasn't the only source on the matter.

"Safe from what?"

His face tells a story. It is not a nice one. "Right now? Yourself."

"That's not an answer."

"Usually children are full of wonder, they brighten the Fairhome, but you?" Oberon crosses his arms. "This is where you need to be. I just need to find a way to keep you from harming yourself."

"Take me home. If this isn't a dream, I want to go back!"

Oberon rubs his nose as if he could wring out a witty comeback. "No." Then his concern lifts, and what replaces can only be described as a smirk. "Or maybe, this might make a teachable moment—we've chatted for too long, and there is much I must do. I think you had best go."

Behind his words a thick ink pours out, parting in two long lines cut by the fairy's tongue. Niena raises her arms reflexively as the moonlight drowns. But now in her hands there is a heavy weight. She looks down and into the pantomime faces of her lyre.

Where the fairy stood is only a smudge.

There are many things we must endure in life. The fairy's words rip through her mind like a knife through silk. *Lack of knowledge is a curse, true, but a small one. And for you, there is a greater: whispers of hatred, passed from the dragon's last breath, to the one it cursed to be its heir. A true curse of a scale, you might say.*

"Oh chords, bleeding riddles? I'm bleeding terrible at—"

The smudge focuses. Eyes glower into red beams, sharpen inward. File towards two points of crimson knives. And Niena swallows, as they too are eventually engulfed by the returning forest.

"Wait!"

Again she is alone. A breeze ripples her dress, coaxing the trim towards the glowing trail. *The mushrooms!* They still pulse with power but are also slowly fading—moment to moment. Niena counts, watching the nearest glow drift and settle. But with that loss comes the return of the fear. Stalking. Caressing the hairs on her arms. Creeping up her neck. With no other alternative, she follows the path, all the while hoping to either find a way home or to wake up from this fantasy.

Seconds *crackle* with each step. A minute *snaps. Time eats, reality fasts.* Niena tries to shake these thoughts from her head. Now isn't the time for writing. Bubbles of light pulse and arc from the mushrooms. Faster. One step. Faster. Each step. Hair by hair, inch by inch, her feet bathe in the silvery luminescence. Time seems to dance around as she follows the trail, tilting to a distant music.

Until it does not. The end of the trail brings no sudden change. There's no flash of light. No spiraling darkness, like her trip through the pool before. Only a retreat—the withdraw of silence against the return of life. Once more

Niena is surrounded by the dark forest, but this time she is not alone. Cicadas string their love, frogs croak, and night birds flitter through the expansive canopy. And where she walks, the crisp crunch of the undergrowth pitches.

One step. Two heartbeats. Niena slides over a small boulder, and her feet sink into the mud below. Three. Four. Closer to a panic, closer still. Now brought to a hush. Wonder is betrayed by fear. And fear washes away her courage.

"What the bleeding chords is this?" she shouts, fingers pulling at her hair. Smells and sounds flow towards her with the wind, dashing any thoughts of a reunion with her grandfather. Maidenhill is not on the horizon.

Chapter 9
A Way Back

Raindrops slipping on pine needles, critters asleep in the hollows. And a young woman in the middle. Between roof and hearth, root and heaven. But everywhere there is night, and everywhere the possibility of danger. For the careful and the strong, or the careless and scared.

A droplet falls, and Niena wipes the reminder of the last hour's shower from her face. A breeze whistles past her nose, and she thinks of Maidenhill. The rain is not too cold, and the wind tickles with the pleasant scent of lavender — a flower that does not grow in this part of the Weld. The storm swept from the west, and if she knew better, Niena might seek to go that way. In that direction there are fields, fields that blunt the fist of the mountain ranges, where flax, heather ale, and young girls are raised.

Three chords, her curse and prayer. Fingers tighten as another peal of thunder shakes the branches of the tree she is climbing. A few seconds more, and again the sky crackles. Her lips are broken, with the taste of blood trailing each inch as she tries to stand. *One, two* — Niena squints just as the first rays of dawn squeeze through the canopy, interrupting her counting. *Four?* One last hurrah from the storm in retreat. Now a red glow, orange crest — morning really is coming. She pulls, and lifts her leg up to the branch, scraping the inside of her thighs against the trunk in the process.

Dawn. Fire dances on the trunk: the work of the light and wind, through a puppet of leaves and branches. Niena squeezes her eyes closed. "This was stupid; I'm stupid." The hours before buzz around her head like flies. "It's morning, I'm halfway up this stupid tree, and what do I see? Leaves and branches. Stupid book."

Alamand climbed. She recites in her head. *Pinning his hopes on finding the mission. But from the old tree, he could only see the beginning of the Willywin River. A week! A week mo—*

Both of her hands grasp the next lowest branch, until she is able to push up, and plant a foot. Niena's legs now span this, and the last. So she leans, letting her back press against the trunk as her left arm reaches for another hold. Bark breaks, needled loose by long fingers in the first attempt. The second gains her a firm brace, where she is able to turn and grasp with the other hand.

"I can do this," Niena believes she says. What comes out is more of a mix between a groan and a whine. A tangle of branches, needles, and more taunt her above. *This is just like climbing the Kimbesh Tower at the Overwatch.* That was a lie; the tower had stairs.

And what about this whole situation? Meeting a fairy, being kidnapped by said fairy — fantastic plot points for a new story, but dismal settings for reality, which the painful cuts and the growling in her stomach make clear where she is now. But they require more lies. Layers upon layers of them, and the biggest of them all? That she is not going crazy.

I hope some of it was a dream. Niena inhales and presses her wet face against a mesh of leaves and twigs. *Maybe somehow, something happened to me in that tavern. Maybe I was poisoned and turned everything into some sort of walking dream. But then how did I get out here?*

Time drips by, and she spends the next hour with her eyes either closed or keyed into the trunk itself. All other distractions eventually disperse, carried away by a wind that rocks her cradle in the canopy. But that itself is a problem: the shaking. The branches are getting thinner, and her knuckles whiter. The trunk of the massive pine itself is becoming as slender as some of the limbs before. Down, she needs to start thinking about down, but before then, the reason she climbed in the first place.

"Marny, chords, but you're wrong." Light stains her eyelids. Niena winces, stirring up the courage to look, then turns. "And sort of right: I don't know what I am doing, I don't know how I will get to Taledric's. I…I'm…" She laughs sadly, eyes still closed and fingers entwined around a clump of leaves. "I don't know how I'd get home either. Or even out of this bloody tree."

Wood creaks, cracks. Her feet slip as the limb below snaps, but she is able to cling to a cluster of branches and climb just a little further. Then she looks down. A stew of dizzying height dashed with a chaos of leaves and branches is bound in a bowl of agoraphobia, served in copious amounts as her head falls back against the trunk and her eyes rise from the ground to the sky.

And a whole new world opens.

From the treetops to the sky, the green of the leaves shines and moulds the horizon around them, like jade secreted under a blue scarf. She looks to the east. A flock of birds sways into the clouds and passes beyond a massive outcrop where fingers of stone poke out from the canopy — or smudge into the line, grey and rough. More trees ring this top, and the sheen of the green seems to circle a peculiarly high and straight wall on the east side, that could, if she uses her imagination, be an old watch-tower. But right now she can't shake the mental painting of a hand holding up a particularly rough-cut jewel in the sun. The light's rays fall all around the white stone.

A bird cries behind her. That's north, and not where Niena wants to go. That way lies more forest, but darker and thicker than the spread of the east. Green turns to black, and black eventually ends in a gnash of seven jagged red teeth. Mountains. There's nothing further wanting there, and she in truth can't see much beyond their caps of snow — or clouds? She swallows, hands shaking from the strain after a sudden gust. A strong fragrance follows, but the flowery odour is so laced with the pine that it tickles, and she sneezes into the trunk.

"Nothing," she says, remarking on the view west. The land rises, giving way to a fence of forest that controls the horizon. Niena sighs, clutching fiercely to the tree. She can see barely a mile that way. "It's all so beautiful," with a hopeless tone — a graveyard can be beautiful.

What's wrong child?

She bites her lip. "Everywhere is just more of the same! Trees, trees, and oh look. More trees! If I was a ranger, I'd be ecstatic!"

Well, at least here it is safe. You have much more control...wait, that's not true, is it?

It's finally happened; her inner voice has started talking back. Niena doesn't know what it means precisely, and she can't help but answer. "I am going to die alone out here." Shades of her grandmother, phantoms of dinner now dance before her eyes. "I'm never going to leave this forest."

Oh, you won't die alone. There's plenty of woodland beasts out here, and me. That's better; at least her voices have their usual dark sense of humour. *Where's the dreamer, where's the imagination?*

"Imagination?" Dreaming! While it is easier to dream amid darkness, it can be harder to see the light. "Maybe some sparrows will find me, and make a nest out of my skull…Then, hah, then I'd really be a bird brain!"

Are you crying?

"No," she says, burying her head in pine needles.

Do you see the scar in the Weld?

Niena wipes her eyes while shaking her head.

Just beyond the shade of the ruined castle?

She looks again. Waves of leaves ripple in the early morning breeze. "Just more trees, what do you want me —" They flow, flooding the expanse in a sea of varying hints of depth: dark greens, light greens, and all in between. But where the voice told her to look there is a hole that the light does not fill. Niena cannot believe she didn't notice it before. The hole is more of a gash, a scar as the voice put it — but marring only the view. For the girl, however, it is hope.

"It's a town!" Her heart racing. "Or the ruin of one." She squints, seeing something else. "Those are clouds, black clouds. Or not clouds, but smoke? I can't believe I didn't see it before!"

Niena risks stretching out with one hand and uses it to orient herself to the scar in the forest. "It's south mostly. Barely south west." She straightens against the trunk, energy rushing through her body with a wave of hope. "If it's a town, there's got to be a road. Even if just a ruin, but…"

She looks down again, and her knees begin to quiver. "There's no way I can climb down that," as she ties a daydream of herself doing just that. The imaginary Niena has now died in a broken heap amid the roots at least five times before she says: "If a girl falls to her death in the forest, will she still get grounded?"

But then a foreign thought bubbles up and over: *don't think too much girl, just put one foot below and use your legs to support you. Use more of the trunk, until those branches get thicker.*

One foot feels down, while the rest of her clings to whatever she can. Pain flickers with each movement: thorns and bark disrespect the lining of her dress and dig into her thighs at every opportunity. That inner monologue may have been full of enthusiasm, but, if she is honest with herself, it feels harder and harder to grasp at each tenuous foothold.

"No." No more tears. "I can do this." She closes her eyes, remembering the tower. Sure, there were stairs, but it was a sheer drop. Below her, she pictures the town of Kimbesh rising in splintered darkness; torches, cousins of larger watchfires on the gates are sprinkled around the city proper. The huts, shacks, and few great houses cluster together in the light. Niena remembers climbing down the last rung before the eastern window and the full view of the town that the vantage gave. While there were a couple of farms out in the hills, most of the community was tightly packed around a half circle. The old foreign quarters, and the remains of the castle shine onyx like a second night.

Marny was so angry at her for climbing up there. And she can't help dredging up the image of him tossing his hat, cursing at the soldiers, cursing at everything. She smiles, and her laughter begins to swirl with the wind around the tree. "Old goat," she chuckles, and then quickly remembers where she is.

The memory of the town's lights march away. "I wonder if my father gave him as much trouble as I did." Niena bites her lip, tasting blood and the dry, cracked skin. That's one thing she wished he would talk more about.

Mentioning his son Graham was the only thing that ever shut him up.

The way back is difficult, and the rush of energy flees almost as quickly as it arrived. Niena is left with weakening limbs and a growing headache — one last parting gift. She feels cheated somehow, but at least her daydreams don't come true. One hour brings her midway, and the fence of trees she once saw to the west is everywhere now. There are other things though, more birds, and more sounds. The wind isn't so strong here, and it no longer carries away the forest chatter. Another hour, and the last before noon takes her almost to the ground. Below she can see her lyre, and she pauses at the final branch. For a second, Niena swears the carven faces wink at her. But at this she shrugs and leaps down.

"I made it," she says, exhausted. The satisfying crunch of a fern. A brief flash — delicate, but hopeful tickles. "I made it!"

With the sun as the stick, and the town a carrot, she continues on. In her arms, the vine scrollwork of her lyre is sharp against the white. The dark red of a stylised rowan berry bends along the edge of the black lacquer and carven faces, moving together in a mockery of frozen festivity. Niena stops, pushing aside the young limbs of a small beech. A few words, perhaps even a speech, begins to play in her head for this moment. But it is the grumble of her stomach that speaks first.

Chapter 10
Green Eyes

Early afternoon. Blue eyes stare back at Marny. Sunken but bright, worn yet whole. He has seen a lot, the man with those eyes. Yet what is his tale? He must be old; those wrinkles have their stories; faint scars attest to a younger life spent fighting. Dueling. This is someone who might have had some measure of pride to uphold. But who also knew how to laugh, and weep.

Both men stroke their days-old beards, but Marny reaches out and wipes a line of dirt from the glass window. Everywhere grey and black flakes settle; this is not snow. Soot and smoke from the earlier flames drift through the town.

"Not much here either. Only a burned-out shell," he says, walking past his reflection.

"Pot calling the kettle."

Marny sighs quietly and looks over his shoulder. There she is, hovering nearby with another shawl — *wait, where did Deliah get that one?*

"The granny house still had a hope chest that wasn't touched," she says. "What's wrong?"

What's wrong? Where do I start? Three days with no sign of his granddaughter, while every town has been like the last. By now all the destruction flows together, and at this point, Marny is no longer even sure he left Maidenhill. He stares through Deliah.

"Nothing, Mouse," reading between the furrowed lines on her forehead. "Nothing's wrong. I'm just tired."

"You're worried," she says, walking over to tug on his coat. "It's alright; I am worried too." But Marny gently pulls away.

Deliah tilts her head down and then looks up at him. "Do you think she could have already made it to Hornhold?"

"It's a week by horse from here, wherever-"

"Umaut," she interrupts. "It means 'river point' in old Kimbeshi, my mother's father was from here. Remember?"

"Right," with a click of his tongue. "The short answer is no, no I don't think she has. She can't be much further than we, and there's not a lot standing between Maidenhill and Coppercreek."

He becomes quiet, mindful of the forms shambling around the periphery. Not creatures, monsters, or other such fantasies, but people — survivors from the other villages. The reason for his silence appears in the rubble of a watchtower.

"We are moving out!" A man ducks below a knotted beam, briefly disappearing as he crosses the remains of the tower. Marny watches him weave between the other families, his comments and attempts at cheering people up having little effect over the grey of the surroundings.

The man pulls closer. Strands of conversation flitter; the man's boisterous voice throws it all up. With each moment Marny becomes increasingly aware of the small talk worming its way along and decides to throw a foot before it.

"I wasn't aware of any consensus being met," Marny says with a curt nod as the man, a poacher by his own admittance, swings around to meet him. "Last I heard everyone was still arguing about which hole to shit in."

The young man pulls on his hat, revealing stretches of clean skin underneath. "Emyrh's rallying them folks, says he has some new word of a town that hasn't been wrecked yet."

"Mrm," Marny groans. "Where'd he get that little treat?"

"We…I think we found a couple of soldiers."

"The same you've been yapping about before you got to me?"

As Marny's glance drifts, the poacher follows it. "Yeah, maybe. I got a big mouth, don't I?" The lack of gainsay leads him to clear his throat. "Emyrh says the two we found are bakers. But I think, soldiers. Militia maybe…"

"Spreading rumours isn't smart, boy." Marny looks over his right shoulder, but Deliah is already gone. "Sides, what gives you that impression?"

"Look yonder."

The captain struggles to distinguish dirt from drab, the land against the soiled garments. Yet, even with the obstructions, he catches enough—by manner and at-tire—to still his tongue.

"I don't know many bakers who need a hide jerkin like that. I don't see it as that sort of dangerous profes-sion, if you know the bones I'm tossing, that is."

"You've never experienced my wife's cooking," as Marny bends to rest on a barrel.

They share a small laugh. "Wouldn't you like to have a closer gander? Seeing as how you are a captain and all. And a captain might know better than a priest."

"No," quietly. "I don't think I am going to get in-volved."

The man smiles with a nod. "Alright. Well, we figure on clearing out before midday. I'd tell you to travel light, but well? I'm going to go help Widow Cary. Look to

Emyrh if you change your mind, I am sure he will be around them…bakers."

Wood cracks in a nearby fire like a whip as the man makes his way. "Did you listen to that boy?" Marny says, staring after as the poacher climbs up and over some debris and on towards another crop of people. "I know the road that leads to, and I've got enough problems of my own without faffing around with everyone else."

"Will some of the routes take us into the mountains?" Deliah's voice stretches across his shoulder. "Pipes?"

Marny picks up a shawl lying on a nearby fence, one he found in a small house earlier. "I don't know, that sort of depends. But it wouldn't be unwise to take that bit you got there after all. Yes, maybe we can sew them together to make an extra blanket. Or something to line our boots. Your feet are terribly cold at even the best of times."

"You always tell me you love my cold feet."

"Did I say that?" Standing now. "I lied."

She sighs. *Or was that the wind?* Marny's mind is a mess, much like the remains of the village, which takes his attention away from his wife. Sweeping vistas of green, of yellow and red out beyond, settle into a quiet death at the blackened edge of the town. Like his mood, despite the brief levity. With one arm he hefts the shawl onto his shoulder, and then a small pack over.

"We might as well go," he says. But she has already disappeared, and it is the wind that follows him out into the open, past a cluttered street that hugs the tumbledown buildings nearest.

His movement spurs others to join. Together with another family, he skirts into a southward alley, where the smoke and shadow plays tricks on the eyes. Everywhere the skeletons of former businesses and hovels lean over.

In one, the remains of a tavern, a pop of timber frightens a small child, and the girl drops a trinket into the husk of a trough.

I can smell it already. Even through the soot. There's no mistaking what they are walking towards, and he unfurls his handkerchief to cover his face. In this instant, Marny's eyes fall upon that dropped trinket, which is, in fact, a doll. He stares as the shadows swirl around it. Here, for a short while, time holds still as a painting. The eyes are…alive in a word of death. Candles in a tomb. It does not last. A gust of wind stirs up, splinters and dust fall around.

Marny rubs his eyes. Dark lines of clouds streak underneath a late sun. "At the least we can gain some supplies, if Emyrh's information is true," to the air as he daubs his handkerchief with his canteen. Another change in the wind lets him unbury himself from the coat collar.

"And maybe a night's rest," someone adds. Marny casually nods, pushing past a crumbling post as they turn down the street. The action makes him loose the handkerchief from his face, while the sound of water speaks to them.

After a quick corner, he can see the priest and a wide blue band that must be the river. The air is still thick, choked with fear. Yet no disaster can be as depressing as the clergy who see it as their divine duty to inspire. Some do it with loud clothing. Others with wild gestures, and sonorous voices. This fellow, Emyrh, tries his hand at all of it. And while the snippets of questions around Marny keep repeating, he would never feel right sending them off to this man for answers. They pass the priest on his pulpit without a word.

When they turn another corner, the view of the bridge opens up fully. Everywhere Marny looks the meagre possessions of the peasantry lay under trampled arms, or crisp bodies. It is grisly, but no worse than the shapes bobbing like corks, caught in branches, snags, and rocks in the river below. The measly few that join him in this stretch do not make eye contact at all. But despite a vocal pall that has fallen over the travelers, each of their steps echoes. Drum on the wood. The sounds rally up old memories for Marny, a time when he was younger, and the sight of the dead affected him more. Before the beast came down from the Hakaal Mountains, and uprooted everyone's lives like weeds. Before the wars. And Marny was only twenty when they drove it back, back into the new wastes.

"Wastes," he chuckles. Back when he was a boy, the terraced hillsides of the Alamari Valleys were awash in wine and wealth. That was the capital of the Empire. *After the dragon, little more than a nightmare. And*, he remarks to himself, *now a recurring one.*

Wars followed, the Emperor's death made sure of that. This led to other present problems, not of beasts, but men. His tongue clicks the back of his teeth. *Those soldiers. If they are soldiers, where could they have been stationed?* More flakes streak his face, which is already chalky as the ground.

Still more people join him on the other side. Men, women. Children. Some worse off than others, but all silent with a sort of rigid determination. And at the crossroads, there is a man waving people along. Marny stops only twenty feet from the signpost. "Livemoss," he says, looking past. "Is that a town? But that is east. Hornhold is south-by-southwest. Where are they leading us?"

What's changed in the last few hours? Where could Emyrh have gotten his tip off to this 'untouched' town? The answer ties a knot in his stomach, a knot connected by a short bit of string to: *of course, those soldiers*. It is an easy confirmation to make. But then why are they here, and not there?

Crows circle a ring of brush at the water's edge. Marny's thoughts circle too, spinning around these fears. But another problem sinks him: doubt, doubt in himself. It is a deep hole to fill and plagues him at every step. Even now, he can feel his failures walking with him. At the corner, and in the water. Green eyes plead with him. Green eyes judge him.

He jerks to a stop. Between the lap of water and the beating of his own heart he thought he heard something. Marny holds his breath, straining to listen over the river and the plod of boots surrounding him. There! Just below the rustle of leaves.

The bushes quiver and his hands find their way to the hilt of his sword. A rustle. Then nothing. Marny leans forward, ignoring the other refugees as they pass. Moments creep without any change. The wire of the sword's grip presses into his hand. *Shh! Quiet!*

Leaves shudder. Steel rings in the air as he draws his sword. Then returns it with a weary sigh. A river scavenger pokes into the open, and back to the shroud, its furry tail disappearing in a blur. "Chords," Marny says. A few of the other refugees, who had stopped in the middle to watch, turn away. Some even shake their heads.

A woman's voice separates from the crowd. "What were you expecting to see?"

"Mouse," he whispers.

Deliah smiles at him, and in that instant, the words on Marny's lips are lost. Cut away, by two emerald daggers. "You were expecting to see me?" she says with a laugh.

"Yes," he says. "No. I had a thought…a thought that we are being led into a trap."

"Really? By whom?" When he answers 'the soldiers,' she smirks. If her eyes had a bit of cloth tacked to them, they could have cleaned her skull. "Didn't you say you weren't going to get involved? You haven't even met them yet. The word of a *poacher* guides your hand now."

"What are you saying? Are you saying I *should* get involved?"

She shrugs, and Marny stumbles off into whispers. His eyes turn from her, to the road, and to the path before him. The sun emerges from a bank of clouds, and he looses his hand from the hilt of the sword. At times he stumbles, unsure of each foot. And at times the purchase of two steps forward requires the selling of one in retreat. Still, he continues. Eventually, the trail winds up through rock and beech. More than sun and wind accompany him: the press of villagers, of survivors, who, if he was paying attention, look upon him kindly. Expectantly. For a few of them know he was once the captain of the Bluecoats. The others, by now have heard.

So onward by an uncertain way, and with few questions. For somewhere ahead, beyond the sylvan sprawl, spreads the village of Livemoss. Marny tucks his shirt back into his trousers and wonders.

Chapter 11
The Misses and the Missus

A high sun follows the refugees into a low stream. It's the second of two river fords they've made, on a trail that promised to take them to higher ground. It lied. Muddy waters swirl around Marny's pale legs.

"Don't mind him," Deliah says. "He always gets this way before a move."

Over his shoulder, two children play. Splashing, swimming — or as much as they can in two feet of water. But with each splash, they become a little cleaner. "Move?"

Emyrh is the one who answers. Ash cakes the fringe of his hair, making the olive-skinned man look like a powdered eccentric. "We can't stay forever? No, no, no, no. We get the supplies, we trade for. Then we go to Carnuma…Care num — "

"Cairnumastali, just call it Cairn," Marny says. The forest embraces the river on both sides. Even as he watches, others of their party disappear through curtains of green at the crossing.

"You middle-worlders and your words."

And Marny stops to look left. White water hops over submerged rocks just beyond. The winter melt will soon fill this river, and swell the roads. Now is the time to start planting. Now is the time to also be careful, for the mountains of the border country are alive, and spring rains may yet tempt them to move.

He takes a deep breath. The air is warm and heavy, and even if he was not old, Marny could tell that rain approaches. And to this effect, up and in the direction of the wind, a sheet of clouds roil. In a few more hours the sun will retire. It is a good thing they are crossing the river now, he muses. At the opposite shore, water rushes over a sunken log, digging a hole into the silt. If it were any darker no one would have noticed before they fell in.

Together with the wagon, he makes the final crossing, but at the opposite side, they part temporarily. Marny shifts his cloak and boots underneath his arm. The river bottom is muddy, the shore rock strewn, and now pebbles plaster his feet.

A boulder serves to assault his tailbone while he scrapes inches of muck from his boots. Someone behind is humming. He doesn't recognise the man but does the tune. It's an old one, a sea shanty. *Not a one here has seen the sea*, to himself as he shimmies on one foot. But realises that the last time he heard that song was in a Breach Point tavern a few years back. Several of the lines had been cast off, changed. He didn't care too much for that version but still finds himself humming along to it as he moves to catch up with the wagon.

After the river, the land dips even lower, and the state of the road not far behind. With the light retreating, their feet find the ruts before their eyes do. True to his prediction, the rain comes, threatening to turn the holes into puddles, and the puddles into lakes. With each plod and platter the way becomes less manageable. More and more hands gather around their one wagon to steady the horse and save the wheels.

Cloud speaks to cloud, through the thunder and crash of the lightning. Marny's coat finds its way to the cart, to cover their meagre supplies. All the while the rain fights its way through the canopy to get to them. His grey hair is slicked, and the rest of his clothes cling tightly. The smell of wet horse pelts him with each gust.

"Keep her eyes on the road," he orders. "She's young." They do as he says. Deeper into the forest, where a queer feeling strikes Marny. He ignores it, though occasionally it will pop with the lightning, and he thinks of the two men that Emyrh found in Umaut.

With the rain eventually comes the darkness. So too, do the stories, in the few moments of time when the storm slacks. Griff is the main provocateur of these. With him the firebugs become ghosts. Devils. The lights upon that hill? Marauders. And they gleam wildly as they draw close, their short but brilliant red bodies beckon the tired with long, flickering arms. Marny knows though that several of their pack are already hours ahead of them. They too should look to make camp.

"This castle, and…" Emyrh tries to look at the captain purposefully while an elderly couple squeezes between. "Are you sure this is the place to go?" But Marny ignores him.

Ahead on the hill, he can make out a man where a torch in the periphery casts a long shadow. Elsewhere gloom creeps; the sun's rays are as faint as a lantern covered in tattered cloth.

The spread of trees momentarily relents as they near the remains of an old caravan camp. Exposed stone foundations offer respite for tired legs and the opening of the woods for their mood. Still the rain falls while laughter flies with the wind around them. Marny pulls the collar of his coat closer. The smell of burned beech meets the hiss of water and flame.

Now Marny looks at the priest, who has passed the last hour with him in silence. "I don't know if the castle is the best place," he says, tugging at his wet linen tunic. "I don't even know if the castle still stands. But it's where I am going."

Pans, pots, and other odds and ends crash to the ground with a sudden jerk of the wagon. Marny manages to steady the frightened horse, while a young boy scurries between the wheels to collect the dropped supplies. Emyrh meets him at the reins, oblivious to the danger of the struggling beast.

"But what are we to do then?" Emyrh is incredulous, even though this is the second time today the priest has posed this question.

"You want a fresh source of water? Cairn has it. You want strong walls? It has those too, and more." A few choice curse words come to his mind, and then his lips. But the more he does so, the more Marny notices Deliah. Again, she is at his side, her eyes prying at him better than any chisel. "Everyone in these parts knows to head to the Cairn for trouble, but nobody's been up there in years."

"And it's a border castle, but not just any border," the word flies from Marny's lips as he continues, but this time, Emyrh catches the meaning, and they both say, "The wastes."

"Dragon fire was a real concern in those days," Marny adds quietly. And that statement seals the conversation. The rest of the way they spend in silence. But as they slow he notices some of the others are already at work making lean-tos, or staking bed claims. Their action moves Marny to do the same, and he nods a farewell to the priest with the intent of assisting the rest of the handlers with the horse.

But before he does, Emyrh steps in close. "Marny," he says quietly. "You are looking for someone?"

A child somewhere laughs. To his left. No, just ahead. "Mind your—" In the middle of the road, between two families, there is a little girl. Long black locks drip over small shoulders. A mother and father are taking turns tickling her.

"My granddaughter," after the pause. He then looks to the priest. "My aim is the Cairn, you should know. You understand, if we have any more detours, I'll leave you all behind. I don't know these people; I don't owe them anything."

Emyrh's lips pinch in a knowing smile. "But they know you. And they will want to follow you like—how do you middle-worlders say it? Ah!—like the puppy."

"That's their problem," as he helps unhitch the wagon.

"We'll see, my friend." Emyrh's smile doesn't leave his face. Elsewhere the chatter pops and crackles with the new fires. Sizzles with heated words. "Words and scriptures fill the heart but leave the belly empty. They will look to you. It is better that way."

"Emyrh." The horse's whinny cuts off the rest of what Marny is about to say, and a part of him is relieved. He watches as the priest gives him a short nod, and departs. The question about the men, the two soldiers Griff mentioned, can remain buried for now. *Stay out of it,* Marny reminds himself. *You have your own problems.*

The whinnying dwindles as he walks back towards the ruins of the old caravan camp. Right now his problems involve finding dry bedding, and there are few spots left under trees, or amidst the stone foundations. He may have to go hunting in the forest for pine to make a lean-to himself.

"Bleeding chords," remembering what he left in the wagon. Marny turns back, but sees Griff there, coming from the cart with his blue coat draped over his square shoulders. He makes a quick salute in thanks, hoping it may cut the conversation short.

"Found a good spot yet?" the poacher asks cheerfully.

"Those rocks over there look good to me," with a curt motion of his head. "Think I can get some of that horse shit over there to make a real nice pillow." When he sees Griff's flat face pug up in contemplation, he smiles. "I am going to cut some pine saplings if any are there that aren't soaked."

Griff nods. "No need for that, my wife went ahead of us and set down with the other families. Told her to make a space for you." He bows curtly, holding his hat. "Hope I am not too bold. You can bed down with the rest of us. That is, if you don't mind sharing a tree with a few gamesmen."

"I don't know if I can handle the stink, but I'm up to try."

The poacher shoulders shake as he laughs, and he motions towards a lady as thin as the sheen of rain. Marny shifts his weight and takes the bundle from Griff. The captain's mouth opens as if he wants to croak a snide remark, but he holds his tongue. The drive to stir up a fight just isn't there.

A fine mist chases. And the camp is divided, both by the storm, and a small ridge between the ruins and the forest. On this side are most of the older households, those without young kids to slow them, and as such were the first to set camp. Marny looks at this rag-tag group. It is dark, but the mood of the people here is brighter than the morning in Umaut.

"Misses," he says, passing a family of two. "Miss," to a teen barely his granddaughter's age. He must have passed by at least a dozen families today, all in about the same state. He adds two more here, on his way to the tree. Marny stops and nods politely to Griff's wife. She shows him to a spot in the shadow of a live oak where pine needles have been laid, and some straw — and immediately understands that someone must have saved it and shared their bedding with him.

"Thank you," he says to her softly. She returns a smile before wandering back to whatever tasks making his bed took her from and leaves Marny there to think and appreciate the dry place to sleep.

The sky twinkles down, parading before a myriad of moons which glisten in each droplet. But nature cannot ease his mind or body. His old back finds the rocks underneath the bedding, the uneven ground. It has been too long since he has been out on a campaign. There is much he has forgotten. Still, he closes his eyes.

And opens them. He never passed any men like Griff described. Where were they? In the little time he has known Emyrh, he knows it's not like him not to try to introduce every riff-raff that comes along. Unless of course, the priest gets distracted. Marny lets out a deep breath. He always accused his Squirrel of having an overactive imagination, and yet here he is.

"What did you mean by 'move'? We're coming back, aren't we?"

Marny looks to where the voice came from, but there is no one there. *Squirrel*, her name stuck in his throat. "Thought you wanted adventure?"

There is no answer, but he wasn't expecting one. He closes his eyes again.

"Something is wrong isn't it?" Deliah says. "After forty years. This is more than whatever you grumbled at me back in the house."

"Mouse." He bunches the sleeves of his coat to give him a little more cushion and lays his head down again.

"I don't like secrets; you know that," she says. "I may have more wrinkles than when we first met, but my eyes and ears still work fine."

Marny shakes his head on the pillow. "Only you could keep a sense a humour in all of this. Do you remember the Coilwood Campaign? Chords-awful mess, with everyone losing their bleeding minds when the rebels gutted our supply line. Do you remember what you told the captain then?"

"I do. But I wasn't trying to be funny about it."

"He must have weighed only two stone," Marny says through a forced smile. "And you told him to tighten his belt. If the man had done so anymore, he'd have cut himself in half!"

"Love? Quit trying to change the subject."

Marny reaches out to brush his fingers against lips, lips that are not there.

"No lumps in my tea, thank you."

"Where are my men?" finally able push the words out. But there is no mistaking the strain, fear, and doubt that scratches out of his dry throat. "Why have you not asked me about my soldiers, Deliah?"

"They're not real soldiers, sweetie." That wasn't it. "What are you trying to say?"

"I..." he stutters. "It's the Castra Alm problem all over again. Only this time..."

"This time," his eyes open, and slowly find their way back to the sky. "I fear he's more than just hunting. I fear he's seeking a new lair. The beast is on the move."

Chapter 12
One More Time

Two nightingales sing. *One male, one female.* Somewhere nearby a child snores. *No, a lady.* After a time, Marny is able to separate the men from the women, the young birds from the old. And as he lays on his back, the myriad sounds of the forest fowl and human fouler naturally mix into their own rude musical.

He listens intently to the nightingale's song. Even though the little bird's happy tune pelts him like stones thrown by an angry mob, he listens. He continues to do so through the hour, while the evening dips its feet into 'chill.' Until finally, when dusk arrives, he is settled enough to roll over and close his eyes.

The fires are behind me. I must stay focused. This bleeding cold is…bleeding into my bones. The sky, I must stay focused. Where is the damn beast? I can't see—there! Come on, Traveller, it's leaving us behind!

He's struggling, I think, I think he's not going to last. Please, one more time!

Grumbling. Cursing. He shifts the coat underneath his head.

It's broke. His leg is bleeding broken. We must have hit a hole; I don't know how far. Is this hay? Yes, it's hay. The sky is a bleeding mess, and I can't see shit, but I can smell the damn hay. I might be a little more than half way. Maybe near Tucker's farm?

Can't leave Traveller like this.

Marny's face opens into the night; then he turns on his side. The dream steps into these moments of half-sleep. He sees himself, and the sky — always the sky. Out of the divine, the wyrm coils down, and down, trailing ash and fire in a terrible wake upon everything below. He sighs, exhausted, and pops his knuckles before forcing his eyes shut once more.

I must keep moving. I must keep moving. I can see the fields. I wish I couldn't see the fields, but I can see everything now. Chords, it's all light. Damn the light!

Old hands tremble as he wipes the sweat from his forehead. Frantic moments quarantined by each breath flash one by one. The dash to the street where he lives. The eruption of flame and smoke. But the screams, it is the screams that burn.

Marny sits up, no longer interested in sleep. The air is cool, quiet. He however, is hot. Anger fast sweeps away the shakes and hardens his hands around the grip of his sword.

The feeling of helplessness in his dream is replaced by the firm truth of steel. The dragon. The beast, it's still out there; perhaps it waits for another day to come, salivates over yet another town to destroy. Victims to torment. Or maybe it is just a beast. As he is just a man. But there are some things he can fight, some things where 'just a man' is all that is needed. Here, and now. His mind wanders back to his gut feeling about the soldiers Griff spoke of. Marny shoots to his feet and redresses his sword to the side.

"Emyrh," his voice rolls along the ground. "Emyrh!"

People stir when he shouts, but he doesn't recognise any of the groans and curses that answer him. Marny grinds his teeth and rummages through a stack of faggots piled nearby. After a few moments, he pulls a long branch, still green and ply, and makes a torch with a rag as the cloth.

It works like a charm, but those nearby don't find it at all charming. More curses, and some threats come his way as he searches for the priest. Peering inside the lean-tos, around the campfires, and even a tent, before he finds the man at the edge of the company, on a small mound overlooking the others. Emyrh is not asleep, and strings of his chatter unravel the more Marny listens.

"You need but lye—"

He climbs up behind. Shale and gravel break away, but still, the priest doesn't appear to notice. The man remains engrossed in the story. Wild hands, wild curly hair. Whatever it is he is telling, his powerful arm-waving speaks to a climax.

"Can make your own charcoal soap—" just as Marny's hand lands on his shoulder. At this Emyrh snaps around, look of shock spinning into a wide smile.

"Marny!" with arms wide open. "My friend! You are in luck; I was just about to tell these gentlemen how to dye their own linens white! Maybe you'd—"

But he is cut off by Marny's gnarled hand over his lips. "Those men, those soldiers. Where are they now?"

Emyrh's jaw wobbles. "Soldiers? What is this you are talking about? I—"

"The two men." The priest's babbles shorten into a squawk when Marny pulls him up. His own tone is far more fierce. "The bleeding bakers! The ones you found in Umaut."

"They are asleep," he says. "That is to say, I would think so? No?"

"You and you," turning to the priest's company. "Start pulling people up. When you wake someone, have them do the same to someone else. Get everyone in the middle of the road."

"But they are asleep!" the priest protests.

The torch's flame whisks behind Marny as he turns, and the pits of his eyes sit like black coal, slashing back towards the three, waiting to burn. "You will do as I say." The two men don't hesitate.

"By the seven suns, what devil has gotten into you?"

"Seven suns?" Marny says, surveying the camp. "What happened to the Triad, of...There aren't seven suns in the," mumbling something inaudible. "Sky."

"But there are seven days in our calendar." The priest shifts on the grass. His robe of dirty white and red appears pink between the torch and his own fire. "Seven days. Seven suns. For each day should be bright to us!"

"Enough with the poetry. I want to see these two bakers of yours. The poacher, that lad Griff, seems to think they are soldiers. I want to have a look at them."

"But why? We are all brothers in arms under the—"

Marny leads the priest down. "Save it for later. These men, this supposed untouched village. It just stinks to me. Oh, I could be wrong, and then you can make me your fool." He looses his hold on Emyrh to direct another man that one of the two just woke. "But everything is equal to the maggots."

"And when you find the men? What will you do? What are you so worried. Are you yourself not militia?"

"How long have you lived here? Lad, there wouldn't be militia up in these parts. You might have a constable, but not two." *We've traveled east, west, then southeast along the main road. The south shires are a long ways from these lands, and there's still the blasted wastes between.* "Who are they going to protect people from, cows? Ugly farm girls?"

He waves the torch, using it like an extension of his arm. As he continues talking more and more refugees gather nearby, some becoming surly. "This land had been pacified before there was even an empire." The two farmers that accompanied the priest return.

"But people, they move? Maybe they were going to your Kimbesh."

"And they just happened to have armour lying around," Marny says. "Stick to your sermons, let me deal with reality. Now, I want you to point them out."

Weary faces. Angry faces. Hopeless faces. Emyrh leads them through the gallery.

"Why couldn't this have waited until morning?" he says, receiving the torch from Marny. The priest has a method, which the old captain silently appreciates. A tap on the right shoulder dismisses someone, a tap on the left sends them to a line to be looked at again.

"There's no morning for us," Marny says, as an elderly man is checked to the left. That one he's already mentally dismissed himself, however.

Emyrh holds his thumb up to a small child and presses it against her temple. A small sign, an old blessing that everyone knows. "You worry too much. What sort would come for us? What do we have that they might want?"

"You have food," he says. Twenty-three, that's the number of people he's counted so far. "You have women, and I have steel."

"You are a very sour old man," Emyrh says, looking back at the captain with a raised eyebrow. "Do you see death in every corner?"

"Only when I want to live."

Seventy-four. Forty women, even. Twenty-three men, the rest are children. Of those men, Marny has dismissed every single one of them. If any of these are the rumoured soldiers, well, he figures he may need to invest in a new hat and learn to juggle.

"Might there be more, beyond this camp?"

"I don't understand," Emyrh says as he shakes his head. He swims through the line of people again, bringing the torch to their faces, left to right. "No. No my friend, they are not here. But seven knows I am sure they came with us this far. Maybe they are out far in the woods?"

Marny sucks his teeth. "They are either shy then, or that's one hell of a piss." He takes the torch from Emyrh, and yells over the short man's head. "Where's that poacher, Griff?"

A tall man separates from the crowd. Still dirty. Still carrying half the world in his long beard. "I'm here."

"You are about to become a popular man, Griff," patting the poacher on the shoulder. "Do you still have a bow?"

"Yes, I...yes I do," he says groggily. "What's this all about?"

"I'm going to need someone who can kill a deer, and not get caught by the constable for doing it," Marny answers, then uses the torch in his left hand to address the gathering. "If you can hunt, I may need you."

A few answering cries pipe out from the crowd. But a more general murmur of disquiet builds. Several calls for some sort of explanation multiply and grow in clamour. Marny asks for quiet, using the torch again as a baton to symbolically beat down the noise.

"What's this? What's this?" someone yells after the initial ruckus.

"We've apparently lost two men. Two soldiers that wandered into our camp this morning. You do not need to be here when those men come back. Because, dead to rights, they won't be coming alone. And they won't be interested in having a sing-along."

Most folks understand; several lived through the times immediately after the fall of the Empire, when raids and general banditry were as common as spring storms. Again murmurs and questions arise, but this time they are more frightened than angry. Should they run into the forest? Should they fight?

"Leave everything behind," Marny says, and the suggestion is immediately unpopular. "Leave it all! There's no time for arguing here. Leave it, and make your way quietly into the forest. Stay together, stay quiet!"

"No, no, no, my friend," Emyrh pleads quietly, grabbing hold of the captain's arm. "How will the people eat? how can we ask them to lose everything again?"

To Emyrh: "Goal one is to keep them breathing." Mothers begin picking up their children. Fathers, brothers, daughters all hesitate. A few of the more seasoned push them along and keep people from lingering around their belongings. "I know what you are thinking. Robbers? Raiders? The same. Deserters? Bandits? More of the same. Men? Men everywhere are the same. Bandits, deserters, they don't want a fight. They will be happy enough to paw through the baggage. At least for now."

"What are you going to do?"

He chews on his bottom lip. "I'm going to kill them all." And before Emyrh can protest, he looks to the hunters and poachers who have come to meet him. There are six in total, including himself. "Anyone here by chance seen where our bakers were last? Griff?"

A few seconds of quiet brew as man looks to man, then one of them, a balding gentleman near Marny's age, speaks up. "I think I know. Two men, one wearing a kepi, the other hide. Had two long dirks between them, and if my eyes right, one had on his right leg a billet with the white rose of Arlin."

There are nods of approval and some quiet laughter from the others. Marny's eyes narrow as he stares at the wizened grandpa, but he seems more than that. An old soldier is before him, an old scout. "Where were they last?"

"Yonder," he says, nodding to the northeast. "I thought they might be going for the nature walk about, oh, an hour or so ago. But they'd not come back, though it fled my mind since. I try not to think about things. Things like that bring trouble."

Griff pulls Marny aside. "The white flower? What do you expect us to do? We can't fight an army."

"And you won't have to," loud enough for all to hear. "Arlin men, this far north? I would wager they are deserters. Opportunistic enough to waylay stragglers, but not to attack townsfolk. Until now. We are going to try and find their camp."

"And then what?"

"Kill those we find, better than they kill us? What do you want, a speech?" Marny points to the bows, and knives the men carry. "We'll get their stragglers at the camp, and lay in wait for the rest. Or we'll get them along the way."

A shout from one of the hunters snatches their attention. "Boots!" he yells, having already separated from the small band. "Hobnailed boots! Only one track though."

Someone yells back, "What are you on about?" but Marny already knows. Good boots. Hobnailed boots, might be the men they are looking for; few farmers here have need of such an addition. As one they move towards the discovery.

"Hobnailed, that's certain," one says.

"Got a broken heel," another.

Griff finds the second set, but those are not boots, just common shoes. "Could be them," he says. "They do head off into the woods like the old man said." He glances at Marny, then back towards the prints. "The other old man. But it could also be someone else from camp. It's not like we've done a counting of every shoe 'tween man and beast."

"It's them," Marny says, pointing. "Look how the weight is all at the heel. That's a soldier."

"If you are sure, then these are more than an hour old," the poacher adds. "More the like of two, or three."

A couple of the men shake their heads and fidget. Marny straightens. "They're pointing northeast. Livemoss is still southeast of here. We'll find their camp that way, I suspect. Means they aren't stupid enough to sit in town." He scratches his neck. "And Livemoss might need to change the first half of its name."

"We're going to run right into their return party if we follow these."

Marny rubs his chin. "Not if we are upwind. Once we know their direction for certain, we can stay hid and quiet when they pass."

"Can you be quiet, old timer?" Griff gestures towards Marny's own boots and sword. "With those, and that."

He shrugs and looks around. After a few moments of backtracking, Marny returns with a rag from one of the beds to wrap up his sword. "Don't worry about the boots. Not my first knifing."

Quiet rules, as they make their way into the forest. And up above? A yellow moon. Each knows what that portends: storms for the farmer, evil times for all. The mood is thin as the light.

Chapter 13
Fair Way Come Again

Wind rattles a broken fence, rakes Niena's dress. A southern breeze, carrying warm air and hints of smoke.

One of her legs brushes a fern. Morning fell behind the wind earlier and aged to noon before catching. Now sunlight too has found her, where a ruined wall anchors the shadow of leaves to its blank slate. "Oh." She gasps. Niena wonders at the scratches that criss-cross her arms, legs. Over these lay the shreds of a dress.

Another shout escapes from deeper in the ruined town. She looks left, right. Old wood and stone hide under years' worth of growth and neglect.

A cut's a cut? Repeating a snag of the conversation. Two men at least, but where? She flattens herself against the wall and listens.

But as the wind turns the voices of the men are lost. Niena shields her eyes. Light caught by green maple leaves slips through. Slip. Slip. Onto a broken roof, and along the gutters. Around the cracked plaster, down the wall. Slipping. Slipping. All the way to her face. *Maybe I can get closer.*

There is paved stone here; it peeks out from between patches of rubble and moss. She squints. Another alley too, just ahead and after the corner. Yet the way forward is harder for Niena than the forest; stones slick with dew and crumbled walls are obstacles greater than bough and thicket. She carefully nudges a pile of debris with her big toe.

"What do you think we can get out of 'em?"

A soft thud as her back hits the wall. *What do you think we can get out of them?* she repeats. *They're right here.* She wonders if she is about to be discovered. Her heart races, she freezes.

They're killers, as the chatter unfolds. Definitely two men, but they've mentioned more. Niena inches her head around the corner. Sneaking around ruins, spying on men—no, bandits? This isn't exactly the sort of adventure she was hoping for.

The alley is empty and must have acted as a funnel for the noise. Her hands tremble against the wall with relief. Splintered voices, chopped strings of prattle, *and I'm in the middle,* as she pushes off. Leaves crunch underfoot. *Forget this, I need to find the road.*

And she quickly shifts right, away from the wall, into the shade of a gnarled old tree. Its thick roots crack the street and eat at buildings on either side of the alley, and its bark feels thin as she steps into the foothold made between the wall and the tree itself. Niena climbs up and-

The lyre! She wants to yell "chords" but the strings of the instrument beat her, as three notes ripple where it slides against her leg. And now? She flies along the street. Rubble and debris scatter her attention but don't slow her. It is impulse, not reason, that drives her finally to stop, and climb through the arch of a collapsed house to hide.

Mortar crumbles at the intrusion. Niena peers into the dark, immediately noticing the broken back wall, and the clearing she can see through the mesh of saplings and bush. Panic catches up with her rushed breath. She crouches and retreats out of view of the larger gaps in the wood.

Minutes pass, and no one comes looking for her. She settles in, listening for the men's conversation, but hears only faint traces. Other sounds though, closer and crisper, make her pause. Niena holds her breath and kneels. Someone or something is moving in the clearing behind.

Holes in the thicket fill up as the light is slowly blocked. Niena scoots closer. Her every move crinkles with the sound of debris, leaves, broken masonry. Between her toes something wiggles. Momentarily distracted, she watches the strange bug. A bulbous head gives way to a long slender body bristling with legs, and as it scurries away, she bites her lip. *I wond-*

Light invades as the figure departs. She covers her mouth. The sound from before, which she now knows to be water sloshing in a bucket, disappears. Niena leans with her arms against the wall. A peek through the holes offers little: glances at a fire, flashes of pots, kettles. A knapsack.

I've stumbled into their camp, as a sparrow trills from the bush. *Chords*, her lips spell. Fear pushes her further into the corner, while the bird beckons her out, singing from somewhere midst twig and leaf. In a cage.

Where Niena sinks, the sparrow's song flies. It flitters and breaks as she tilts the lyre on her knees. The pale faces of the instrument return her stare and speak to the moment. Their eyes, dark. The dual mix of smile and frown, exaggerated. They are visages that meander between jovial and sadness.

Unlucky girl, the lips of the painted faces mime, and Niena stares wide-eyed as they do so again and again. Then their whispers follow. *Unlucky girl. Unlucky girl. Unlucky girl. Unlucky girl. Unlucky girl.*

She recoils, and a battle plays out on that floor between shock and fear. It is terror that wins, preventing her from tossing the lyre. All manner of thoughts circle, but are shot down as the whisperer says her name.

Niena. It is the same voice that masqueraded as her own thought earlier. *Niena.* But now, with each utterance of her name, it changes just a little. *Niena.* Until it is unmistakably that of the creature from her dreams.

"Oberon," she taps the cadence of his name on her lips.

Did you think I was gone? Lost? His thoughts play over her own like a trumpet in a library. *What is lost is found by those who seek. Stay awhile. Buried answers long to live!*

No, not him! This madness isn't the answer. She just needs to backtrack, return to the forest, and get out of here. But Oberon quickly snuffs out these thoughts.

Run? Where will you go? Right into the arms of one of the men here? You are not quiet. You are not a fighter, and they heard you, they heard you before, but have not found you. How long will an unlucky child like yourself last? You have only the one advantage.

Niena cradles the lyre, then opens her mouth to answer. *Not me.* Oberon says. *But you. Your magic; the one true thing that sets you apart from these cobswagglers. It's the story of your life and the writing on your tombstone. Tell me, child, what do you know of the three chords?*

She has had lessons. This lyre isn't just a family heirloom, she can — *Not your rude yawps, the melody of being! Everyone and everything have their own piece of a song, a sheet that is theirs, and theirs alone. Know the harmony of the forest and the madness of the seas and you will be a power the world of men can't reckon.* Oberon's timbre then changes. Calms. *But for now you only need safety, and I know just the song. Do you remember?*

No.

Back a day ago?

No.

You don't remember Fairhome?

A sigh sinks into her stomach. Where they were before? That insipid little piece of madness.

The Fairhome lies conveniently behind the curtain. There are many things you might accomplish there. It is a safe place. And harmless.

Harmless? She remembers something entirely different. The strange lights, sounds, and the spiders. She would have to be crazy to want to go back there. And why should she listen to him, he, the one that put her in this position in the first place?

Do you have any idea what those men will do to you when they find you? His answer makes Niena's skin crawl. *A salve can heal a cut. A splint, right a broken leg. But some wounds...There are harms that will leave a person's soul to bleed, but linger. Forevermore in pain.*

"I can handle myself," she growls, confidence budding. The tread of boots in the clearing stops. "I don't need you, this is all your fault!" And she closes her eyes.

Grey clouds break in the sky, slowly pushing against mountains of blue in the distance. But those are only her imagination, as she tries to drown Oberon out. Now, the figure of the fairy is diminished. And Niena starts to inhabit an escape plan coalescing in her head.

I can see myself running to the entrance and grabbing the arch. My fingers slide into the grooves of the mortar, but I use the leverage to pull myself up over the wreckage of the door, and into the street. The face of a man careens around my right, and the rest of him skids along the gravel and onto the ground. He cries out, which makes me hesitate just long enough to see his friend come around and nearly do the same thing. With the thud of the man's shoulder hitting the wall, I spin, and run.

I follow a stream I found earlier. Weeds wave as I pass. Saplings and briar shake their fists. And the reeds of the bank whistle until I plunge into the mud-marked waters of a creek.

Stop! the fairy's voice thunders and rips her away from behind the eyes of her dream self. She watches now, over her own shoulder. A soft splash echoes briefly in the back. Then it wanders. Behind, to the side. Beyond, and behind, repeating again and again until the image of Niena spins around, and comes face to face with… "You," she says, just as the eyes of the fey disappear into a rustle of leaves.

Niena stands, shakes her head, and the tattered banner of her daydream is lost to the wind. The leaves of the bush buck and sway in a dance, almost, tiptoeing in and out of reality.

What you are doing there is dangerous, he says. *It always has been for one such as yourself. You can't just wander aimlessly into dreams anymore. Not without training.*

Drizzle begins to fall into the open roof. "And you," she whispers. "You are a fairy. Why should I believe anything you say?"

Because the man from the clearing is coming to nab you. And you've run out of time, and options.

The last few moments of their conversation bring reality home. Panicked, Niena lunges for the door.

Do not worry, I am with you. His comment more menacing than comforting. *You need not fear them, or Fairhome any, or no more than you might fear yourself. We are only going to step through for a moment, and for this moment…listen. Listen to my tune. Feel it, know it, and sing it.*

Memories can be a strange thing. The cadence of the music, the pulse of the urgent beat as it flows and froths inside her, triggers a pint or two of them. Of times sitting in a bar with her grandfather, watching as the mistress of the tavern poured his drink. How it bubbled and foamed. With each droplet. At every shake of his hand. That glass could only hold so much beer before it would spill over. Every container has its limits.

Air breaks, still winds snap. Not with a thunderclap, or the crash of a dam. The moment the magic spills over is quiet, a scream choked with rags. Indeed, if the bandits in the ruins could hear, they would think more of a mouse in a field than the awakening of a dragon.

"Oh chords." Niena shudders. The sensation flows down her arms, legs. Into her hands, and circles the balls of her feet. She grabs the lyre and slides the back of her hand down a solitary string. Phantasmal fingers overlay her own, setting fire to nerves with the feeling of something near, but far.

And the skies flow grey... "As the sea, and the night till morn." Their voices merge into one song. Niena dips forward and then stands. Black locks dangle over exposed shoulders. "Light carries the days, like leaves lost in the wind."

A barrage of dust batters the walls of the room, pumping out and away from Niena with the rhythm of the lyre. "Fair way, come again."

A silence that chokes lurks around, but for her, and the music. The air in the alley becomes cold and thick as muddy water. And the bubbling feeling, the sensation of being the glass, continues, only now there is spillage. Spillage that might drown her.

Blue eyes flutter open, expecting to find sense, reason. "And the waves crash, against shores, heaven bred," she sings as reality bends.

Shh! Oberon warns. The leaves on the brush wall quiver and vibrate. Out of this reality, and into the beyond. As Niena completes the verse, the last roars of a distant Nearearth fade into the fair: Fairhome.

"Fair way, come again," she gasps.

Chapter 14
Lurking Near the Surface

Lichen crumbles in Calem's hand and his gaze climbs to the sky. "That's not possible."

This land's magic is strange, yet even so... The evening prior his spell caught a chance trace of Niena. He thought then this escapade was almost over. Miles have been traversed towards that end. Enthusiasm spent. Strength, too. Calem clenches his fist. *How can there still be so much distance between us?*

"I fear—" A well-timed nudge at the elbow from the cat spills the rest of the lichen from his hand. He exhales. "I am sorry, my friend, we can't rest yet."

Calem strokes it, finding stronger muscles and healthier fur than the day before. He smiles after another pulse of magic elicits a sneeze from the tabby.

"Let's go."

Mountainous terrain descends into craggy forests and the sun welcomes him behind blue-green needles, waving in a morning breeze. Orange fur flashes on the periphery. Calem looks on. The lie of the land is removed from his sight. Only trees, and green-hazed sunshine beyond the tops. Yet this doesn't bother him; retreating from the open spaces actually feels more natural. Safer.

Nearby, he can hear the trickle of water, and on cue his throat parches. A few minutes of searching reveals a small spring, clean enough to fill a canteen, but dirty enough to make washing his face pointless. He does so anyway.

"She couldn't have run all of this way." Calem wipes grit from his lips and entertains the idea of resting, but there is an unspoken meaning to his words that hangs, and even urges him to continue. Instead of a pause, his pace quickens, and quickly another mile parts ways and deposits him into the low country, while above the canopy thins, near, the trunks of the trees slim, and then all at once he stumbles into a small open field. There are no buildings close, but plenty of felled timber without cut marks.

Heavy storms, he thinks, to keep the silence unbroken. This field lies even lower, between the crests of two small inclines. Calem, because he is either too tired, or because he misjudged the conditions, steps on, and in, mud. It clings to the soles of his shoes. Threatens to take them. He spends twice as long passing through than he would have taken to circumvent it. Every foot of progress seems to require two curses in payment.

How many days have passed since I rescued Niena from the Drel'nu? The count takes all of his fingers. *How many days before she starts to change?*

These thoughts have been lurking near the surface since the evening before, but now his frustration acts like cheese dangled above the noses of frightened mice. One by one, they poke out, sniff the air, and scurry into the light.

Didn't it take a long time for the Drel'nu to get her? Months? No, years I think. Yes, I distinctly remember there were years between. But she said they found her right before she changed. Might have only frozen her at that moment.

"Oberon would know the truth." But under his breath he asks: "Would he care?"

A low branch frees him from the mire, and a clutch of beeches lean close. The smell of wet leaves and grass meets him on the verge. He pulls himself over another hill and recognises the young forest for what it is. Calem looks past the slender lines and sees the touch of civilisation in the change.

His fingers dig into a sapling's bark. "He cares, and he knows." Everywhere he looks the branches of the beeches dip in answer as if to whisper 'betrayal.'

"If he thinks he can get the better of me, he will be sorely mistaken."

Chapter 15
Wind Between the Stones

At night, there are many creatures that stir in Fairhome. At night, they often cannot be seen or heard, unless they do not belong to the forest. Niena, it is always night in the Fairhome. But this is no reason to fear.

She pulls the lyre close to her body as the hum of Oberon's words leaves her. "But that's me, I don't belong here!"

Don't be so sure. That is a special instrument you have, Wyrmspun. Your father never had the talent to use it, but you? The Fairhome will listen to you.

Hush falls as a cloud passes before the moon. Niena climbs over what she thinks might be ivy and crouches. Noises in the background put her on edge, and her eyes bounce between the sky and the forest ground.

Notice how different the forest is this time? You are in control, not me. The power has always been a part of you. Ever since the beginning, and the ending.

Her hands set upon something smooth. Immediately she begins to imagine crumbled pillars and fallen statues. But on further exploration, the rock proves to be just a rock.

Dreams, desires and nightmares, they all have their play.

The smell of decayed leaves and dank moss hits her as she climbs up and over a boulder to find a dull expanse of craggy rocks and stubborn shrubbery. She can somehow imagine this being the leading shore of a canyon's river, where just over the next set of stones the two would meet. On cue, the sound of water reaches her.

The human, the wolf, and the wolf with the rabbit. Time hunts them all, but do they all fear time? The sound of Niena's clothing ripping on a branch is followed by the fairy's smug laughter. *No, only the human fears that. Humankind worries over all sorts of harmless things. Be better than that.*

Darkness pushes out the dreams of castles, forests, and adventures that normally fill Niena's imagination. They have been fading since her entrance here, but now they are finally gone, replaced by emptiness, and the feeling of being watched. Yet there is hope of a reprieve: nearby, pockets of green and grey stand out. A hiding place, just what she was looking for.

Grass rustles to the left. *Don't waste your time with that,* even as she moves that way. *Instead, think of some place familiar. With the lyre, we can use your imagination to take us anywhere. But beware, do not think of home.*

A light flashes on the right. Niena gets on her knees and crawls towards a gap beneath a boulder. The space is wide and almost as tall as her. She looks up at the great tree that crowns the mass, whose roots birthed the crack, before stepping in. "Why shouldn't I think of my home?"

A lot has happened since you left. Or did you think I stole you away to keep you safe only from some future peril? There is a *tap*, or slight rap, on the stone above. *And it seems we aren't safe here, from you! Quickly, we have bickered too much. Think! Before the threads of the magic unwind!*

The sound skitters. "Alright, I don't—"

No, Oberon's voice booms. *Don't bring death into Fairhome!*

"I can't help it! I always think of my dad when it gets dark like this." A line, like a stick, whose black, segmented length makes the night look pale, sets down just in front of the opening. Niena's breath catches in the back of her throat. She can't scream.

Another leg joins the first, and the air struggles against Niena for each breath. Pebbles scrape and roll against her legs as she retreats deeper. Her only light now comes from a split in the rock above.

Think, child! What about your books? There must be some place you can picture.

Niena bites her lip. "There…There is actually, but it isn't from my books."

It doesn't matter now. Hold onto it, Niena, and sing. Try to fit the rhythm of the song that brought us here.

The legs bend. *Tap, tap, tap.* Three at once, as the rest of the creature lands on the floor just beyond her feet.

"No!" She shakes her head vigorously. Niena, deep in that little hole, finds her fingers drifting to the strings. Terror strains into words, and the words pull out the terror.

"The hills hide our hearts," she feels the chords thrum. "Where the roof, and the sky are one."

And Niena stands, forcing the song in a hardened timbre. The words come to her naturally, from a wellspring deep inside. "Stone crowns earthen brows, where pilgrims pass into the waste.

"Let day come again."

Good, feel the music child! You must believe!

"Let day come again." Her hand moves away from the lyre. The strings become silent, the last of their music disappears with the forest. The fairy's commands shrivel away too, and the seconds slip into moments. Around her the world changes.

Lilacs. The first thing she sees, the first thing she smells, are the lilacs. They wave against a violent wind, stand defiant in a broken trail, and proudly perch on grass-covered mounds here, there. Upon rock-strewn tops.

"I don't believe it," she whispers. She shuffles the lyre under arm, and her fingers reach out. Touching the grass, the dirt, and the aforementioned flowers. But their purple faces are the only colour she sees, the rest, the vast expanse of fields and mounds, is visible through a grey veil–like a room lit by a candle behind a bedsheet.

"It's…" her stomach twisting. "I'm here. After all this time."

That was very close. I worried for a moment that you'd remain in your creation, and be lost. Next time we will work on control.

She blinks once, twice, and rubs her eyes. It takes several minutes, but the light returns from its hiding spot. Gleaming, blinding, and beautiful. Colours follow soon after, and the last pieces of Fairhome peel away. There is calm. There is peace, and the untainted spread of a countryside cupped by mountains, green and gold re-emerges. Those mounds dot every corner of her sight straight ahead until they don't—ending in a blast of red sandstone, and the castle mounted upon the apex. A beacon on a blue horizon.

There is only one tree and she is under it. Leaves shake, and the light is caught with the movement. Their shadows set the ground on fire. Niena takes a deep breath and looks out over the vale. Those mountains squeeze the castle as if it were the meat in a sandwich. This is the Sallow March, the gateway between the north, the south, the east, and the lands that once made up the capital of the Empire, now are only a wasteland.

"So you chose a cemetery," Oberon says, appearing next to her upon the grassy mound. "I am not surprised. Are you always so morbid?"

The impromptu appearance of the old fey doesn't faze her. "You're here? I thought...I assumed you couldn't do that outside of..." She takes a deep breath and twists away from him. "There's nothing morbid about this place. Not like your home."

He paces. "I think it is best we talk, face to face," Oberon says with a bow. "Mano e mano. Just you and me. No more twitting about in that cobweb-breeding ground you call a mind. No more empty cupboards, and I don't even have to clean the outhouse now!"

"Chords..."

Oberon waves his arms manically. "Hurray!"

Before he can say anything else, Niena squelches the fairy with one raised finger. "I don't understand what you are trying to do. One minute you are all on about fear, dread, and things hunting *me*. The next, you act like a fool."

The fairy's glasses slide down his nose, revealing two crossed eyes. Niena hides her smile. "Tell me, girl, what are you feeling at this very moment?"

"Irritated, bored," she says. And Oberon presses even closer to her, forcing Niena to either back away, or stand her ground. She does the latter. "*Angry.*"

His finger pokes her on the nose. "You were smiling. Now tell me, when you look out over this graveyard. What do you feel?"

"Hopeful," quietly.

"Your lies may fool yourself, but not me. I sense emptiness, fear, and hurt. But look at the banners on that castle," he says with a sad smile. A quick rain earlier has freshened the morning air. The breeze is sweet, and free of pollen—as if servants opened the shutters of this world to let out the dust from the rooms. "Look at them flutter! There's nothing sad about this view."

"It is beautiful." And she gazes back out over the land. "Here is a hall, whose splendour and wealth dances under waning light. But music will never play here. We call it Cairnumastali. Or 'the kingdom's mound'."

"Quoting your father?" Oberon's nose twitches.

She rounds on him. "Stay out of my head!"

"If you are to know the three chords," he says. Niena's eyes look past him as he places his hand upon her shoulder. "You must bury this, or it will you."

Her gaze flies past the mounds, to the red gash of a pillar the castle sits on. Flags there flail white upon white, except at the tips: the bloodstained banner. These edges — tattered now after years of neglect — cut the sky in a long line on the battlements, tower to tower. Like a scar from ear to ear.

"I just want." She looks at Oberon, and whatever she was about to say breaks apart with a sigh. With a shake of her head, she walks past him, and sets down against a large rock, not realising it is the top of an ancient cairn. "I don't know what I want, alright? But it isn't this."

"Then I suggest first finding out what you need. Or what you don't need. But do so carefully, here." Niena's eyes flash as she looks at the fairy, and he coughs and runs his fingers into his white beard. "The easiest way to get rid of me is to take care of yourself."

"I'll have to remember that," she says. "Coming here is the last thing I needed."

"Then why are we here, Niena?"

Her eyes absently slip up and to her right. "There's a town on the opposite side. I believe I can get on a caravan to Taledric's there. Or back home."

"That town…That is where you incur the wyrm's curse. The only thing I should have done was to keep you away from it. And I failed. You mustn't enter Shenan." The fairy's shoulders slump. "My attention is divided, I must watch all, to keep you safe, and I…am not what I was. Whatever it is you need, you must find it elsewhere."

"I didn't ask you for that." Niena turns away. "And I can take care of myself. I'll be careful."

Afternoon is here, and Niena savours the sweet smell of the grass. And the horizon: blue, deep and haunting. Waves of sky break against the red rock as she watches, while below spread a handful of cairns. Yes, it is a grave-yard, she admits with a shrug. But between the cracks and the monuments to the fallen, the fields are alive, welcoming them with a chorus of birds, cicadas, and the sound of the wind spinning between worn stones. For a moment her fears are far away, still stuck in Fairhome.

"I want to keep moving, get some place where I can make sense of all of this." Almost unconsciously her hands snake between the cracks of the shattered cap-stone. Her pale face is graven, frozen like the stone she leans against. But her bright eyes glint in the reflection of the fairy's own as he stares into her, and she is be-trayed.

"Your father is buried here, isn't he?"

Cold. Warm. Cold again. Her fingers glide over bro-ken stone. She gestures with her head to a small pile of rocks, basking in the sun, not but a stone's throw away. Rough hands brush back the tangled weave of Niena's hair. Her own. She trembles. "What do you want me to say?"

"Nothing." Oberon's face is kind. Gentle. He smiles, sunlight wrapping itself around his profile. And as she looks at him, a breeze picks up. Under his wide-brimmed hat, silver hair flitters. Then fades. Niena squints. So too does the black rim of the hat distress into grey. And his vest? It is pink now, the sunlight not only frames him, but peers right through.

"You have time now." His voice drifting, slipping away with the breeze. "And no excuses not to visit. Just heed my warning, for both our sakes."

One quick breath and he is gone. Niena, now alone on the hill, looks out over the waves of grass, the islands of stone, and the hearts of men and women sunken there. She fidgets, knowing that the fairy is right, and in a few hours lines of red and purple clouds will whittle away at the afternoon. It is still early, but sooner than she would like, it will be evening. Niena sighs and walks down the side of her little hill, as if everything from the past few days has landed on her shoulders at once.

"I should have visited." Her mother's plans to return every summer were laid to rest the following year, in Maidenhill. Now the city of Shenan, in the shade of the castle, is a strange place. And his gravesite is overgrown. Still, they could have come, she could have pestered Marny. But he, for his own reasons, never wanted to go, and she never fought it.

Rocks tumble down with the weeds and dirt as she makes her way to his cairn. The long grass parts left with the wind, and right, with effort. And there it is, one lonely little stack of rocks at the top, almost overshadowed by the flowers that ring it. Peaceful and quiet, much different from the man that lies beneath. Niena crushes back some of the grass encroaching on the grave. Many of the rocks have fallen in the ten years since.

Her face is pale. "You've let yourself go."

Lilacs shake in the wind. She looks out past the other cairns that guard the way to Cairnumastali and wonders: why do her thoughts keep coming back to him lately?

"Marny says I'm just chasing ghosts." Ghosts; the word tastes bitter in her mouth. "That I'm trying to live your dreams." Niena toes a small rock. It might have been part of the larger stack, once. But it lies now on its flat head, dwarfed by the weeds and separated from the rest. She picks it up.

"Maybe he's right," so quietly, the wind takes it. "Maybe I don't know who you are, and I'm sentimental and silly. But I wish he were too. I wish he were more like you."

He is a stern man, her grandfather. Cold sometimes. It always seems he only has smiles for her grandmother. And those slip into the cracks of his wrinkles, where they become like stone. Because Marny to her is a statue. A statue of discipline, with the occasional rude word thrown in.

"He's an arsehole," she laughs, then chokes. "He says you were one too."

Niena tosses the rock on top of the pile. She winces. "You did leave us. Maybe he's right."

And the wind whips between the stones. Throwing her hair back to a raven flag, testing the strength of all the flowers on that hill. Niena bends. Without another word, she leaves her father's grave.

Dirt crumbles underfoot, and the sun meets her on the southwestern slope. The mound is steeper here, having been washed away not long after completion. Her family wasn't rich, and the construction of the barrow was left mostly to them. Quick rains and summer floods took away most of the topsoil. Niena stumbles near the bottom and lands on her hands and knees.

Anger swells within her, but not from the sting of the scrapes. "What do I want?" She flexes her hands and stands. "What the chords do *I* want?"

Niena runs. Where? Towards the castle, towards the town. Grass reaches out and marks the remains of her hem. She leaps over a rotten log, over clumps of dirt and debris from her father's grave. Past the shadow of the mound, and into the field. Faster. Her breath peppers the air. Faster. Until every exhale feels like she is trying to cough up a stone.

Flowers, grass, trees, graves. They live on the periphery of her sight and pass with cursory attention. She struggles, stumbles. Nearly a day of no food and little water catches up, no matter how hard she tries to outrun it. In the end, it only takes a few hundred yards for her to fall again on bruised knees. Coughing, spitting. The castle still stands in the distance. Proud, aloof.

Niena gets up again and adjusts what's left of her dress. Her shoulders are burnt, or 'sun-kissed' as her grandmother might say. She looks down at the black harp, between the smile and the frown of the painted faces. And then back to the horizon. What she wants, and needs, may be found there: a future of her own choosing.

Chapter 16
To Adventure!

The city of Shenan is known as 'the Emperor's Signet'. A peculiar name, for it is not now, or has ever been, the capital. But stories live here, and stories die here. Its location has always been important, and the city is a trade hub even to this day. Merchants from the south, east and north pass through in a constant stream—but their money, mostly, remains.

"Oberon? What happened here?"

A tide washes towards Winter's Gate, not of water, but of people. Niena retreats further into a corner behind the main postern. The smell of stale urine sprinkles the mass of bodies. Young men, women, old men. Tattered clothes, blackened and forlorn faces. Some are clutching valuables, precious things, but not a ware meant to sell between.

Where are these people coming from? But Niena is left to puzzle this question alone too. Her fingers grope blindly for her secret way into the city while she watches the throng.

She shortly finds it and squeezes into a gap in the wall. It is tight, but with care, she manages to fit both her and the lyre into a passage that childhood recollections whisper should be much larger. Though memory can be fickle, at least it is loyal. After only a few feet the light scampers off, leaving only fuzzy remembrances and the chill of the stone to guide her.

Behind there is darkness. Forward, mostly darkness. Niena's breath rebounds off the wall, and the mist of it sprays her face as she squints. There's an opening ahead! She doubles her effort. The thin ribbon of light lengthens into a bar, stretching with hints of a street in its fabric, rumours of a corner. And as the yellow band lightens, so too does her smile. Now she can see buildings and details. The light carries with it the famed hue of the brickwork that dominates construction here. Niena chuckles dryly. This is the real reason for the city's name; it has nothing to do with an ancient battle or the myth that the streets are laid out in the pattern of the Emperor's sigil. Shenan appears as a yellow jewel from afar, set within a band of sandstone. The rock around is so like rose-gold in colour that locals have—for as long as memory—referred to it as simply 'the Ring.'

"Have you seen so many—" The conversation stops when Niena turns a corner. Concerned faces twist into sneers of disgust when they see her and disappear back into their little nests. It's quickly apparent what the locals see in her, as she regards the remains of her clothing. Tree limbs, rocks, and briars have all performed little alterations.

The lyre's faces look up at her. They catch what light they can find in the alley, and spit it back. Niena nods as if that little sparkle along the edge of the instrument were a distinct set of instructions. Stairs lead up, past dark little holes and grease-stained windows.

"I need to get a new dress somehow," she says, but the grumbles from her stomach quickly correct that notion. She needs food first, food and water.

Niena's eyes climb, followed not long after by the rest of her. The stairs lead up into a wider street, one which she is familiar with. But where memory sees stretches of tables, chairs, and bustling wenches, eyes encounter only closed shops and empty flagstones.

A window once filled with treats, pastries, and smiling children steals her attention on the right. *Something terrible must have happened here too*, she tells herself while shaking her head at the blank face of a boarded-up door, and the frown of shattered glass. Niena tucks the lyre against her chest and continues past more of the same.

Former restaurants, livery stores. A butcher. In a long street of broken dreams, only the inn remains open. The strange facade stands out: whitewashed, over a thin yellow overcoat. Wooden walls and a curved roof further announce that the Seven Sisters Inn is a holdover from the days when trade from the western isles was new, and anything so foreign, trendy. It sits on the edge of her street and looks out over an old fountain.

"And now everything changes." She looks down at her lyre, then stuffs it under her arm confidently. With one deep breath and one shallow push, the green gabled doors swing open.

Tired eyes veer her way. From the tables near the stage, from the patrons at the bar. Even the barkeep stares her down before rubbing his meaty jowls with a dirty hand. But Niena turns to the aforementioned stage. Snags of song, wisps of cheers still dwell there. Ghosts of laughter. They all present themselves with one theatrical bow.

And then the glow from the fireplace pulls out full memories. Niena bumps into a dark wood table and runs her hands along the edge. Gashes in the wood that could be from her misuse of a fork as a child, or just random marks. This isn't the finest inn they ever got thrown out of, but it was one of her favourites. The former owner was soft on children, and would save some of the midday stew for her.

"What are you here for?" The current bartender's question rolls over Niena. She does hear it, but the ghosts have her attention.

Old Tabbard, she thinks with a smile. His voice always scratched along the seams of the floor like sawdust. What was his favourite topic? When winter knocked on his door, doom was on his mind.

"The land is old and grey," he would start with, while his daughter scraped dishes. Niena would listen to his slow shuffle. His family's bored rebuffs. She would listen and take. A comment here, a cough there, they would mix well with the pop and crackle of the fire. Imagination turned an empty bar into a thriving port of call. A place where adventure began.

His son Bran would then remind him that it was winter. To which the old man would repeat all of his usual. Rarely deviating. Though if it was a special day, he just might add, "It creaks along like an old dodder."

Then there was that one day. That one day—vaguely she remembers what lead to it. And vaguely, she recalls why her father bade the man to forget himself, and come sing with him and her mother.

Oh how the rain drummed against the western wall then, and when she looked at the grizzled man, she swore his back stiffened, as if her father had touched on some painful memory. He told them, there were no more songs to be made.

"Even the birds grow weary of it," his voice ringing in her ears. "All our stories have flown away, and left an empty nest in our hearts."

Niena blinks. It was poetry, something she had never expected from Tabbard then, and something she had forgotten since. Poetry, but wrong. She now knows there are always more songs and stories to tell.

"This isn't a soup hall, girl." Like a plate dropped in the middle of the room, the current owner's booming voice centres everyone's attention once again on Niena. She starts, shaken out of the daydream, un-welcomed back into a room full of drunk and leering men.

She looks from face to face, trying to find a friendly one, but the effort is futile.

"You heard me," as he tosses a towel at a server. "You take yourself elsewhere, I won't have you driving off what's left of my regulars."

Niena steps up to the bar. "I'm not looking for a handout," she says. "I'm an entertainer."

The man steps back, and eyes Niena up and down. "We aren't that sort of establishment."

She takes the lyre and sets it down on the table. "How about ten songs, for bread, water, and you let me sleep in your stable for the night?"

The man's eyes flash, and he stares at the lyre. "I'll give you five copper for it, but that's all."

"I don't think you understand," pulling it back. "I'm a bard and—"

His hand slaps the table, making Niena jump, and everyone else laugh. "Do your eyes still work? Look around, who are you going to sing to, the rats?"

"But I can bring in more people."

The barkeep's voice—loud, and harsh as a bull—beats the bustle down. "I don't need more of your kind. But look, girly, I am not without heart. I tell you this, if you can catch any of my rats, I'll get Molly to cook them up."

A round of snorts and guffaws follows a snide answer from the kitchen. The barkeep shrugs, and throws her an apologetic look. The floor erupts again, and their jeers follow Niena as she turns away.

"Here's for you," a man's voice slurs her way from a nearby table. Bits of cheese fall out of his slack maw when he tosses something at her feet. It's a copper piece. Niena's eyes narrow. She kneels down and presses the lyre as close to her chest as possible, picks the piece up, and flips it back into her hand without letting go of her stare. The drunk, realising he is not going to get a show, tosses something from his plate at her.

Niena runs out before he can think to chase. The green doors close shut behind, and she slumps against them while the cheer of the tavern rumbles through the oak.

This isn't the warm, inviting inn she remembers. What happened to Tabbard's family? These people seem to have forgotten the old customs. Traditions that a fifteen-year-old girl shouldn't have to remind them of. Or was she mistaken, and those only existed in her books?

"They think I'm…" And now, another man's voice interrupts her. What did he say? The whispers of this memory are only meant for her, both then and now. Her father's message though is clear.

If they think you are their fool. "Be their fool, but remember." Her hands wrap around the brass knob again as she repeats his mantra. "The real fool is the one who laughs first."

Be the one who laughs last. Niena returns to the door and throws it open again as bits of food fall off her dress. The barkeep's groan greets her entrance.

"Have you ever heard of the five chords?" Her voice thin, but rising.

The barkeep rubs his neck-beard. "It's three chords, girly. As in chords this, chords that. Stuff the chords in your dirty little," the rest drops into a mumble, but he finishes with: "get the bloody rag out of here!"

Niena sucks in a slow breath. "Five chords, and five fingers."

The heavyset man wipes his hands on his apron, and hovers over a loaf of bread he just laid, planting his elbows wide. "If I have to come over this bar, girly —"

"The three chords are nothing. Child's play." She looks at the man who tossed the penny. "Fool's play. In Taledric's they teach us about the five chords."

"Taledric's?"

She nods and straightens her neck. "Yes, Taledric's." There is a commanding tilt to her head now, and the nervousness that touched her words prior has died.

"Five chords, eh?" With a snort. "Can't be much help. You are the skinniest, most flat-chested bard I've ever seen."

Niena resists the urge to hit him with her lyre. "With the five chords, you can summon anything, anything at all out of thin air."

"Then why ain't you the Queen of Shenan?" he snorts.

"Watch," she says. The barkeep leans back against his stool, and motions for Niena to continue. Chuckles and coughs echo all around as she approaches the table.

"Five chords, five fingers," she repeats, waiving her hand over the bar top. "Before I had no bread, and now?"

One barstool topples into a second, and that into a third from her kick. Men and drinks crash to the ground while the bartender lunges, only to have his hands, and his head, serve as stepping stones to the counter.

Other men rush to his aid. Arms reach out and try to grab her, but she is too quick. Their cries of pain ring out almost melodiously as Niena knees, stomps, and jabs the faces, fingers, and chins that dare come too close. The whole bar is now roaring. Men careen towards, around, and into the tables, chairs, and even walls in their attempts to grab her.

"Looks like I'm going to get my tickle after all."

Niena looks up from the floor to a man standing between her and the door. Sturdy shoes rise into well-made pants, and then a coat that was once neat and pressed, but still fine. Yet it's his dropping mouth, and his face—slapped with an alcoholic's purse—that tell her who this is. Her own twists into a sneer. "So it's you, Bran." *Tabbard's eldest.*

His red eyes widen when she charges forward and he moves to act, but Niena slides with ease underneath his awkward lunge. The air he does manage to catch doesn't hold him, and a quick boot to his behind keeps him going. Towards the table. And into a group of chairs.

But for Niena that move takes her into a roll, and the roll into a hop, and the hop into a straight dash. Out the door. Out into the streets. Once there, in the darkening hour, she tries to catch her own air. A breath, and a moment of pause. Yet that isn't to be. The green doors are thrown wide and from them emerges the bartender, roaring like a dragon after a burglar.

Niena continues her flight, steering down alleyways almost blindly, as the heavyset man's footsteps drum behind like a monster. The empty ways begin to fill up. First with just a few people, then more, until the stamp of a crowd drowns out the pursuit. Then that fades completely, and soon after, Niena's run turns into a victory walk under the moon and starlight.

"One, two, three coppers and a silver crown." The drip of an upstairs outhouse pipe forces Niena to cover her nose. "That's more than Dad got in a week."

The moon, that old companion of thieves, sits snug behind a blanket of clouds and watches as Niena argues with herself.

"Why can't I have a normal life?" Niena's voice bounces along the stonework. "Because my head's in the clouds, or as Grandpa says, my mind's so high up, he'd need a ladder to reach me."

"I guess life just isn't normal anyways." Over, over, and then under. The echo of her feet on the cobble fills the narrows of the old town. She skirts past the tottering buildings that make up the old market. Away from the ragged men and women that crowded the other streets. There are many, so many. Even here they fill every line of sight; wherever there might be a fallen or decrepit building, she seems sure to find them.

The noises of the city herd Niena away from the less poverty-hit areas, and into the parts of town where there are guards, and where her baggage could be noticed. She takes extra care to veer away from these patrols, or posts. Finally, after nearly an hour, Niena returns to a neighbourhood that hasn't changed much since she left. Down, into a square dominated by a temple between the rows of houses that still hold the wealthier merchants, clerks, and other wage workers. She follows an alley that curves around the foundations of a ruined tower, then slips through a crack into the rotunda.

Hay and sawdust kick up everywhere. It is difficult for her to see, save with the help of one vagabond moonbeam that has snuck through a hole in the roof. But while this plays along her raven hair, and down her left arm, it isn't bright enough to be useful.

"To adventure," weakly. Niena sighs, and breaks off a piece of the bread. One long day. Two, maybe three new questions. But also, at least a couple things she needed.

Her thin smile returns. And this time, she thrusts the loaf into the air: "To adventure!"

Chapter 17
Smoke in the Air

Early morning. A murmur smoulders among the six. Old Bip saw it first: smoke in the air. "There, near the ruins."

Marny cuts between him and Griff. All hush, eyes drawn towards flashes of steel and iron.

"We must move," Bip says, and his gaze wanders to the right. "Yonder I think will do. I'd like to get behind old wood."

Griff and another hunter nod in agreement. Step by step, as the wind rises, they move together. Bip gives the order to fan out. One man keeps sight of another, and he the next, their little party sweeping through the forest garden like a wing of geese. Within the hour each has repositioned himself. And the camp is only a little more than two hundred yards away.

Twelve men in total stir at the edge of the ruined town. Many of them have similar equipment, and some still have the white rose displayed firmly on their right thigh.

"Deserters," Marny squeezes through clenched teeth. "Not all the same regiment. They are about to leave, would put them back at our camp before dawn."

Marny turns to Bip, and whispers something in his ear. Then to Griff: "We'll pinch them once they get into the brush. Bip will be up behind that rotten log, on the hollow. If they run, they won't be able to get past the briar quick enough, and then they're out in the open. Preserve yourself until fifty yards, then loose, and put the scare to these devils!"

The word passes through the ambush party, followed by a renewed hush, and anxious stillness. Each man Marny brought with him is of unknown quality. Poachers and hunters are quiet enough, but will they get jumpy in a real fight? So far the group has exceeded expectations. The old captain has a feeling that he isn't the only one with highway robbery hidden away in the cupboard.

Starlight wanders down through the leaves and the moon that leers over the camp is yellow-toothed and angry. The last mutters about that from Griff were settled nearly an hour ago. Now he only fidgets, running his hands up and down his bow.

"First time I've ever done this," Griff says. "Tried to kill a man, that is."

Marny rubs his chin. "Haven't been married long, have you?"

"No," with a nervous chuckle. A rustle of leaves ripples through the brush near. Bip's sign. Each man looks to the other and readies. The deserters approach, making neither haste nor caution as they tramp through the edges of the forest garden.

"Steady," Marny warns, setting his hand on Griff's bow. "Fifty yards."

In the heat of battle archers often forget they can't hold a bow for long. In the heat of battle, others forget that their enemies aren't targeting dummies; real soldiers shoot back. Marny spits, his teeth locked otherwise. Specks of the green foliage sparkle with silver, then bronze.

Twilight in the forest. A quick breeze takes the cheer from the approaching party and scatters it tween each ambusher. Nine, ten—the twelfth deserter breaks from the bush, cursing and angry, to his fellows' amusement. Just about every one of them to a man has bows. Twelve, to their five.

One more step—Marny throws his fist into the air and a whistle of death answers. Five arrows fly, three men fall. Two bandits then attempt to fly, and three arrows follow them.

A clumsy return volley sings over Marny's head, so he stands defiantly. The sound of the arrowheads breaking against hard wood crackles all around him. "Malar tu Caras!" And a wave of hunting whoops answer, punctuated at the high yelp by the unsheathing of Marny's sword. "Don't let them find cover!"

Poachers, hunters, old captains. Young men, old men. They erupt from their holes like hounds after a fox. Marny leads them, six against five still standing. Then six against four. Three. The deserters return fire, and there is the crash of a body rumbling through the underbrush on Marny's right. And that is the last of it. Before they even reach the field the twang of the hunters' bows silences the remaining combatants. The screams of the two who fled die soon after in the briar.

The bloody work done, the men exchange few words. Most look to Marny, but Bip to the forest behind. "Think it was Gregory. I'll go have a look, and put it right if needs."

Marny nods and regards the others. "Cleanup work then, let's see their camp."

"What, us four only?" Griff blinks. "There could be who knows how many in there."

"It's not bleeding fair is it?" The old captain whistles at the retreating Bip, who is helping an injured Gregory to stand. "Shadow Bip, and help him and Gregory back to camp."

Griff looks between the other three men there. From stern face to stony mask. He then stiffens and nods. Cicadas return in the silence of his departure.

Marny spits as Griff and Bip join the shade of the forest beyond. "Good man with the bow, but this isn't for him."

"They've heard us, no mistaking that." A young man, that one. Bip said he calls himself Brother. "They'll be waiting."

"They're probably taking turns shitting themselves around the fire," Marny says. "If they thought they had the number, they'd be out here now."

"What's the plan then?" Brother asks.

Marny cocks his head. "More murder."

Under the starlight they spend a moment to rummage through the fallens' gear, passing by the awkward armour, and picking up swords, or unspent arrows. Marny motions for the two remaining hunters to wing him, and then they too traverse the briar field.

Marny spits at an arrow-pinned corpse. "When I was campaigning, so long as you gave a man a coin and spun him to the nearest whorehouse, he was alright. Now? Can't guarantee much with just a whip."

"Own fault for breaking the prostitutes' guild," Randall adds. His face then lightens, as they break through the last of the briar. "I've stepped in that shit in the past. Can't say we didn't have our fair share of deserters though."

"Not in my regiment," he says.

"Do you see 'em?" Brother asks.

"Not a one." Marny looks to Randall, who gestures towards the smoke snaking from near the middle.

"They won't be there," Randall says. The man rubs his index finger against his thumb and holds it up to the layout of the ruins. "That's the high ground, a fort used to run east to south near that ridge, if I am right." He squints. "Looks like a temple or something now. I suppose we will find guards near."

"They're hoping to ambush us in the streets," Marny says. "Not a terrible idea. Keep your eye on that tower at six. The topless one, between the inner and outer wall. Let's stay low."

Herbs from forgotten gardens grow wild. Basil, thyme, and sage wrinkle the men's noses, and none of the three gains a yard without sneezing, or holding back a sneeze. But the cicadas and night birds cover for them, acting as a fourth man. Dew slicks their bellies as they crawl. Soaks their trousers.

The three hit the wall, and kneel down with their backs to it. Randall rolls his head back and stares up at lichen dangling from the ruined battlement. "So now what? Up the stairs?"

"Yeah," Marny whispers back. "But careful; up that way I saw a breach where a house used to be. They catch us in that hole, well, we might as well carry a handful of dirt with us."

"So," he adds with his hand on Brother's shoulder, "I need you to watch that bleeding tower, while me and Randall here cross the divide. Put a hole in anything that pops out."

"Don't know." Brother shakes his head. "You think they'll be up there?"

Marny risks a glance over the broken wall. "I'd say so. Now they might also have someone at the top of the stairs. In that case, when you hear me yell, you drop flat."

"Then we'll just be dead ducks," Randall says. "You think we can just leave them?"

"Not going to risk it. And it's more than that. They got weapons. And almost sure to have food, clothing. How long do you think our people back there are going to last like this? There's no telling when or where the next meal is coming," he says. "Now we have to out-bandit the bandits."

"Chords," Brother curses.

"Come on." Marny swings around the corner, through the toppled gate, and into the pass. Randall follows with his bow ready, while Brother hangs near the entrance.

They slide up along the left wall. The path is free, something which has them both on edge. Openings to villas and townhouses gape, but none of these represent the breach that Marny had spoken of before. That remains a stone's throw ahead. A full thirty feet of open space up the incline.

"That's some bitter ale," Randall whispers into Marny's ear. "We're going to raise the whole town, running through that."

Marny whips his head back. "You afraid of ghosts?"

"No, just of becoming one," he answers. "You think you can run that, you old bag of bones?"

"Meet you at the top."

The moon lights their way, giving the ground and the white plaster beside them a strange tint. They climb with weapons drawn until they reach the edge of the breach. Here Marny has Randall lower his bow. The hour is late, but dawn will be the thing sneaking up on *them* if they waste too much time.

The fingers of Marny's left hand feel at the edge. Plaster, mortar and rock break off under his touch, and he and Randall both flatten themselves against the wall. He looks back, lips mouthing a countdown. One. Two.

Shoes clatter against stone, echoing through the passage like a dinner bell. Randall lets out a cry at five feet, as their worst fear takes aim and fires. The first flies wide, over the hole to their right, and becomes one with the ruins. But the second, that one slices just at the cuff of Marny's thigh, sending him briefly to the ground.

Behind them a twang answers. Ten feet. Fifteen. Another loosed arrow from Brother whistles past. The two trade shots, until Marny and Randall are twenty-five feet through hole, where a last arrow from the tower shatters against the stone stairs. Two seconds later, a wild volley from Brother ends the conversation. And there are no more after.

The sound of a sword being drawn rings ahead, and Marny raises his own when two men appear at the top of the stairs. A pikeman, and a swordsman. Fifteen to twenty yards lay between them, with the reach of the pike extending a full half. The old captain and the hunter stand their ground, while the two ahead press with the obvious intent to push them back into the hole.

Marny raises his sword in salute, then quickly flattens to one side. Randall's arrow sinks into the neck of the pikeman, who falls, crashing down the stairs. The swordsman retreats around the corner just in time to see an arrow strike the wall behind.

"Should we wait for Brother?" Randall steps over the body.

"We take the top first." Together, they crest the final few stairs. The alley now corners left.

Cuts of light dance upon the wall opposite, starlight caught and thrown from the blade of Marny's sword and the dirk that hangs on Randall's belt. They step softly, and every so often they hear the scratch of a gauntlet, or maybe chainmail, against the stone ahead, and the approach of Brother below.

"I'm going to take a look." The plaster is cool against Marny's neck and his sword hangs low, parallel to the edge of the wall while he is still flat against it. To look only takes him a second, but the exhale when he returns seems to last forever.

"Two," he says. "Archer behind his shield."

Randall sucks his teeth, then unfastens the dirk, the belt — everything that might carry the light with him. He hands these to Marny and places his bow up on top of the wall. "Whistle, and I will pick him off; he'll have no cover with me up there. But you're going to have to get on them quickly and draw their attention first because I'll have no cover from him either."

"Gods' speed," Marny says. Randall slides himself up just as Brother comes at their rear, breathing heavily.

"What's it," panting. "Why'd no one think to cover me just in case?"

Marny silences him with one finger, and with the same directs Brother's attention. "Don't aim, just fire."

He nods, and Marny pushes himself off the wall. With his sword raised, he careens around the corner and rushes forwards. A shot slices his tunic, misses flesh, but draws the captain's signal. There's a shout as he closes the distance to the swordsman and an arrow whips through the air overhead, followed closely by another returning in answer; by the time Marny crashes into the man's shield, grappling for his sword arm, the bandit archer lies with an arrow through his eye, and Randall is bleeding out somewhere behind Marny and above.

They wrestle. When Brother joins, their combined strength proves to be too much for the swordsman. Marny removes his dirk and stabs the screaming man prone beneath him until the stone runs red and the blood chokes him out.

"Check on Randall," Marny says, crimson matting his tunic.

Brother pulls himself up and hangs there for a few seconds before falling back. "Blessed is the music, and hallowed is the song of the first strings."

"I see where you got your name."

"Until paradise comes," pressing the tip of the bow to his forehead. "And all may sing together, anew."

Flies find the corpses, and all the two men can hear outside their own shuffling in the darkness is the buzzing. Debris from the crumbled walls of the temple complex litters the narrow road. It appears to continue straight for some way, but a break a few paces along hints at another street.

"Come on," Marny says. The duo meet no resistance at the junction and continue on past. Twenty paces further the wall opens up onto a small grotto which holds the still burning campfire. Most of its colonnades have collapsed, and the few remaining outbuildings that touch the courtyard are little more than dank holes.

Movement catches Brother's eye, and he taps Marny on the shoulder. In the far corner, there are stacks of bags and rows of barrels.

"Come out now or die in your hole," Marny shouts. There is no immediate response, except for the shuffle of a bag. From behind the burlap, a hand extends, then legs, and finally the rest of the sack-shaped man.

"I'm just the cook." Palms out. "Just the cook. Please, I have no weapons!"

Brother checks, while Marny keeps him at swordpoint. The latter's eyes study the man. "You're no soldier, or no soldiers' cook."

"I was part of a caravan," he says. "They had a knife at my belly just like the others, but I told em I could cook and they kept me. Taking as, they liked my cooking or else I'd be thrown back to the trees."

Brother's fingers rap on the bow. "Are there any others?"

"I don't know," his eyes flitting up, down, then to the left. "There's always one in the tower, and when they head out I can usually count to twelve or thirteen. Three? Maybe four? I don't know where the others might be but—"

"Dead," Marny says. The cook swallows. "No one's going to kill you; we're going to need a cook ourselves, I think."

"What? No, please, no more marauders."

"No," Brother says, his voice dripping with menace. "Worse. Women and children. What's in the barrels? What you got stocked up?" Marny walks away.

"Some pork, mostly potatoes..." The conversation drifts as Marny makes his own account. The bags contain most of what they were hoping for: food, mulled ale, scraps of clothing. Some bolts, even, of the better stuff. His hands flow through a small sack holding a fold of papers, what looks to be a journal, and then various small sticks, until they come upon a bottled dark liquid that he subsequently holds up to the sky.

"Ink," Marny says to himself. A cloud passes before the moon, removing the touch of yellow around his feet. Now, there is only starlight and the red fangs of the campfire behind. He wraps up the contents of the pack and tucks it under his coat.

Chapter 18
What Lies Buried

Life once again returns to the ruin. Real life: laughter for some, tears for others. A city to call their home if they were to stay. By now the refugees have been able to scrounge up a second wagon, and are midway through loading.

"Must we go already?" Emyrh asks.

Marny rubs his now four-day-old beard. "Well." Several faces turn to him, expectantly. He sighs, and those gnarled hands slip to his forehead. "Yes, we can't risk a night here. Not with the size of this group."

"I see," Emyrh says. He pats the head of their one horse and then looks back up at the captain. "The other one, the wagon, she will need us to tow ourselves. I don't think our little girl can pull the two."

"We'll take turns." Dawn peeks annoyingly through the columns right into Marny's eyes. "The stronger of us. And Gregory will have to ride, so there's no way around the fact that some sacks will have to be carried."

"Of course," the priest says. He taps Marny's arm as if testing to see if the old man will explode. "But why must we go? This place is good. It is a good camp, better than the rock or the road. It is almost a city. No. It could be a city."

Marny spits. "Yeah, that's what I am afraid of, Emyrh." And the priest's head cocks at his name. "That dragon. I've dealt with the same one before, back in the wastes. Back when I was half as young and nearly as dumb as you."

And he raises his voice for the others to hear. "When a dragon starts putting towns to the torch, it means only one thing: the beast is looking for a new lair." A murmur stews among them, and he pulls Emyrh closer. "The waste follows the dragon, lad. You pop a city in its territory, and sooner or later it will notice. You don't want wyrmkind to notice."

"You are right, Marny, you have the right." His blue eyes weary. "The people are with you. Where are we to go then? To this Cairnum…astali? I got that right, didn't I?"

"Yeah, the Cairn," he says. "There are two things dragons respect: hard walls, and—"

"Magic?"

Marny sneers. "No, a ballista with thick iron bolts. Sharp enough to pierce the scales, and hard enough not to break in a dive. Something to really sink the bleeding bugger."

"And this Ca…this castle has these?"

"I helped stock it myself," he says quietly. "Once upon a time, it was going to be the staging point to retake the capital. But with the Emperor's death, well. I don't need to elaborate."

Brother slaps the horse's behind, which nearly causes the priest to jump out of his frock.

"We'll stop once we are back on the road, the right road," Marny says, addressing both the priest and the refugees.

Hooves strike amidst the crowd, and the wagons roll on. Their spokes spin away the morning, turning day into night, and night into dawn. It is only when the last crow cries in the overgrown fields, and the ruins are a memory behind, that they stop.

Randall's body has finally been prepared for his journey. The priest tends, but the sermon everyone seems to remember after comes from the hunter called Brother, rather than Emyrh. His words have a more grounded quality that finds resonance among the folk. That isn't to say that cheer—such as the priest can supply in his own distracted way—is unwelcome. With full bellies, and a place to finally rest, some measure of joy or contentment is purchased. But while the fire of Randall's pyre dims, so too does their patience for flowery phrase.

The second day brings news; holdovers from another burned town tell the refugees that their own traveled the same route and that the way is clear as far as Rivenholt, where one of theirs turned back. A few of this town's leftovers look to join the caravan, and there is some consternation over who gets to guard the stocks. The newcomers eagerly offer their turn at the job, a little too eagerly for Brother and the other hunters. Again, as has often been in the case in the last while, they look to Marny to solve the problem. His decisions lead most of these new refugees to turn back, but three families remain, along with twelve river men and a mercenary named Brock. He and Griff form a quick camaraderie.

Morning brings another stop. They choose this time to wait in between the shadow of two hills, off the road. In the Kimbesh tongue, these are known as drimmern, or 'sleeping men'. Some were born when the glaciers left this land, long, long ago. Others are manmade, and under these families still lay. Later tradition brought the addition of stone cairns to the burials.

Marny swings past their new cook arguing with a half-deaf farmhand over which barrel to offload first.

Their conversation drifts over the cooking times for potatoes, and the importance of not disturbing the ale casks. Normal talk of sorts, in a crazy world. Neither this nor the children playing in the meadows strikes him as odd. Everyone is looking for something familiar to cling to.

"I hate to tell them what their new normal will be," he says to the sky. The sun is really upon them, and it feels like the first spring day in a month that has teased at it. The old captain turns and straightens a straw hat he bartered for. Brock and Griff wave to him from underneath a hickory. He stretches, steals a glance to his left and right, then when sure no one is looking, settles onto a barrel to rest.

From underneath his coat, he removes a slip of paper. It's been years since he has written anything, letting the junior officers do the paperwork as he got older. Now though, he has a different mind. Marny sets the ink down on a second barrel. The words come slowly. Clumsily. The first sentence ends with more strikes than a drunk tied to a tree.

"Where's Deliah when I need her," he mumbles. The stock of the paper is crude, and his handwriting is barely legible. He folds the first half down and uses his arm as a table.

A shadow underlines his script, and Marny looks up into the bearded mountain that is the poacher. "Griff," he says, laying the manuscript down.

"It's such a fine morning, isn't it?" Griff pulls off his hat and begins to fold back the rim. "Can we talk? If you are free, I can always come back later—"

Marny fans away the stuttering with his papers. "Don't bleeding lead me around the water, boy."

"It's just…let's take a walk, shall we?" Griff says. He gestures away, and Marny obliges—even though every inch of his back protests. The thrill of the fight hid a lot of his age from him until late yesterday, and now the creaks and pains are out and having a little party.

Lavender plays in the fields. The sweet tones mix with the rustic landscape, painting a picture of lovers, and picnics. And of strolls with a different end in mind than the one he's having with Griff. Marny looks at the poacher. He's babbling on about the fight with the bandits—leading him around the water, just as he warned him not to. He cuts the young man off just as he is about to go on about his one shot, the shot that nearly went wide. Marny has the measure of where this is going now.

"Look lad, I'm not lying when I say I'd take you over any of the recruits back in Maiden," he says. "You're a good shot and a steady hand. But you aren't a real killer."

"It was my first fight." Griff places his hand on his chest as if what he says here was a prayer. "I just need more practice."

"Practice?" Marny scowls. "I'll not contribute to that, I think. Look, what's this about? That merc's been filling your head with stories?"

The poacher steps aside. "He thinks I'd be good in a spot. And chords know I could use the money." Griff then steps in and puts his hand on Marny's shoulder. "I misjudged you before, but you proved me wrong. Let me prove myself to you. The others, everyone here respects you now, if they didn't before. They'll listen to you."

"But my conscience won't," Marny says. "You've got a wife, and soon will probably have a tike or two. Mercs aren't family men, Griff. Most of them don't even end up with a decent burial."

"Do you know what's the difference between a poacher, and a hunter?" Griff uses his hands as if the conversation is a piece of cake he's slicing. "Hunters pay for their licenses, licenses which I…I'm wanted in three cantons now. What do you think the constables have waiting for me? For my wife who helped me?"

Marny sucks his teeth, his looks darting from a hillock and a small row of rocks to the man. Somewhere along the way, he picks up the frown he left at the barrels. "I'll think of something."

Griff leaves him happy, as cheerful as a puppy thrown a steak. Marny, for his part, doesn't see what's so wonderful about it all. His mind races with thoughts of where to stick the boy, to keep him out of trouble. In the end, it all comes back to that hillock, and the row of rocks. A fallen cairn, from the look of its.

"Shenan," he whispers. "Graham."

Responsibility. That's not something he's looking for, not since the last—Marny closes his eyes. The morning's heat washes over him, and he is back. Back in Maidenhill, looking at his home, and the outstretched hand that no one can help any longer.

"I'll find this one a wall job," he says. "Somehow, someplace close to his wife." Resolute, he stands and makes his way to somewhere quieter.

Morning spills into afternoon, and the noon flows over the evening. Rivenholt is behind them now, and they have continued on further, making good time, passing more and more of the man-made hills. The horizon swims blue, then red. Then treads from red to brown, as the distant mountainscape melds into the sky and golden hills. The mood of the refugees brightens with each mile, even as the sky darkens. By night, half of the families here could be mistaken for night revelers.

Marny though becomes withdrawn. It seems every stone along the road leads him back, back to a different Cairnumastali. To his days as a young sergeant, leading his regiment out of the wastes. To later, returning as a captain, and the ill-fated expedition to the capital. There pride and valour died between fire and fang. And then, finally, nearly ten years ago to when he received the letter from Graham's wife. It was the last time he ever wrote anything.

"What about Squirrel?" Deliah's voice follows him. Marny pushes the straw hat down lower and quickens his pace. But she still catches him.

"He was out of his mind," he says, refusing to turn. "Or I just heard what I wanted to hear. I'm hearing a lot of things lately…"

And she is gone again. He fingers the ruffles of the papers under his coat. The night is warm, the day was long. Tomorrow, he hopes to find an end to this journey and put more than one thing to rest.

Chapter 19
The Right Fit

Last night there was a disturbance at the castle, and no one seems to know what precisely they mean by that. But the consensus is, there was a disturbance. Whatever it may have been, Niena slept through. Her night was spent in dreams of fresh bread, and a new set of clothes. The former becoming stale upon dawn.

Vibrant reds, patterned blues, the colours of the shopper's clothes as they root around the stalls in the market reminds Niena of a garden, though some people look more like onions than flowers. Her own side of the square is far different, where muted shades, dirt, and the touches of stress and wear are the fashion of the day, as spring seen through a grimy window.

Guards keep a watchful eye. Niena, in turn, watches them as they move through the crowd.

"Hold your own and pray for death." A dirty face blocks Niena's view as an old man jumps in front. His fingers fall to her shoulders, smearing ash upon the tattered strap, as he has done to everyone making the mistake of standing still for too long.

"Find yourself a good place to die, child," he says, smiling. She tenses, and the old man's eyes roll back to the sky as he looks for the next victim. "Don't matter if it's warm, we'll all be warm soon enough!"

She shivers and wipes off his touch. His sort normally thrive on the fringes, but with the stories she's heard this morning, she wonders where that edge really lays. And those tales, what do they talk about? Craziness, that's what. Any other day she might consider them utterly ridiculous. Until she remembers the fairy. But it's still madness.

A **dragon**. *Well,* she thinks to herself, *that's one heck of an answer.* And while it may be important to know who sent the fairy to help her, and how that person knew to do so, just one question really lingers: what happened to her family in Maidenhill?

"Am I crazy? Are we the madness gnawing on the roots of the world?" Niena perks, and the longing for a piece of paper and some good ink wells up. "No, clothes. I need clothes first."

The crowds thin out near the main street. Here there are more guards, and she stops only a few feet away. Men and women pass, but not between her and them, creating a clear break. There is tension, however. Something just beyond that she can't find by looking.

Decisions face her now. Pictures of her staring down the guards and walking straight towards the main, protected thoroughfare, break. They are pure fantasy. Instead, Niena takes one look at those men, with their tense gestures that suggest 'shove off,' and turns away.

Fantasy, she repeats to herself. Niena closes her eyes and pushes the sounds of the city away. Then opens them again. The flowering clothes of the rich mingle with the roots and stems of the poor. She imagines a garden, no a forest, a wild one.

The young druid stretched over the boulder, Niena dreams. *Her mud-smeared body blended with the rock at the river's edge. It was a warm afternoon, warm and humid.*

Niena stands on her toes after climbing the base of a lamppost. The stone is cold underneath her bare feet, and the river of people, wild.

What was that? Slipped between the lap of water and the beating of her own heart she thought she heard something. Niena held her breath, straining to listen over the cacophony. There! Just below the rustle of the leaves on the far shore.

She sees a path among them, and it is the bells of a temple that alert her first to it. Though most of the market stalls cluster around the middle of the square, there is still a thin line that leads along the opposite way of which she came. These traders, and the people there, flow almost directly into a side street to the far left of the guards.

The girl followed the edge of the river, hunting her prey. Reeds whistled in the faint breeze. Niena crouched low among them, hoping to escape notice, and blend in.

"Air stinks down here," a local mutters.

"Always have that, comes right off the ole motte, an right down that new midden."

The wide stream of people narrows as she approaches. But it's not the passage itself that interests her. Some way in, another alley opens. She walks towards this, slowly. With a little maneuvering around private gardens, and rooftops, she can circumvent all of the guard posts.

There, in the middle. Muddy water swirled around the great trunk, where somewhere up above, a water eagle nests. Her prey.

Splinters press into her palm, but she ignores the pain, climbing up and over the roof of a last dilapidated house. Niena's feet slap the cobble of the corner row. She steps lively and emerges from the arch of a private residence's garden, out into a wide road.

The street is lined in both directions by a string of two-storey buildings, in places behind her backed by an inner city wall. It is paved neatly with cobble, and several manicured trees follow the road out, towards the main gate: the Black Fort. Only ruins of the burned original remain, just outside the current and larger city entrance. The name, however, stuck, and the new one was painted to mimic the blackened ruin.

There are fewer people and even fewer rude stares here. "I guess I need a dressmaker," she says. Left, right? She settles on a side street past what looks to be fabric shop. It strikes her only later, that this too, would have been an option.

Even here everything appears new and clean. The gilding on the oil lamps has been freshly polished, and street sweepers work even now to keep the heart of the jewel of the empire clear. Niena can't help but feel them inching towards her with their brooms and scrapers, even if that is paranoia.

She wanders through the various side streets. Past sweet shops, butchers. Several of the businesses here are also closed. Long closed; the decline is not new.

"My husband would never..." The voice loses itself to garble.

Two women chat outside their shops, with a third at the edge of their conversation. A lamppost divides the two shop owners and the third, a customer from the sound of it, looks like she wants a way out.

"Your Xav slums. All husbands slum, dear."

Niena leans against a tree. The live oak's arms reach from shop roof to lamppost, almost touching the latter. "One of those is a dressmaker," she says to herself, looking between the two, and at the store fronts. "The other's a second-hand seamstress, if I am reading the shop sign right." Though she figures with the nature of the work, the two sometimes share clients and stock.

The one on the right. No, left. Both women are dressed in near-identical cuts: a low neckline, high waist affair, with thick pleats to keep the back straight. Black dresses in mirror, with a white fichu. The only difference in the colour, style, accessories, and the fitting is that one is wearing a pinafore while the other is without. Niena focuses on that lady. She is quite lovely, with curled blonde hair tucked underneath a hat. Though while she towers over her friend, she seems to be constantly on the defensive.

"Really? Really? I think you spend too much time reading your penny pamphlets," says she. "And beeesides," she stretches out the word as she crosses her arms. The third again tries to make her goodbyes. "He could have easily got it from your scoundrel."

"Tut-tut. Kieve is a serious-minded man, he doesn't take with talk of dragons and other piffle-paffle. Dragons! You just don't want to admit Xav is silly. *Silly.*"

"Ahh, boosy, boosy!" The customer, an elderly lady, fawns over an old tabby. Where he came from, Niena can't say. Given the ferociousness of the street sweepers, she would think that any stray – especially this raggedy creature – would be pushed halfway to Coppercreek by now. Nevertheless, following the animal allows her a way out of the clutches of the two shopkeepers.

"Now you done it, Alendra," Kieve's wife says. "You've got her loony, and chasing cats."

"Me?" Xav's wife answers. "You are the one who went all brutal. All's I said was, supposedly, it's burned half the towns from here to the river, that's why all those ragged, dirty…Oh dear."

As the two watched their little bird escape her cage, so too had their eyes fallen upon Niena. Their faces pale in terror at the thought that she might have overheard.

"That is nonsense," Niena says, her tongue stinging with distaste at her use of a posh accent. "But it is probably the worst forest fire the midlands has ever seen."

The tall shop-owner forces a smile. "And you are, my dear?"

"Tianna," Niena says. "Tianna of Kimbesh. I was on my way to study in Sunford when I was caught up in it all." Sunford always conjures up pictures of bored scholars and miles and miles of texts and libraries. It's a good practice that if you want to impersonate anyone with decently deep pockets, you pick Sunford as a destination. So came the thieves' saying "always in Sunford." Niena read that somewhere.

"It started at the edge of the woods, and swept over the town in the middle of the night, as if it had wings of fire." This extra embellishment tickles her, and she can't help but to continue, "Like a wyrm! And of course, that's what they say it is when they don't understand."

Alendra's eyes cut a vertical slice in her friend from breast to temple. "A forest fire, Mira, not *dragons*. Now that is right, and that is the proper of it. And we will hear no more of your Xav's billy-bolly."

"Honestly, where do you get your words?" Mira snorts. "And you. Thank you, now she will never let me hear the end of it."

"By the by," Alendra says, looking down Niena's dress to her bare feet, "you're nearly out of your dress, dear."

Niena lips pucker, and her hands fall to the coin purse. She fakes a slight tremble, for good measure. "That's…that's why I am here. I don't have much, but I can't show up at the university like this." Her voice chokes. "I was barely able to hold onto my lyre. I don't know why I thought about it, and not my school books, I—"

Alendra looks to Mira. "I don't have anything ready made, do you?"

"The Meerens brought me a dress the other day that *might* fit," she says slowly. "Trading in for their daughter's dowry. I would need at least a silver and a six piece for it though."

Niena empties the contents into the woman's outstretched hand and cringes as the total only comes to one silver and three.

Alendra picks out the silver and presses the rest back into Niena's hand. "I'll make up the difference for her. You're going to need the rest for a proper bath, I'd say. Else that cat won't ever leave you."

And she just now notices the tabby running between her legs. Every so often the stray looks up at her and flashes the queerest set of eyes, amber, like the glass in the street lamps.

"You don't know how much this means to me. Now I will be able to afford to at least get back to my uncle in Farmott."

Somewhere during their conversation, Mira left, and now she appears carrying a small bundle.

"You'll have to hem it yourself," she says. "But I've included a little thread and a needle." And she smiles, earning a small victory over her friend and rival.

"Well, I wish you good journey then," Alendra tells Niena.

Niena unfolds the dress. White linen and…

"It's a bit, flattering, this dress," Mira says, apologetically. "The Meerens have an odd taste in fashion for their daughter."

There's something about the white dress, despite the lack of modesty – or because of it – that is exciting. It's not covered in flowers or child-like ivy. This is closer to what her mother wore, once. What women wear.

She thanks the two ladies and leaves, carrying the new dress over the lyre, like it is the most precious thing she owns. The rest of the day takes shape in her mind. A bath, a meal, and then a return to the market. She has no real reason to go there, except maybe to buy a cheap pair of shoes. But, just for today, she wants to be one of those flowers in the square.

Chapter 20
At Every Corner

Niena sticks to the alcove, almost nude under the white muslin of the moon. The hour is late, the air warm, humid. And her dress clings.

The night turns cold when a breeze skims from the city canal. Niena shivers, the sweat under her clothing raising goosebumps wherever it touches. Still, she would rather be out here than in the tower. The wind bites gentler than the vermin in the hay, after all.

But while she is contemplating this, laughter walks down from the gate on the opposite side of the canal bridge. Niena sinks deeper into the cut as several figures drift out and over the bridge and towards where she is hiding.

She watches them as they pass. They are older girls than she, but still young, and in their hands each carries a candlelit globe tied to a long stick. Niena sighs, remembering her mother telling her stories about this. Young maids in the dark, crossing the river. It harkens back to the myths of the elves in the marshes, and their queer lights that lead men astray.

When the last of the ladies dwindle into the distance, she too leaves, crossing the bridge and into that fine street. Only the stars walk with Niena this far, every other light has retreated deep into the cosy houses and lofts that make up the merchants' row. And there, snug in feather beds, the wealthy sleep. Away from the un-washed horde that crowds the other districts. Away from responsibility, and protected by guards on all sides. But Niena knows the secret ways through. To-night, this street is also hers.

"I want a lolly, lolly in each hand. Give me two, for my penny mister man."

Her song carries, skipping around the cobblestone, the colourful signs that glow in the returned moonlight. And everywhere that she can't be. It's not her favourite, at least, not since she was ten. Yet it is here, in her head, and for some reason right now, that means it needs to be sung.

"Break it in half, you'll see. It's as dandy, as dandy be. And you'll give a lolly, lolly. And I'll have a lolly, lolly."

The tune falls apart in giggles at the far end of a horse trough. But the night sky still dances on the water's sur-face, and Niena's fingers glide and sweep in place of her legs. She skips with the clouds. Twirls with the stars. Dancing and twirling, twirling, and sweeping until she plunges her hands into the water, just to flip back up and splash an invisible friend.

Her reflection catches the smile when she leans over, as well as her full lips, high cheekbones, and a face that no longer says 'little girl,' but instead speaks of a matur-ing young woman. While she smiles back at her mirror, the moon appears from behind a patch of clouds, and in the image, her head. So that it hovers over like a halo, which makes Niena laugh.

A few threads of the music wind down. Then, just like the calm of the water, they are gone. Niena's laugh also fades into a chuckle. She peers hard at the surface, and memories of her grandparent's bubble. Tomorrow. To-morrow she shall go looking for them. First, she'll talk to the urchins. Then the guards. Last, with the priests. These thoughts take her smile with them.

Her hands dip under again. This time she cups and drinks greedily, and she finds the water to be sweet, sweet to a parched throat. Niena shakes her hands dry. Thunder rumbles the surface of the water, though the rain that pelts it is from her fingertips.

"I already had my bath. Could we come back tomorrow?" she says to the sky.

There is a dull throb and pressure digging into her temple. Niena wipes her forehead and looks out into the street. Still dark. Still empty. A sigh concedes the obvious: sleep can't be avoided, and these streets won't be safe for that. Need requires her to save the last copper for a meal tomorrow. Back to the tower tonight, then.

"At least they're small rats." The few she has seen. Niena's lips purse as she stretches, then nearly trips. And in answer comes a raspy purring, too loud for a daydream to smother.

"Well hello," to the new friend at her feet. With all the thoughts of mice and hay, it's a surprise that she managed to ignore the mouser there for so long.

"I've seen you before, haven't I? So you are following me, huh? I'm afraid you're too old to catch a mouse," she says, scratching its chin. "Chords, the mouse would probably catch you. But you have such pretty eyes. Like autumn leaves, or dried honey."

The pressure in her temple rages, and she winces. It feels almost *like a scream, from the inside.* Niena jumps as the cat nips her hand. "Oberon?" she asks the air.

A footstep resounds somewhere, and the purring stops. Even the sky quiets, as if the very thunder was stolen out of the air. Another footstep. Niena looks down at the feline, watching it smack its lips and stalk expectantly forward. Her eyes follow. Down the street, past the one working oil light. Into an alley that only the shadows walk.

Niena? Oh good, here we are. It's getting more difficult to talk to you.

She stands. "Oberon?"

Listen closely child, you need to find a way out of here. The urgency in the fairy's voice doesn't click. *I warned you against coming to the city. And now he's shown up!*

"He? What are you talking about?"

Yes! He! Him! Your husband!

"What?! What the chords are you talking about?"

Did I forget to mention there were other parts to your story? This is one! .

"That isn't just another part! That's like saying a brain is just an accessory!"

You must listen to me, this is dangerous. He's dangerous. I don't know what his intentions are, but you and him connecting now cannot be a good thing.

But Niena ignores Oberon's pleading, determined to face this nonsense head on. Whatever he might be, he is certainly only human. Isn't he?

"So he's my husband? That would mean he's come from some sort of future? He's somehow found a way to go back in time, just to find me. Me? Why would anyone want to do that? I'm only fifteen, and I can't even do a proper hem right."

When is just like where. Another reality that you can explore, if you know the way there, or then.

"Billy-bolly!" she says, enjoying the sound of the new phrase. "That's magic!"

It's magic all right. Niena stares past the lamp and wills her feet into place. *Powerful magic, girly. Not something to mix yourself up in.*

"I can't believe this. This doesn't even begin to make…But he loves me, doesn't he? That's why he's here. Why else would he come all of this way?" Every approaching footstep jostles her nerves.

I am not certain if it is love that motivates him. I think it is, at best, a zealot's resolve towards what he feels needs to be done, and worse, the desire to hold onto a possession.

Out of the black, a shape materialises. She swallows, and the darkness falls back from his cloak to reveal a very human man, with a shaggy beard, and rough clothes. He doesn't look like a powerful magician who could chase a girl through time and more. But it is that very appearance that loosens Niena's nerve. They stare at one another. Her into the recess of his hood, which remains shadowed despite the oil light. And him at her, at the length of a white dress wrapping the thin lines of a teenage girl.

The man throws back his hood. He regards her with a tilt of his head as the tabby weaves around his legs. "What is this? Who are you?"

A steady rain begins. The fall, the soft *splash* of each drop is the only thing separating them now. And it is just a sound.

"Don't be frightened," he says, taking a step forward. "I'm not interested in harming you."

Out of the sheet of rain, a familiar face emerges. Niena's breath catches in the back of her throat as Oberon dances between them. His feet move in time with the emerging thunder and lightning. One step forward, one back. Pirouette, pirouette, and then a long stretch to her side.

The man's eyes steal her attention back and push away the rain, peering at her, into her. "Do you know a woman by the name of Niena?"

She blinks, as Oberon's hands cup her ears. "Tell him yes, and that if he closes his eyes and counts to a hundred, you'll get her for him." The corner of her eyes crinkle as she looks at the fairy, and shakes her head.

"I know, here I am, a stranger asking you all of these questions," this man, her husband, says slowly. "You must be confused, and so am I. Niena is my wife, you see, and I've tracked her through forests, fields. I've taken on the forms of beasts and ridden with monsters. All to be here, now."

"I warned you, but did you listen? Oh no, what's the worst he can do, leave the toilet seat up? Wait," Oberon says as his hands clench tightly around Squirrel's sleeve. "Don't tell him I'm here."

"I don't know…" Niena says, trying to ignore the fey. This man doesn't seem to have the same problem. He doesn't even notice Oberon.

"You don't know? What don't you know?" His nostrils flare, and his voice is heavy, like a wolf getting ready to snarl.

"No…no…" Oberon's mouth drops as if he were hanging on a hook. "We shall always be free!"

Her husband continues, "The whereabouts of my wife? Or how to explain how you ended up with her lyre? Or is it something more practical: are you merely uncertain of what lie you want to tell me?" His tone boils over, then settles back to a simmer. He relaxes. "I don't care about the instrument. Let's go back to the beginning, shall we? Who are you?"

Wait, why doesn't he recognise me? The sheen of the moon disappears beneath the clouds. And somewhere, behind her, comes the sound of shutters being closed. Niena stands tall.

"I am the teller of riddles, and the keeper of books," she says. "I ride wagons into dreams and give form to nightmares. I sing and the worlds listen."

He flexes his hands and blinks. "Please, enough of that. What do you think this is, some sort of fairytale?"

"Fraud save the Queen!" Oberon grabs her by the shoulder. "Cod save the Queen!"

"Spider-slayer, I laugh in the face of giants," she says.

"Stop talking like that," the man growls. "I've had enough idiocy for—" and his eyes narrow. "What is your game? Why are you acting like this?"

Oberon pauses, so terrified that the metal latches on his boots jingle. "Gourd save the Queen? Wait, that doesn't even rhyme."

She pulls the lyre against her chest and slides her hand in to play. "I steal the bread in their hands, and pluck their manhood from between."

"Damn you!" the man yells. "If you think I won't harm a child if it could lead me to my wife, you will find that mistake costly."

"Liberation!" Oberon cries. "Liberation!"

The man moves closer, his approach deliberate, menacing. "I am done being pissed on. When did you steal that lyre? I want answers!"

"Freedom! Liberation!"

"Stay back or I'll—"

"When fairies, cursed, at elven command, rose from the sombre main."

"You'll what?" he says with a smirk. "You're just a bleeding thief and a child at that. What can you do?"

"This was the permit in our hand, and the babbling twits sang..."

"I'm not a thief," a lie. "I'm a bard, and I know the three chords."

"Rue, Britannia!"

"What do you know?" His laugh unfriendly.

"I…" she stammers. "Britannia?"

"Britannia, rue the fey!

Niena rounds on the fairy, who is busy rubbing up against a lamppost. "Oberon! Shut the bleeding chords up!"

"Oberon?" His eyes flare wide, then sharpen to a knife edge.

"Fairies never, never, never…" The fairy sings while he kicks the post. "shall be slaves!"

"Bleeding chords," she whispers, because at the mention of the fairy's name the man's face has turned from annoyed to hostile.

"I knew it. I knew that's what this was. You're in league with that devil, aren't you!"

Almost instinctively, Niena pulls the lyre up, and her fingers glide towards the strings.

"What did he promise you?"

She feels a rush to her head, as if all the blood in her body is on the move. And then a tingling sensation winds up through her. From the toes to the knees. Up, and up. Niena head tilts high, she inhales deeply.

"Little boy, oh little boy. Where have you been all last eve?" Niena can sense she is touching something special. Something, powerful. And it flowers within her.

The man tilts his head, startled, but she keeps singing. Her eyes flutter, then close, as a wind sweeps hard rain into them both. "You disappeared at twilight, and left me to wander alone."

"How are — No!"

Footsteps shuffle. Then stop. She can hear his curses, but nothing else. Niena slowly steps back, towards the bridge. "Little boy, oh little boy. Why can't I walk with you now?"

The darkness throbs, within her head, around her body, what she can feel and not see. "Your footsteps are gone, and I can no longer remember your name."

Her eyes flash open. Both the fairy and her 'husband' are only feet away now. The man staring into her. No, through her!

His fists clench, flushing red, before eventually relaxing. All anger has left the man's face, and he looks towards where Niena was, but moves no further. "I did not need my eyes to find you the first time. I won't need them now."

Finding her? She can believe that. Catching is a whole different prospect, however. And Niena slowly steps away.

"So you are more than just a thief." His face does not follow her. "You have put yourself in a very dangerous position." He takes a step forward. "I don't know what price you paid for the knowledge he gave you. But it won't be worth it for either of us."

Niena watches him take a breath, and then close his eyes. Deciding that it is time to take her leave, she backtracks quickly to the temple on this side of the bridge. A rim along the edge of the alcove's roof provides her a hold. Niena pushes up with her legs and pulls the rest of her body over. Water splashes.

"Whatever he told you, he's lying!" she hears from behind.

Over, over, and then under. Niena uses the echo of his shoes as motivation as she runs along the colonnade. Pale frescoes of battles stand in frieze to her left side; silent preachers of the Knight cult's faith. She kneels and looks over her shoulder at the corner. Nothing. Then peers up, and to her side. The floor on which she stands is near the height of the neighbouring buildings. The columns though, they tower above Niena.

"This isn't just my life you are playing with," his voice echoes along the cobble. The man is near, but Niena is unable to see him. "I don't want to harm you, but I won't fail my wife."

Left. Right. Back to left. At another thirty yards, the wall must turn. There she knows the street becomes a mere alley bordering the one-storey barracks that the Rose Guard now uses. Niena looks down from where she came and sighs. Whatever the truth is, she's not interested in risking a conversation with the man. One step. Nothing. She takes another, slowly—and then she's off, rushing down the lane. Faster, faster still.

Flies scatter as she leaps above and over the refuse of the alley and lands on the thatch of the old barracks. Niena jerks around. At the sudden announcement of the man's approach from behind and below, her left hand hooks into a knuckle of the straw face. She smiles to herself; he's not moving.

Thanks to a well-timed flash of lightning she can clearly see his face. Confusion touches his brow now, but with every parting second, it begins to slip. Slip. Until realisation must have hit him. Behind her comes the sound of him climbing the thatch, but she is already up and over. She rolls as she hits the ground.

"I must be absolutely mad," she says. The barracks courtyard spreads out before her. Tents butt against the rectangular walls, and there are soldiers, members of the militia everywhere. Oil lamps hanging on shepherd hooks give plenty of light, but none of the men notice her presence. Niena nods, satisfied that the spell is still working, and looks back towards the roof whence she came.

"Go ahead, look for me here," she says to herself, eyeing the crouched figure. "Try and find your needle, and don't get pricked."

He disappears beyond, and she lets out the breath that feels like she has been holding since running. Another round of thunder follows as she looks to the tents, the men, and to a nearby door leading into the barracks proper. Niena shakes her head, turns, and walks, hoping to find her way through. But now, danger lurks at every corner.

Chapter 21
We Will Have Answers

Cart wheels creak, the groans of men replace the snorts of the cavalry's horses, and the tread of sandals is not as orderly as the marches of Marny's memories. Again through those rose coloured gates.

Someone to his right asks him a question, but Marny can't understand a word. He looks up as the late afternoon sky converges with the gate's ceiling. Then ahead. The stone walls around the portcullis drive almost every voice, every sound, forward. He pulls his cloak closer. It's no longer just blue; days of travel have imprinted their tales.

Where are the other guards? Bodies press tight. The smells of the horse and the other refugees mingle, and Marny's eyes dart from one man to another. Their faces, which had lit up in awe when the walls of Shenan first came into view, are now tinged with concern.

The soldier in question stands at the right corner, furthest from the opening, with his back up against something. As the crowd pushes along, that something turns out to be a set of stairs. Marny peers past him. *Are there more on the battlement? There should be at least a few on the gate.*

And the answer doesn't ease his fears.

"Not bad time, but if we had cut through the mounds like I suggested, we would have been here already,"

Griff says. Brother, Bip, and Gregory join him and Marny. "At least the taverns will be open. I can't be the only one thinking of crawling to the nearest hole."

Those men mutter amongst themselves, but Bip adds something that Marny also noticed. "Doesn't look like we have the first of it here," he says.

A few farm folk push past the little group. They are strangers, having joined only upon the approach to the eastern gate. Marny watches them go, his mind racing. It seems to him there are a lot of stories playing about right now, and the dragon is only one of them. Kimbesh had long been concerned about the war in the south spilling over. Yet it is the eastern provinces, if these folks are to be believed, who have apparently had to live through that fear.

"And we won't be the last," Marny says. Around them, the faded husks of merchant stands and guard posts lay against the walls like bodies after a siege. "Let's get the women and children to the market."

A couple of people chuckle until his concerned look catches, spreads among them. Only Griff is still smiling.

"Brother should probably go ahead and try and keep us together," Marny says. "Just take any road you think we can; everything leads to the market. She's an old soldier, this city. And Shenan's stomach is that bleeding place."

Griff shakes his head sadly. "We are now behind the biggest walls in the Empire. Can you not relax? There's nothing more you really need to do for the next while."

Above rests Cairnumastali. Stoic, ready. The blood-stained banners of the ill-fated Second Crusade of Reclamation still ripple, up there, up on the battlements. They have stood guard for the last forty years, while the city of Shenan's own are empty.

Marny licks his thumb and gestures to the castle. "That's our goal, not this shit bowl."

"I don't see why it matters…"

"You think they'll let us up in that?" Brother interrupts Griff, and everyone's eyes climb the steep rock side with him. "I doubt that we can just call on them."

"We need those walls, so you better hope we can talk to the commander, and convince him too," Marny says. "By the looks of things, they need more soldiers. Perhaps we can deal." And he grasps Griff by the shoulder.

So they move on from the gate, flushed out with the rest of the tide. Space opens once the barracks and other small outbuildings disappear behind them. But it will be evening soon. The cart wheels roll on, their grind barely audible over the collective excitement—which makes it even harder for Marny and the others to keep them together. Several of the refugees have broken off or melted in with the further traffic. Bip drags behind, to check on the other wagon, but Brother skips ahead. A half hour has to die before the swath of their families begin to pull in on themselves and move as one solid flock through the rest. After some confusion, it's Brother that leads them down a side path at Marny's direction.

There is more life in the streets beyond. And more clutter. Here, tents and hastily constructed shacks squeeze the traffic even tighter. The stores and houses themselves appear abandoned by their original owners, some even hollowed out. Squatters and fellow refugees fill these, swarming to and fro like ants in a kicked mound.

Where are all the bleeding locals? And the guard posts? Whereas the ones near the wall were merely empty, the corner stands here have been completely removed. Marny stops, hands on his sides. *Maybe the young Griff is right, and I need to relax.* But still this doesn't loosen his grip from the pommel of his sword.

"Look at this fabric I found," Deliah's voice reaches him. Marny turns, but only to push away a beggar that has come too close. She is there when he looks forward again, bright eyed, and younger, much younger; gone are the happy wrinkles created from a lifetime of smiling. In her hands there is a bolt of blue wool. One end is loose at the top, and it drags behind Griff so closely while they walk that she and the bolt could be his cloak.

"I think it will make a smashing coat for you." She smiles. "It will be so warm! Not like the threadbare linen the quartermaster gave you."

Marny nods, trying to look past her. But her laughter fills his ear, and she leaps forward and wraps him up with the fabric.

"And there might be enough left over for a blanket…Tonight?"

He staggers into a tent pole. The weight of her breath, the feel of those lips against his cheek, is too much for him to carry. Brother and Gregory see him stumble and reach out to lend him a hand, but he swats them both away.

"Keep on the cart," he growls at them. Marny struggles to stand, tripping over boxes, bottles, and other refuse in his way. The pole itself clatters to the ground. He grudgingly accepts a second hand from Griff.

They stay together along this street, past the remnants of an inner city wall, and around a fountain fronting a tavern ground. Both him and Griff's hands are on their pommels here, and all eyes are on the mercenaries that mill around a broken statuette in the centre. Marny's own slip from one to another, to a third, until he counts twelve, with three probably employed by the inn itself. Two guard the entrance, with spears at the ready.

Horseshoes clack rapidly: theirs, urged on. One. Two — in quick secession. They are followed by the noise of a rabble confronting the third guard. *Keep them tight, chords, keep those boys away from the other wagon.* Marny prays to himself as he sees a barrage of rocks clatter into the third mercenary's shield. *Bip is back there*, he knows. His head subconsciously veers to look behind.

But shouts bring him back with time enough to catch a red headed little scoundrel rock his cart, and scare the horse.

"Fatten his nose!" one of them yells.

The horse lurches to the right. Marny tugs on a woman's shirt, and gets her to switch places as the curses fly from the gaggle of youths. More thrown rocks follow. He shouts back his own stream of profanities, but that's all he can do.

"You got him!"

Marny growls at the second topknot that careens around his cart. And the chaos continues, with the captain ready to draw on either the mercenary or the boys, as a third follows his friends. All three of the youths retreat into the safety of an alley where cheers greet them.

"Little faster now," he says to the woman holding the reins. Marny rubs his chest where one of the missiles had planted dead on. "They're going for it again." Because the boys know he won't leave to catch them.

And they do, forcing him to draw, and walk the length. But here, unexpected help comes from the harassed mercenary, whose shield provides welcome cover. And a target for the boys and their rocks.

It's nearly a half hour before the last of their train passes the grounds. Marny makes sure to thank the mercenary in the only way such a man appreciates: a copper pressed into hand. The tavern's problems with the gang, however, will likely only continue. At least that's how

Marny sees it, as both the sounds of trouble dwindle, and the facade of the market gate teases in the distance. Between here and there the squeeze really sets in. If it wasn't for the carts, they would have to walk single file. Marny finds himself isolated at the back with their second wagon.

"Sausage," Bip says, nose to the air. "Smells nice and greasy."

The lines of scavenged open beds, refuse, and dirtier families now begin to taper, as if the refugees and downtrodden along this street have created their own little tiers of class among the newly classless. The people here are no less dishevelled, but there are more tents and scavenged shacks than before. And a sense of order. The last worries Marny.

"You can smell that over all the perfume and…whatever the chords that other filth is." Marny shoves a man away to make room for the cart behind them, then turns, and shoots a quick glance back at the old scout. "I'm only getting shit, shit and more shit. Unless that's your sausages?"

"Might be," Bip answers from behind. "Don't see many cows around here, anyhow."

Marny shrugs. "Rat then, can be a bit too stringy for my tastes. And too greasy for my constitution. Deliah used to say greasy food gives my outhouse nightmares."

"Might come to it," Bip says. And Marny knows that to be true; there were plenty of times where he had no better.

The talk stops once they pass under the arches of the market gate. A large field of cobble widens after. Perhaps once the market had been full of stalls and vendors, but the majority of them have disappeared. As Marny and the others make their way into the square, they find most of the stands sit in the middle, where they ring a series of small statues and stages.

But it isn't empty of people. More shoppers — *no, more like us*—stir along the outer edges, where the full stores, built into the wall itself, were. As he looks out, he can see where all the guards are now. At least six men meander through the crowds at the centre, and another three towards the entrance that leads to the main gate into town.

"That's far too few," he says.

Brother, closer now that their front line has compressed, looks back at him. "Should we take them towards the guards?"

"Not on your life," Marny says. Even from this distance, he can feel the tension between the two sides. The shoppers and merchants left in the middle, whether they realise it or not, are circling their wagons. "If there's trouble, that's where it will be. Piss in the wind, and it will rain."

"I'd like a corner," Bip says, but Griff disagrees. The two argue, and the discussion spreads to the rest of the hunters. Then to some of the men and women around, until finally after a half hour, the outer edges of their group have already begun setting up their tents only a few yards from the gate itself, in the middle of the rectangular bullseye of locals and outsiders.

Marny is listless during this conversation. His mind wanders. While they discuss Brother's suggestion of segregating themselves from the main rabble, he is thinking of his granddaughter. *She would be here. Maybe even somewhere in this very market.*

"Removing ourselves will make us targets for them, eventually," Marny says, rekindling the debate.

"It's good that you agree," Emyrh says. "We should all move together, for we are all lost. These men and women don't need to be strangers—no, I see their eyes from here, they don't want it! We could relieve them."

Marny rolls his arm back, popping his shoulder. "And that would just make us a target for the guards. We'd be instigators, maybe even insurgents, but definitely trouble. And they'd try put a stop to that quickly. I…"

He looks over their expectant faces. This was important, but somehow it just didn't have hold of Marny's attention. Or heart. "We are going to have to move by morning anyways." He looks to Griff, to Brother, and finally drifts back to the real priest. "Brother, organise the camp if you would. Griff, I think you should look to Bip, let him show you how to patrol discretely."

"And what about yourself?" Griff says. "I'll see if my wife can go ahead and set you a place if you are tired."

"I am going to go see who's in charge, and get us some answers," Marny says slowly. "I'm taking Emyrh with me."

"That crazy bugger?" Griff says, then shrugs at Emyrh. Whether or not the priest is offended, he shows no sign. "It will be evening soon. Shouldn't you take someone who can handle a sword?"

"I am," Marny growls. "Myself."

A cloud passes before the setting sun, and the strange shape casts a shadow over the square that spurs whispers. "We've not much time to argue." The last chatter around him dies away. "It will come. Tonight, tomorrow—I don't know when. But it will come, and we must not be in the streets here."

And everyone follows his eyes as he stares off into the returning light. "Or we'll join Randall in his pyre."

Chapter 22
A Temple Without Faith

Brown, unblinking eyes stare at Marny. And needle. Prick. They aren't jewels, belonging to a writer's soppy analogy. Nor are they coals, or dark and heavy slits. Just eyes in a sombre little man. His pose is rigid: back straight, hands clenched to the armrest of the chair he doesn't fully sit against. He is neither pale nor tanned. Old nor young. A wide forehead accentuates his slicked hair and the practical cut of his coat. You could almost tell time by the symmetry of the embroidery.

Marny looks away from the painting, one of four men in this establishment. "It was a long shot," he tells the owner, who despite the lack of customers still busies himself by cleaning the mugs and plates lined in front of him. "You're telling me everyone just up and left?"

"'Cept for the most stubborn," the barkeep says. "Or who's got the most to lose by running, I think. No one wants to end up like these poor dregs."

"I'm not keen on being a lawn ornament myself," Marny says. "Where'd they go then?"

"North I think. Might have passed some of your folk on the road too. Now that would really be something. Can you imagine the talk? One man says to the other: why you heading North? And he says back: to get away from the shit. Then he too asks: why you heading South? To get away from the shit!"

"A chorus of shit," Marny says and winks at Emyrh. "What happens when you get too many priests together, too, am I right?"

And the priest's hand grips his shoulder. "This is the second beer, and the second tavern you've come into. Should we not find a way to the militia?"

"Old habits," Marny answers. "I don't like walking into a pit full of armed men, militia or not, without knowing a—" His bushy left eyebrow rises like a grey flag, and he snaps back around to the counter. "Where did the rest of the army skitter off to?"

The barkeep looks from him to Emyrh, and then back into his mug. "Well, since you're paying." His voice drops off briefly into a mumble, then he clears his throat. "One morning they marched out from the black gate. That was a little over two weeks ago, and no one has heard. Though some are saying Arlin's men wiped them out to the man."

Marny chuckles into his beer. "They probably just dropped their trousers, and ran." The captain takes out a copper coin hidden in a pouch at his neck and slides it across the counter. He thanks him, and nods at Emyrh to depart.

"They aren't here! Whole city is ready to fight, and they're gone!" The barkeep says to their backs.

Doors slam shut, cutting off the barkeep's goodbyes. But other sounds stumble forward to fill the gap. Marny looks past the guards at the threshold.

"Where now?" Emyrh asks. "To another tavern? One beer a bar, we will be walking, stumbling all night."

"Normally I'd have found what I needed at the first one." He grimaces. "But normal's buried and rotting, and we're going someplace different next."

His sword brushes against a leg as they descend the stairs. The crowds are right where they left them.

In the streets. *I'll go track down the twit in charge here, in the morning. If he's still—Bleeding chords, can't these bastards find some other hole to die in?*

Almost wherever he steps. *Alright, this ass is not going to move unless I move him. I am also going to lose Emyrh in this. I need a damn leash.*

Huddled against both walls. *Tallow Vine Lane? When the chords did we walk past Wick's Down? Oh, I am not dragging my arse back through that.*

"We're going to have to cut through that alley. That one, there," to the priest. *I hope that's an alley and not just a crack in a wall.*

Even right up to the doors of the few open businesses. *But not further than that, thank good—shit, it's a bleeding crack in the wall.*

And as the last light of day escapes, Marny and Emyrh must fight back, and through. Clamour grinds. The wails of children battle for attention amongst laughter, the prostrating of priests and doomsayers, and even the spiel of peddlers trying to make a quick coin.

It's Emyrh who spots the real alley behind a tent. But it is also he who, after observing the decline of the noise from the main streets, decides to try to fill that void with his own. Marny ignores the majority of the talk to instead focus on the artificial canyon of yellow stone that engulfs them. Moving shadows tell of hidden presences.

"I'm not listening, lad." And some flowery prose wiggles its way out of the priest in answer.

"So you want to know the reason why I brought you with me?" Marny says. "It's because those people back there listen to you, chords, they even respect you."

A shabby grey cat passes from one hiding hole to another. And the captain leans on the opposite side, looking ahead and away from the priest. His fingers needle around a patch of weeds and into the crumbled mortar that was used to cover the former window.

"And that absolutely terrifies me," he says. The priest's happy resolve splits like the seam in the mortar. Marny laughs. But then that smile, just like the cat before, flees down its own hole. "There is a point, a purpose to all of this. And I brought you along because I thought there was something you might want to see."

"A street of rats?"

"No. What, are you trying to become a smartarse now? Stick to your prose." He stares ahead. In the alcoves that freckle every odd building, there are people. But he doesn't believe these are refugees. "Yeah, we should be able to get to the circus from here."

Marny's eyes sweep from hole to hole while they walk, stopping whenever the street bends, or they come to another darkened bricked up door. But the people don't seem to desire confrontation any more than they. The urchins, the homeless, and everyone who didn't fall into the narrative of the trade workers who refused to leave, or the rich who were too stubborn, shelter here. Their clothing, while not much better than the tattered remnants his group now dons, carries a local flair. Pieces of drapes, wider necklines. Old fashions, true, but exotic when compared to the rest of the canton. They have been driven from the main streets by the tide of mouths; they hide from the outsiders, the weather, and the guards—in that order.

"Circus?" Emyrh says. "Do we have need of a performing animal?"

His answer is to point to an empty alcove. "Not that kind of circus, not really. Use to be for statues," he says. "I think..." From here the alley splits. One path climbs up a short set of stairs, then turns. The other curves left.

"I know where we are. Right will just take us to a closed gate." Marny pivots towards the priest. "Just follow me, you'll understand soon enough."

Their alley eventually opens back into a street where the space is less filled with people, and more covered with refuse. It costs him time here to remember and regain his bearings. Time they mostly spend listening to the coughs and curses of the homeless. The rest they give to caution.

"This is an old squatter dump," he says, speaking of the other foreigners. "Means we're getting closer to the slums. Guards would have forced them here first."

Emyrh's worried look is brushed off, and cautiously — a quality which turns out to be time well spent — the two skirt the remains of buildings that have long given to dereliction and into another street. The time is late, and the sun only a memory. Moonlight throws back the shutters of clouds and greets them on its lawn.

"More alcoves, we're getting close," Marny says. The way has risen since the buildings on this new stretch were young. The captain, led by his shadowy memory, brings them around an old guard station and jail. It's boarded up now, dark and silent, but in the moonlight, the rare white plaster walls almost glow. And their steps echo here; the street folk seem reluctant to cross this part of the alley, as if the memories of imprisonment still chain them.

Crumbled frescoes and lines of old decrees paper the way through. It grows darker as they turn and front into another alley, where the narrow walls further confine Emyrh and Marny. The latter covers his nose with a handkerchief. Having grown used to the smell of sweaty humanity over the last while, the dank rot of the wood and forgotten papers is unpleasant.

"There," Marny says. The light from two torches makes it only a few feet from a recess in the path ahead. But it is enough. "That's it."

"This is a circus? I have seen many such things in your countries, but why are there columns, where is the roof?"

"Dust, with the people who made it," Marny says. "It was once a place for heroes, but opinions change, and they became a joke. And this pantheon was used for races, bloodsport." The clack of his footsteps doubles. It's another second or two before Emyrh's follow him.

"What will we find here?"

Marny stops, but does not turn around. "Our hope, maybe," he says to the air. "Now come on, I am going to need you to get—"

The smell of the pitch from the torch coaxes a nasty sneer onto the captain's face, but it is the stream of words in Emyrh's native tongue that makes him spin around. His eyes ricochet off the stone walls, play along the edges of the priest's coat, and then glance off his eyes. And in this pale light, they sparkle like broken glass in the street.

Emyrh walks past him, to the threshold, staring off into the night. Marny follows him, up to the torches that hang loosely in their sconces.

"What's bleeding gotten into you?"

Silence. Marny tries to follow Emyrh's movements, to see what he sees. But the torch stands so close to his own height that the captain's vision is marred by spots.

"Look!" And Marny does, while both Emyrh's shout and finger pierce the air and the quiet.

Clouds ripple over the moon as the night tosses and turns in its bed. There is movement where the priest's hand meets the skies, but is it clouds, or something else? Marny's own falls upon the priest's shoulder.

"Come on," his calm voice seemingly unsettling Emyrh further. Somewhere above, starlight, or perhaps moonlight makes its way to them. But the priest's eyes are locked on Marny, as he turns and moves through the archway.

When there is no answering shuffle behind him, Marny stops and looks over his shoulder. "Can you fly?"

"I know what my eyes see," Emyrh says.

"That's not what I asked." Torchlight flickers at his neck, and the sounds of distant laughter drift past. As Marny walks backward through the archway, his attention flits between the sky and his friend. "Whatever it is you thought you saw, unless you start sprouting wings out of your arse, there's nothing you can do about it."

"Maybe I should try," Emyrh says, joining him.

Distant, the last sounds from the old town lessen to only a murmur, overtaken and lost between the weeds and fallen columns they see. Even the priest is quiet, and having stepped up his pace to be even with Marny he now spends his time trying to arrest their progress after every rustle. But the captain pushes this away with a variety of snorts, sighs, and manhandling.

Ahead there is another set of torches, and the soot-laden face of a door is apparent even at this hour. Twenty paces from it, Marny turns to Emyrh, who has spent the last minute complaining about giggling he heard in the grass.

"They're just children," Marny says. "Filthy, nasty little brats. But brats nonetheless."

"What is this place?"

The grounds near the door are unruly, unkempt. "An orphanage of sorts," he answers. "But more like a field where people drop off unwanted mousers. And the woman you are going to see is the local cat lady."

Marny turns to the priest and speaks to the confusion he sees peeking on the man's olive-tanned face. "Only a few hours ago you wouldn't stop boxing my ears about wanting to help people and all that fluffy nonsense. Well here you are, these kids will need it."

"Children? An orphanage?" Emyrh and looks at Marny as if just seeing him now for the first time. "This is about your granddaughter, isn't it?"

"One of them might have seen her," he says honestly. "Or maybe she is even here, among them. Either way, this is the place to start and…" He motions to the sword. "They won't let someone like me near."

Emyrh nods. "Yes, yes." His face alight. "But what of the other children? Will this…cat lady let me among them?"

A bitter wind breaks around the two, and the worn edges of Marny's coat flitter like leaves on an old oak. He steps back, closer to the door and the fire.

"You're a priest. She will not turn down your help." He looks at Emyrh, and his next words seem to almost bubble out of him. "But there's more. If the worst is coming, you are going to have to find a way to lead the children out of here, and to come to me."

Shadows cast by the torch dance again as another breeze swings past, and this time the priest smells it too. "Is that—"

"My granddaughter should be wearing a white dress," Marny says, interrupting. "She is tall, nearly two hands bigger than you. She has long, black hair, and blue eyes. High cheekbones." His voice begins to wander until his mind finds the path back. "She will answer to Niena. Or Squirrel. Try Squirrel first!

"You can find me at the beggar's cemetery," he adds. "But I will send someone here for you."

"I will find her if she is here," Emyrh says. "But how long can have we got?"

And both of their faces turn towards the sky as Marny answers. "With luck? Morning. No more than bleeding morning."

Chapter 23
No Help Will Come

Riddles. *How much longer will I have to ponder in the dark?* Calem stands and slips to the edge right above the clock face. The ground is probably only four yards below him, but there's no use trying to peer through the grey soup that rises almost to the hour hand. With a bow, he tumbles off the ledge. The air rushes, bringing him the image of-

"Oberon," he huffs. It is more like six yards. Calem straightens. His feet and legs both throb from the impact, but he ignores that for the anger. "Who else have you pulled into your web?"

The girl. *The girl with Niena's lyre.*

There's a stall to his right that was filled yesterday, but today will probably remain empty. He idly looks under the sacks covering the bins, hoping something might have been left. No such luck. Calem taps his nose. It's taken him a few days to get used to having his mind to himself. Days spent confused, trying to piece this mess together. He's far away from the Mirepoint, nearly a world away. How did Niena end up here? Then there are the refugees, and the violence that has tumbled into the streets.

But it's that girl who continues to bother him. To pop up in his head, just like Oberon used to. Trouble has ways of doing that. Calem puts the thought of her away and slips into the main thoroughfare that leads towards the armoury and palace. Rubble from a statue he lunched under yesterday now spreads out over this street. Further, he can see and hear a mob's protest. He's content to stay at this end for now.

"Idiots," he says at the distant figures. "What the chords do they think the Queen will do for them? If she's not already long gone."

There are regular people here too: merchants and home owners. These poke out like scared birds, looking to pick up the pieces of their little nests after a storm. Calem turns away from an elderly couple rummaging through the remnants of their potted garden. More than one accusing glance is thrown his way, and not just by them. He skirts around the remains of a broken cart and heads west.

The mountain commands the skyline. Alone. The sandstone bleeds red into clouds that wrap around the base. Defiant. The castle at the apex challenges the very heavens to crash upon its walls. Calem stops, both in awe, and troubled.

"It's about to get worse," he whispers. Within those clouds something stirs. There are blushes of colour. Interludes of movement. Calem rests himself against the yellow brick side of a guild house and closes his eyes.

And opens them to a different sight. Tall grass parts left and right. A weed, flowering yellow, touches just on the periphery. In two bounds the view pulls over a ridged brim. It's a flower pot. Calem smiles to himself as he sees the back of a townhouse open up through the eyes of his furry friend.

The girl. The one from before, with the lyre. Remember her smell? Calem's thoughts fill the air like static and cling to the creature's mind, forming a gallery of pictures and emotions therein. He inhales, and imprints a last comment on the mouser.

Two neighbours argue in the background over broken furniture. The cat, after cleaning its paws, leaps off the balcony and into the small garden between the houses. Refuse, windows, and finally pillars pass by in gargantuan proportions. Calem's will pushes the creature away from these and towards the other side of the street. From a windowsill, a half-detached rain gutter gives access to the roof.

South. White clouds carry the yolk of the sun in a sky that ends in the cliff face of Shenan's Ring. As a bowl, or perhaps, a pan. And like a pan whose contents are set over the fire, some of the fog froths around the castle grounds, hinting at orange, yellow, and red. Calem reaches out with his mind, as if he could do so with his hand and pluck his breakfast from the heavens.

West, and north. But if any place were to have a fire lit underneath it, the militia's compound would be one. The field of vision swings that way and then accelerates. Chimneys tower to the right. Clouds to the left, and the roofs of the townhouses provide the way towards the forum, onward to where they last encountered Oberon's thief.

Calem stumbles forward and falls onto his hands. The air thunders again with a tremendous roar, and both him and the ground quiver in answer. He blinks. Nearby, a family comes into focus in nauseating lurches. The mother does not move, frozen. The child and the father though—Calem follows the boy's hands as he points to the sky.

No! The dragon's scales shred threads of clouds like bronze sheers. A wonder, a terrible, terrible wonder grips Calem as the beast's wings thresh and push a foul wind down, and down.

"Niena!" Fingernails tear on the cobble as he claws his way to stand. "Niena!" His shouts move the people in the street like a hornets' nest. The family that had been near frozen now pull every which way. "Niena!" The first building to taste the dragon's rage is alight in mere moments. Stones and brick crack like whips, clamouring above the rabble in the palace square.

His limbs tremble and his stomach heaves worse than the day he arrived here after the fairy's spell. Calem stands. Around, the terror takes hold. In every face, he sees a decision, and in almost all of them, that choice melts into a puddle.

Rage. Not terror, sadness, or hopelessness. Not that, but rage is what envelops him. The roar of the beast rocks the buildings behind. People cry out amidst the collapse, their words clear in the mist. "Help," they plead. But no help will come, and least of all from Calem. His will sharpens into red-stained knives.

Find the girl, he forces through the connection between him and his familiar. The anger imprints the animal fiercely. Calem closes his eyes again in the middle of the chaos. Through the cat's senses, the world is again an entirely different place. The screams, the fires, and the destruction differs little from the rioting before. The scene from the rooftop is of light blooming in the fog, and the cries could just as well be a celebration.

The cat turns away and dashes forward instead. His yowl carries in the air as a murderous intent drives him towards the forum that rises in the distance, just over his road of tile and thatch.

Chapter 24
Rumination on Power

An early mist stalks among the columns of the ancient forum, where grey smothers the green and brown of the grass and the trees that have overtaken the ruins. It is morning outside the walls of the militia's compound.

"I don't understand why I can't…" Shouts erupt from the direction of the palace, and Niena looks up from the patch of weeds. She holds her breath until the clamour dies. "Why don't I just use the lyre to make myself invisible again?"

Oberon paces inches behind where she kneels. "Fairy magic," he holds only the last syllable, then quickly: "Or things close are dangerous. You don't want to rely on them."

Fairy magic? A check goes next to an entry in the corner of her mind. "How close are we talking?"

"Close," he whispers, then rounds upon Niena just as she speaks again.

"I'm done mashing up the foeberries and stuff."

"Foeflower and temple berries," Oberon corrects. "Foeberries sounds like something you put in your oatmeal for a balanced breakfast."

Lights spark and roll silently against the fog in the south. Vibrant in the murk, the display reminds her of lightning in a thunderstorm, only the clouds here are far too low to the ground. Perhaps not for much longer;

they grow, and pulse, mushrooming. It is only after a moment of this that the silence is broken.

Niena applies the salve and whispers the incantation Oberon gave her. But when she sits up, she sees the back of the fairy's legs. He is caught by the distant chaos in the city, while her attention switches between him and the faint glow from the concoction on her hand. "This is starting to look a lot like your home," she says. "That place is so dark and dreary."

And the fairy snaps around. "There's no time for nonsense!" Oberon takes a step towards her. "You said the words, you said his name?"

Niena nods. "Good," his face softening. "It will be your warning should he come near, for when it burns it's time to fear."

There is a change in the lights. In the south district, where the clouds had flared the brightest, a smouldering ember remains. But now those same disturbances begin to appear elsewhere. East, southwest, but not north or west. The angry shouts from the palace begin to turn. Jumble.

"And now, you should go." Oberon shifts uneasily. By the time his gaze falls upon the castle, his profile and voice have taken on a bitter tone. "Head towards the cemetery on the southwestern face. You will find a passage that will take you into the mountain, and from there, the castle."

The edges of his coat are touched by a wind that should ignore him. He looks at the girl, and once more she catches a hint of concern about him that tinges his outward expression. And while he fiddles with his hat in both hands, and opens his mouth as if to speak again, Niena immediately reasons what is about to happen.

"Wait!" A strong breezes bursts from the south, driving the grey away and her to the ground. By the time she is able to recover, he is gone.

"Again?" Angry that every time she gets him normal enough to ask questions, he flips off, she inhales deeply to let him have it. "Bleeding..." *chords*, in a cough. The breeze brings with it a foul stench, one which almost rips the breath from her lungs.

That stench follows Niena out of the old courtyard, into a nearby alley. The way here crawls both towards the water and back to the camp, where the noise of activity—horses, men, and women—is more distinct. Through the fog and up a slight incline, she can see why: glimpses of carts, flashes of steel. The soldiers are moving.

Clack. Niena tries to breathe through the fabric of her sleeve. *Clack-click-clop.* She sees the outline of a tawny coat. Brown. White. *Clack, click, clack-clop.* Nostrils flare, steam in the cold air behind. And then those hoof-steps from before ride closer. She throws herself to the side as a horseman breaks through. Grey streams cling to the man like a phantom cloak.

Niena punctuates the air with more coughing. The smell has now settled in, and where she stands, the curved cut of the road doesn't help; ruins and newer buildings stack upon the debris of thousands of years on each side, while the roadway has been kept the same height for centuries. Higher ground teases, but that is also dangerous. Somewhere out there Calem is looking for her.

And now she crosses the street, placing her hand against that wall to follow until the alley spills into the walk facing the canal. Right or left? Left would take her to the main bridge, the one that crosses at the widest point, and also leads to the palace grounds. Niena scratches a back-itch against the corner. The way right spills into a smaller bridge, she notes. The talk in the soldiers' camp was filled with fear, fear of rioters. Both might be treacherous paths, and left—even with the air thick, she can make out shapes moving. What's more, she can hear them. Niena shivers.

Calmly she steps forward and peers into the water below. A thick groove separates the worked stone from the rough rock used to tame this stream. There is no railing, only an angled drop, but sometimes, at irregular paces, a pipe will protrude from the face and dive into the canal. One such is near.

Another crash of wind nearly flattens her. She looks up, and out, but from here the rooftops are hidden, not so much by the fog, but by the buildings beyond. Niena covers her ears as the gale returns, carrying again the shouts and screams from the old town.

She leans over the top and sets both feet on the edge of the thick pipe. Nothing moves, and she is able to inch down the lead roots. Below, the water trickles through a small middle channel, no more than two yards wide. Its shores consist of dirt and refuse piled against the stone canal walls. These banks are thin, but there is enough for grass, some weeds, and perhaps her feet.

"Left, or—" Shouts reach Niena, and her grip slips. The angle of the facing wall catches her, but the stones are slick with moss and algae. She slides seven feet down onto the shore, losing a shoe in the process.

Something large hits the water as she lands. She focuses ahead and braces her right foot against the wall behind for leverage. There's another splash. And again. Then her own, as she misses the bank, but manages to keep her waist and lyre above water until the rest of her body joins them on the crossing.

Voices on the stone just overhead. Angry words. Niena's gaze strays and accidentally catches several shapes bob in the water. She turns away, shaking, then up. There are no pipes near on this side. Weeds will have to do, and by them, and the narrow grooves in the mortar, she climbs. The musk of the moss and the chill of the stone rub her cheeks. Stain her new dress. Her lyre dangles precariously from a makeshift belt.

The edge of the street looms, and if she were to press her arms and push up, she would be able to see the gangs of rioters run by. But the sound of footsteps returns, and Niena is forced to hold herself against the side.

A shadow falls on her shoulders, almost as if…*Dreams starve and die if not fed by imagination.* Oberon's speech echoes inside. *It is always dark in the Fairhome, because it is the twilight of my people.*

"I thought you left me," she whispers back.

I would never do that, Niena. And she sighs, in real relief. *Especially not now. When we are nearing an important turning point. You may cross the road now.*

She takes that push and lifts herself up and onto the walk. Niena scrambles immediately to the cover of a wall, the same whose gate spat out the procession of ladies a couple of days ago. Against the cold stone, the pounding of her heart is almost as loud as the commotion at the nearby bridge.

This sky is unnatural.

Wind rolls and breaks against stone and flesh alike. Following Oberon's words, she scans the horizon. Morning fights against the overcast, and the clouds that had seemed so close to the ground, north looking south, from this vantage butt against Shenan's Ring like tethered balloons.

"It's so weird," she says. "Pretty t—"

I believe Calem isn't the only monster out today, Wyrmspun. Keep moving.

Niena escapes right, following the wall until the defences give way to houses and buildings built into them. There she finds her crack and slips around a manor's side before turning back to peer through the cut in the overhanging roofs of the side-alley. The world behind erupts in an explosion of red and grey. Smoke and fire.

Do you know why I call you that name? I think it is time for me to keep that promise.

Smells of cooking arrive with birdsong. Breakfast or lunch? Niena can't tell, and she suspects the bird is just guessing. She steps quickly. A bricked-up arch closer to the back of the manor provides easy access to a small path behind. The backs of several buildings stretch in a straight line after she climbs over.

"Why ya makin' eggs? I hate eggs!"

That's a child there, she thinks, while ducking behind a rain barrel. His first name is Christian, with a last name of "damn you," she learns, if association marries with repetition. Mother and child hover over a fire built into the recess to a back door.

Wyrmspun isn't a pet name, as I have said before, it's a curse.

The woman stirs milk into a second skillet, eyes forward, blank, and staring into nothing. "Just eat it."

Niena moves closer. White and yellow blend, eggs pop and sizzle on the pan. But the boy's nose scrunches, as if he had never been scolded for turning down food.

"I said eat it, don't make me say it again." The lady cracks a last egg before realising the bowl she was using has been taken for a helmet. Cupping the broken shell in both hands she quickly drops it in the only clean thing nearby: his drinking cup.

Just like being a dragon can be a curse.

"Damn," the mother grumbles, staring at the broken pieces mixed in with the yolk. A nearby spoon teases.

"What are you talking about?"

The ground shudders and crushes Niena's whisper. Something has crashed into one of the buildings nearby, and it came from behind.

Using fairy magic has many risks, none more so than now. There are creatures out there in this world who can sense it. They are drawn like children to candy.

Tiles shatter in the background, and the sound pelts the cobble like heavy rain. Glass breaks. Wood cracks. She stumbles out from behind the barrel, and neither the boy nor the mother pays much attention to her sudden appearance. As everyone turns towards the noise, there is movement behind, and the grind of an immense weight.

Niena starts to run. And they start to run. Masonry crashes down just a breath behind. It is Niena who meets the opposite end first, vaulting onto another bricked-up arch.

From the edge, Niena leans back to help, but they have disappeared into an open door. She quickly throws her right leg over the side. More fog has infiltrated this little alley. And the odour, that rotten egg smell, follows her over. She stumbles after landing on the opposite side and gasps for air.

Her lungs burn. Her eyes water. More and more of the foul white vapour floods into the street. Niena climbs a lamppost, to try and rise above, while to the left the shouts and yells of fighting echo. But between her hacking and the snap of timber, she cannot be further moved. Until, that is, she feels the heat.

Over her shoulder, a gap in the buildings opens. Niena stares in wonder. Flames rush through, smoke follows—smoke, for now she can see the difference. She digs into a small sack she lifted from the militia and tears off a piece of the rag that was her old dress. Face covered, she turns and dives back into the street left, wading through the vaporous sea as fast as she might. The fire swallows the row of townhouses built into the wall.

This wider street spills into a break in the buildings, like a river into a delta. She immediately sees why, and what is causing the commotion she heard a moment earlier. Here is one of the entrances to the Ibis District, a secure zone for those who can afford to live there. She staggers and stumbles through the cobble square. Several families are pressed up against an iron portcullis built into a villa's former stable.

Don't slow down, you are not in the clear yet!

A terrible sound rips through the air behind. A roar. A crash. Both accompanied by a rending, and the press of a sudden heat. But this new thing, the one in the background, the one shaking the foundations, reminds Niena far too closely of the whispers she had heard in the days prior.

One by one, two by two, the backs of those heads turn around. Revealing shock, then terror. Niena staggers forward into a run, not interested in sharing their moment. As she passes the decision to flee seems to spread among them like the plague, and shortly they too are rushing towards an exit.

People are trampled, children left behind in the rout. The narrow cut of this path funnels the press of humanity through the winding alleys, and into utter chaos. Niena, recognising she is about to be overrun, slips into a recess between two buildings.

She closes her eyes and flexes her toes over a bar in the iron gating below. The stampede fades into the distance. Yet a different discord finds her.

Niena coughs into her sleeve as a slow rumble replaces their patter. "It's like a plough," she whispers.

Do you see any oxen here?

"No." Though she lived long enough in Maidenhill to know what they sound like: the low growl of hard wood against unforgiving earth. Only there is the sensation of immense weight to this, and the field being tilled is the heavy cobblestone.

The cold of the iron seeps into her heel. She hesitates. One. Two. There is now a slow and heavy plod along with the rumble. "Shit," she says. Then down, towards the grate, "Shit!"

With a bit of effort, the sewer cover comes loose, and Niena takes the plunge into foul darkness as searingly hot air rushes overhead.

Chapter 25
What You Expect

Quick steps take Niena deeper into darkness where the salve's light is barely fit to prevent a nasty dip. A foul thought, but there is worse hovering overhead. She breathes deeply. Every so often a heavy *thump* shakes the street topside.

Her fingers tremble with the rock. Each stride feels as though it has the weight of eternity. But Niena's interest is taut like a drawn bow, bent and intense. At a junction, she stops and tilts her ear to listen.

Thomb. She presses her cheek against the wall. *Thomb.* Chilled air stabs her lungs. "Shit!"

Light floods and she throws herself against the brickwork in a desperate attempt to keep from falling. *Thomb. Thomb. Crack!* Niena covers her head—

The collapse stops. She opens her eyes. No shadows move. Nothing scurries. When the last of the broken street clatters to the pile, the last of the dust falls too. The light from a hole in the ceiling shows her one remaining path: right.

There is movement through that opening. Cautiously she places a hand against the wall, pushes off and clambers over to the opposite bank. She looks back again, through the gap in the roof. Flames wick beyond. But dust and debris rain again from a tattoo of impacts. Niena clutches the lyre to her chest and continues on.

The shuffle of her feet pushes her onward. Every tenth or twelfth pace is repeated somewhere behind by a deep, but increasingly distant, thud. She swallows and doubles her speed. Shortly, the echoes behind are scarcely louder than the drip of the pipes. It is in this quiet the shadows of all sorts of danger begin to loom in her mind. She finds herself stopping at every noise and sight. Especially when, before reaching another junction, she imagines amber eyes near the waterway.

"Which path now?" Right might be south. Or is it west? How long has she been down here, an hour?

Left, go left!

"Oberon!" she squeaks. "Where have you been?"

When and where you need me, his answer swamps the background noise as she climbs over to the opposite bank.

"This is all your fault," though she knows it's not. "I wouldn't be crawling through a sewer, escaping from a—" There is another crash behind, and the growl of something more living than stone. "It can't get down here, can it?"

This new menace is close. Brickwork gives way to street cobble, fallen and falling into a new gap in the tunnel behind. There is a glimpse, too, of something solid and metallic: a spear, or glaive, but with a thick, curved blade. She cringes as the end tears into the stone ground, and the shriek of the splintering rock rips the air.

You know what is urgent, that is enough.

A cascade of debris tumbles down into the open wound. Glass, metal, and other pieces of the world above scatter into the water in sparks of carried light. The blade—"talon," she whispers through clenched teeth—lifts out of the hole, taking with it more of the ceiling. Niena takes a step back. Smoke sneaks into the tunnel just below it. "It's a bleeding talon!"

Skyless thunder wracks the air and smothers those words. It is nothing like she has ever heard before, and more awful than imagination. Knees buckle, fists ball. Yet somehow she finds the ability to turn around and do the only thing sensible: she runs. Risking a plunge into the sewer water, Niena dives into the darkness ahead. The slap of her feet echoes. Ten yards. Twenty. The tunnel is filled with the smoke that assailed her before. Thirty yards, a surprise turn almost puts Niena into the soup. She crumbles instead to the bank, breathless.

You must keep moving!

"I don't know where I am going!" Niena's fingers dig into the exposed edge of a brick, and she yanks herself up. One step. A whine-like growl stabs the air. Another step. There is a rush of wind into the tunnel, and two heavy thuds in quick succession.

Brickwork eventually gives way to natural stone. She doesn't notice it at first, not while running for her life. It's when effort has stolen the last breath from tired lungs, and she trips and scuffs her knee, that this changes. Niena's run ends in a sputter and a dry cough.

Get up! You can't afford to take a break now.

No, not when the dragon, Niena breaks into a coughing fit. "Can find me by the lyre's magic," she croaks. "Even when I am not using it."

Of the odours she has been afflicted with today, what comes out of an exposed drainpipe beside her absolutely turns her stomach. On a whim, she waves her hand over a block just beneath. The script is archaic, but she believes it reads 'Court Street.'

She waits and listens. "I don't think it's chasing me right now."

Reality is often blinded by the guiles of want.

"Want?" Niena's voices roars against Oberon's snicker. "I want out of this damn hole. I want to know where my grandparents are. I want to bleeding well know why I am traipsing around here, while a dragon — a bleeding chords-blessed *dragon* — is stomping around on my head!"

You don't need the dressing on the cake to survive, it just makes things sweeter.

That's not the sound of the creature's claw on stone, but Niena's teeth gnashing. "If it's not the lyre that thing is hunting, then it must be you."

There are more —

"And it's not you!" she growls. "You haven't come up with your half of the deal. Everyone knows what that means: you can't touch the world!"

A few more yards pass; a few more minutes of silence endure. The tunnel widens slightly to offer room for an iron ladder. Niena's eyes ascend, but she remains below for a moment. There should be light coming from the holes in the grate above, but it is dark.

Three questions.

"Are you asking me?" The rusted holds complain loudly with each jostle from Niena's weight. She finds herself looking down towards her feet, expecting to see the fairy. "Or are you just being dramatic before you say something silly?"

I just gave you what you expect. Laughter. High-pitched, sordid laughter. *Yet, no, I am not asking...And I'm sorry child. Being so direct goes against my nature. Please understand how hard it is for me to do this much. I will answer three of your questions. Faithfully.* Niena hangs on the fairy's words, just as her elbow does to the ladder. The air below what she assumes is the manhole is neither chill nor fresh.

But the cover radiates a strong warmth, and she reaches out to stop only inches below. Fire, she realises, jerking her hand back from the metal. Her head feels strangely queasy, as if the air itself is thin. Instinct keeps her from getting burned here.

"Another, then. Have to keep going." A rung thumps dully on her arms as she slips down the ladder. Once on the ground, the path sprints with her.

Gradually the air thickens, and the smells return. It is once again hard to breathe, but at least she feels there is enough air to do so. Niena shakes her head, as if trying to shuck off doubt.

Between the drip from a pipe, and the scrape of rats on the walls, she whispers: "Three questions then, my first—"

Around her there is a whirl of sound, of laughter, that reminds Niena of gusts of wind sifting through crisp autumn leaves. Oberon returns. *You want to know all about the deal, the one that brought me and you together?*

There is such a string of madness pulling at the fairy's laughter, that her own response becomes shorter and shorter the longer it goes on, until it unravels into a simple, "Yes."

To understand that, you must first know who you are, or were. The tunnel veers right, and the conversation's tone changes just as abruptly. *You were Wyrmspun, cursed to become a dragon, because you slew a so-cursed dragon only a few hours from now.*

Niena stumbles, grabbing a pipe at the last moment to keep from spilling over the edge. *But no one knew what it meant, and you were alone in a city that was still eating itself alive.*

"Marny," she whispers.

Dead. Your grandmother? Dead too. The grade of the tunnel begins to change. A steep incline. *She perished long before in the pyre that was Maidenhill. And he would join her only a week after, paying with his life to protect you at the summit of the castle.*

The walls are cold. The air lifeless. There is a sadness to the fairy's tone that leads her along as if it were a song. *But you, Niena, you struck the final blow.*

"So you are telling me I made a bargain as a dragon? That…sounds ridiculous." As she wrestles to picture both the curse and the loss of her family. "And why the hell are we heading towards the castle?"

Two questions? I will forgive the first, because it all falls into the second. It must count, though.

"I want to know," without hesitation.

It's not an immediate thing, this curse. It works slowly, over years. After all, what is time to a proper wyrm? A creature who was born when the song was just a prelude.

The hand with the salve begins to itch terribly, but she resists the urge to scratch off the remainder of her light. Niena squints. Somewhere far ahead there is a light. Perhaps an exit?

You left the devoured husk of this city an urchin and set out for Taledric's. Somewhere along the way you were captured and sold.

Grey.

You were passed from merchant to soldier, from soldier to farmer, until the day came when physical changes left you unwanted. The first signs of the curse began to show.

Three perfect holes allow light into the sewer. Also sound, though both are muted. Niena hooks her arm around the next rung in the ladder.

Grey.

"Clear," testing the iron. It's cold, unlike the last exit. Black.

The ladder squeals as Niena yanks her hand back and nurses her trampled fingers. Grey. Black. Grey. Grey.

Dirt flakes off in the stuttering light. A stranger's footstep above echo metallically and once more throw the hole to black.

After the cover settles she twines her fingers between the holes and pushes. The grate rattles, showing her a crescent of the street before falling back into its groove. Niena climbs up another rung, and this time leans into the effort. With the groan of iron against stone, the topside world reveals itself.

"Where the chords am I?" Niena's breathy whisper is lost to the breeze. She can see little yet; the split of the road, the march of buildings down the street, and the backs of the people who trod on her hand at the far end come first. But it's what she doesn't see that has her spinning, and she slides herself out of the hole just as a boy careens around.

West looks a lot like north. "Maybe that's actually south," reorienting herself. The crest of the Ring still towers to her east.

And that's where the Drel'nu found you. Your travels had taken you far south, beyond even where your father had ever dared. Their song kept you whole, kept you Niena. Though, there is a question of how much of you was left by then. In turn, they became both your jailers and your new family. You were once again loved.

A familiar yowl spears her from the right. She snaps around, but the street is empty. Niena bumbles to a run.

And desired. For an acquaintance of the elves saw you, and coveted you. His name is Calem. Over the course of several meetings, and months, you became close.

This is the first district of the city. Ancient buildings rest upon even older foundations. The yellow brick that permeates every other street recedes, leaving behind a growing deposit of the same sandstone that forms the Ring. Niena rests below a towering gable held aloft by pillars that slide from natural formation to carved en-hancement.

Another meow prances along the pavement, but she can't tell from where. The itching on her hand now feels like fire ants. "I'm hearing things," she says. "I'm going nuts."

Calem—

"Let me guess, this is the part where he sweeps me off my feet, and we get married in some big to-do, only to later learn who he really is."

Not quite. The Drel'nu sensed something about your grow-ing relationship and tried to hide you. This infuriated him. Denied, and thinking that they were deliberately keeping the curse at bay, but uncured, to suit their own ends, Calem slaughtered them all, took you as his wife, and used their blood in a ritual to summon me because he believed the fey would have the power to undo the dragon's work.

"That would never happen!" Niena's yell thunders. The natural acoustics of an old palace, now warehouse, make it seem as if she is standing on the stage of an am-phitheatre addressing the crowd. The streets here are empty. "I'd never do that!"

That woman is a much different person from who you are now. Calem offered her the only thing that had come to mat-ter: security. And so she traded one owner for another.

Niena slips down an uneven side street that turns left shortly, following the outside wall of a large building. *He promised her that he could end the curse.* The wall and street continue right. *That's where I come in.*

She stops. "Can you?"

That is why you are here, in the past. There are only two ways to end this curse: for you to die, or for you to have never received it in the first place. I hope you appreciate which one I chose.

"So you came back to the past," she says. Her eyes snake through the opening between the buildings that make up this narrow alley and glance off a sliver of the mountainside. "Then, as I said, it's kind of obvious what I really should do: never go to the castle in the first place."

Look over your shoulder, now!

And she does, expecting to see Calem or the cat behind her. But neither are there. Niena groans, desperate to scratch the top of her hand, which feels like it is on fire. In that moment, looking between the tops of the walls and the street, she sees what Oberon intended. And takes a step backward. The fluted edges of the building's roofs frame a scene that makes her stomach twist.

See what I've been struggling with? I thought the best place was for you to stay in the Fairhome. But with your imagination, my goodness, that plan fell apart quickly. I failed for lack of time, something that is ironic and vexing. Sadly, it is too late to avoid the castle.

You cannot run. A diamond-shaped head splits the clouds. *You cannot hide.* Even from this distance the dragon's talons glint like spears in a phalanx. *You are in danger so long as one of the two of you lives.*

Murmurs from afar distract her, and Niena steals away. The street dead-ends and she is forced to backtrack through twisting alleys that look almost as much canyon as town block. Here there are still shadows from lit sconces meant to burn away the morning gloom, but which now only enhance it. She looks back several times in an effort to shoo away nagging fears. The words of the fairy ever on her mind: "It will be your warning should he come near, for when it burns it's time to fear."

Shouts reach her from the passage to the right. Through an arch, she can see a road curve away and march straight on from the mouth of the tunnel. The end of it is still covered by the insufferable mist, but the voices she hears from there do not sound violent. She reflexively covers the top of her hand. The pain is sharp and lingering.

He's close.

By happenstance, Niena looks once more behind. The alley is slim, allowing only a sliver of the outside world in. Torches speckle chinks in the natural rock, and poor placement means that rarely does the light from any two touch. She walks backward towards the sound of the crowd.

There's nothing, only the faint sensation of being watched. She clutches the lyre and quickens to a run. Footsteps soon join her when she makes it past the houses and into a row of merchants where the torches are fewer and the dark holes more numerous. The mist parts like snow to a plough, and the footsteps are clearer as the passage narrows again. Small shapes bob in the fog: children. Before Niena can understand what is going on she has merged with a procession.

Shouts. Commands, and cries from ahead. Whatever this is, it is one mass group. And Niena is a part of it now.

Chapter 26
A Different Path

A high-pitched shriek from the wyrm rattles the alley. The few glass windows shatter, and the iron bars that cage them clang. A gale follows. Calem watches the torches snuff one by one.

He tugs his sleeve and leaves the protection of the corner. Heat from the fires creeps behind, and his feline companion is cleaning himself nearby. Calem's eyes climb the walls. He can only see a shadow of the castle's greatness from where he is, but it is enough to stir.

Walking after the girl reminds him of more recent hunts. Cobble, might as well be river stone. The roar of the fire, the rush of the water. Different, but similar enough to trip a memory. He takes a corner and waits. Two men cut through the miasma and head his way.

I wait, ready for anything. The men run past him. Just like the Drel'nu did that one morning when he hid in ambush. He had tracked them for six months, half a year after his master expelled him for dealing with the fairy. Four at least before then, since they tried to hide from him. He clenches his fist. She was right, though not in the way predicted.

When their boots have trampled away, Calem moves, casually, up the middle of the street. The road rolls here unevenly, higher on the sides than in the centre. "In a good rain, this would be a river."

"A river." There's a sigh. "No, a moan," he says. A little to the left a thin woman rasps in the alley, recovering from the smoke. Calem wants to warn her—there isn't much time, the fires close in everywhere, and there still is the wyrm—but doesn't. He can't seem to get past her hair.

"Glynfaelen," he says.

"Glynfaelen!" I call as the chant washes over me. There she is. Yellow hair spills over bare shoulders, flowing down her sides like gold. I know her name, but Niena has learned to call her 'mother'. I had hoped she would one day let me do the same.

He shakes his head. But no matter how hard he does, he cannot free himself from the image of that beautiful face marked with terror. What had he done? "What I must," he consoles himself. Calem closes his eyes.

She flails, still alive, but dying. She cannot fight me. Even now, she doesn't have the heart to. I can feel my hands slick upon the spear's shaft. I never wanted this either.

He staggers into a signpost. The procession of children curls around a bend, the next length is wide, and the walls give themselves back to yellow brick and red-tiled roofs. Near, blonde locks dangle over worn hands. The woman looks up and catches sight of the druid. Whether or not she saw his face, it doesn't matter. He retreats from her as if she carries a plague.

Her cry is quickly silenced by a second thrust. Niena sees me now. She trips, and stumbles into the river's flow, just as the other elves ready their weapons. But I make sure no help will come from Glynfaelen. Again and again, my blade pierces white flesh, until she falls into the water, dead. The song is broken. My arms shake.

I look to the rest, and ready my spear. My stomach sinks, and I think of Niena, of our future. I do what I must.

Calem is forced to hold onto a crier's post to keep upright. Shouts follow commands, back from where he just came. He falls back. Fires choke the sky only blocks away. The flames stalk him, alongside the memories of last week.

Now there is a tattoo of boots, regimented. "Soldiers," he whispers. The foul vapours hide whomever it is that approaches. Calem can only see the woman.

Niena's weeping overpowers the rush of the river. She is pushed closer to the still arms of her mother. The water is red, the remains of her family begin to wash downstream.

"Shh." I press my thumb firmly against the dimple in her lips. "Listen close, Niena. Why isn't important. What matters right now is the only thing that could ever matter: my love for you."

A pitiful cry at his feet draws his attention. The tabby kneads into his boots as if he could make pasta out of the shoestrings. "Hope? I sold everything to have her, and now my future has been stolen from me by a lie." Calem points towards where the girl might be and notices the other shapes poking out of the smoke. His brow furrows. "There is no hope. What does the fairy plan to do here, I—"

The sharp prick of a sulphurous odour pins him to the present. "Of course," he seethes, understanding at once. Calem clears his throat before he kneels.

"It's meant to end in Shenan," drool strings from the cat's mouth to his hand. Again he finds himself looking towards the sky. "This was her home. She was born here—"

Pain flies across his face, then lands. "And she will die here." He turns his attention back to his friend. A house falls somewhere in the background. Calem doesn't flinch. "It comes to me to set things right."

"Follow that girl," he says, gaze drifting. "These people move as if someone among them knows of a safe space. My gut tells me it's a secret way into the castle." He can see more of the mountain from this vantage. "I will find you there."

Sparks flow around him with the return of the wind. Calem closes his eyes, ignoring the heat streaming through his spread fingers. There is a yowl from the lonely creature at his feet. "We have different paths."

Shadows are born when the sun pushes through a shield of clouds. Three different shades he can feel, restrained by tendrils of soot: theirs, the vine-shaped lines of a garden gate, the leaflike span of immense and beating wings. They are not easy to ignore, and he presses his eyes tighter closed.

A gauntleted palm jabs outward and pushes him away. He blinks, and is at once face to face with a stranger. Campaign buttons march the length of an old man's coat. Dirty, and as worse for wear as he is himself, they lead like a trail of breadcrumbs up the blue frock and end in a soiled cravat. Calem peers through the folds of his hood and into the eyes of an old soldier.

What is given can be returned. The soldier's neck arches while he stares deep into the shade of the druid's hood with all the intensity of a wolf stalking prey. Calem backs away and lets the shadows swallow him.

Marny snaps around and yells to Brother, "Get ahead to the carts, don't let any of these weirdoes near 'em."

Bip and Griff are already at the cemetery. Brother, alone among his hunting companions, is within earshot. The sound of drawn steel reaches him even over the fires that close in. *Madness*, Marny sees. Flames leap from the armoury. He yells ahead to a throng of grey blobs mingling with the children and orders them to tighten their group. Those soldiers were pickups, just like the orphans.

His men pile through an old gate in twos and fours. Some are unburdened, but most carry supplies. One of the carts did not make it away from the market before they were set upon. Marny shouts encouragement as they pass. It is all he can do to keep their eyes on the ground and not the sky. The air chokes.

But his own? He sees the wyrm. He sees it slice the heavens with impunity, yet not only that. Tower, battlement, and house are blackened as easily as clouds and sunrise. He takes one moment to watch the beast dip below a line of buildings. New fires awake in that direction, and a hawk erupts from a twist of black smoke. Marny covers his face, and he turns and stumbles towards his party. Soot threatens to put him in the ground. Luckily, another member of the company catches him by the arm from behind.

Together they wade through the darkening street. The urchins have already fled, and those they pass now are mostly elderly. Like him. A fresh current catches the pollution and lifts it away. For Marny and his companions, the breeze is salvation. Elsewhere the mood is different. The flames roar as more timber, houses, and lives are devoured.

The moment of relief is taken by the screech of the dragon when they stop near two white marble pillars at an alley entrance. Marny coughs. Several people brush past.

"Get inside," he commands, pushing an old farmer through. One pillar supports him, acting as a sturdy mass in a sea of ash and flame. There are more people out there, shapes bob like buoys in the smoke. But with each passing moment, the outlines and flashes of colour disappear; they melt in with the city street or fade away to nothing. Before long there are just two more people following.

"This way!" he shouts. The two, a middle-aged couple, nearly overwhelm him with pleading questions, but between the coughing and the press of heat, he can give none. "My men know the way now. If they were with us, we got them, but I don't know your daughter."

A crash from behind snatches the conversation away, and all turn. The wyrm's return lights a fire in the three's faces, and upon the roof of the villas they just passed. Marny's growled command of "keep moving," is better than any whip, and the refugees do just that.

Yet he remains. He wipes sweat from his forehead and retreats behind the pillar. In the smoke, just before the appearance of the wyrm, he caught sight of something peculiar. He strains, slowly pulling back into the alley himself.

"Deliah?" Nothing. He calls out for her again. There is a shift in the grey, and a vague shape. "Over here, get on, towards my voice!" But if there was anyone to hear him, the words must have frightened them away. Moments pass, and no one answers.

But a yowl. A stuttered purr, and finally, a flash of orange at his feet nearly make him jump. He tries to laugh as the tabby disappears behind, but it falls quickly into a wheeze. Marny reels. Flames billow from the windows opposite, dance in the streams. No longer able to wait, He takes one last look behind, then he too flies within.

Cobble passes the baton to stone, and stone to rough stairs. Shortly he is joined by a small gathering of refugees at the cave's mouth. They look listless, worried, but his return lights up the cave better than their torches.

"Try to stay together," he tells them. "These catacombs go on all through the mountain, and the countryside. You steer away from the path I've lit and we won't find you."

Screams of men, or the beast? The noises channel down to them in a stream of sound. Marny places his hands on the back of a young woman and gently guides her forward. At the bottom of a set of natural stairs, he chances one last look behind. For some reason, he expected to see his wife there, but the hall is empty.

Chapter 27
Where Doom is Written

Shoulders brush shoulders. The texture of the stone under Niena's fingers changes from rough and natural to smooth and worked, and, in the breath between torches, where the fire is neither too bright or dull, she can see paint. Elbows poke. Niches start to appear along the walls; long, shallow, and rectangular, they are large enough for a person to lie in, but would not be comfortable for the living.

A burly farmer roughs his way through. Women, children and other men are pushed left and right in the tight corridor. Niena's own face gets intimate with a fresco of an ancient monk, while the offender tugs at his collar just below a torch. He gasps for air.

Voices cluck in response. Prayers. Cries. The unsure words of men and women trying to be strong, but failing. And tempers flare Niena's. Twice in one day, she has been left to wander through a dark tunnel.

"You just mind me, young Ellie," a brass, but motherly tone walks up her back. Niena squeezes nearly into a crevice as the lady lifts the child up by the belt. The young girl's dress tickles the stairs as both stretch over and through, and two hundred pounds of maternal instinct throws open the gate for everyone else to follow. She ends up stuck with her new acquaintance, the monk, while everyone who dithered at the cave's mouth drives through with the herd. For the next half hour, the mass shoves her aside, as if just beyond the next bend they might find an out. But there is no immediate escape.

When the last of them disappear, Niena exhales and tumbles onto the stairs. Footsteps depart, and footsteps approach. She is tween two groups, and not having any interest in being trampled, secures the lyre and follows after.

The incline is real and makes her wonder. She lived in Shenan for a large portion of her childhood, and during those years never heard anything about caves in the Ring. Secret passages in the castle itself? Possibly. She taps her lips. No, there are many things she doesn't know about this city. Six years running the streets is enough to find a few of the special hiding places. Ten years leaving, though, is too long to know everything. Passages in a castle seem practical though.

"I'm lucky that I ran into them," she says. The stairs here are uneven and rougher than before. There are scratchings above some of the sconces too. They could be pilgrimage symbols, she thinks; seeing one of the cults here would not be surprising.

Niena stops and traces a carving. "First Brigade, Gerard Veilaroon, Battle of Burning Wood, 455," speaking each word with the pass of her finger. Now the man-sized cutout below the inscription makes sense. She's in a tomb. The thought creeps with her.

Fewer torches grace the passage deeper along, giving just enough light to tip a hat to the other. "They're markers…" Niena's tongue hides quickly. A dark hole opens on the right, where the wall curves and the way inclines. She squints, and her breath leaks out in a hiss.

There's a man that way. Thin limbs bend the darkness and swing with all the regularity of a tick and a tock and the unnatural flow of something both solid and limp. She freezes, scream catching, heart hiding. Niena's fingers clench white against a protrusion at her back. A step: hers, and its. Hers up and backwards, as frozen limbs try to fight fear. Its, lithely onwards.

Distorted shouts, curses reach Niena from ahead, up the stairs, though she doesn't dare turn. The sounds are normal in the light of the last few days. Even reassuring. She stiffens, and stares hard into the blurred shape. It moves steadily forward, with a gait that matches the slide of the moments. With each step nearer, however, its glamour falls away. Terror slips off stooped shoulders. Awe sags around knobby ankles.

A cat meows. Torch light flutters. The flames dance. Really, all the usual atmospheric things happen.

"Oberon," she says, putting a name to the tide of words forming in her head. "I should have—" The fairy smacks his lips, forcing her to speak louder. "You won't let me think, will you?"

She says with a smile. Because thinking is bad. Grunting and random acts of aggression are more her forte.

"Stay out of my head," and pauses. "You've come by to check on me, haven't you? What's about to creep up and eat my head, then?"

Oberon smiles an unpleasant crescent and beckons for Niena to follow. She sighs in answer, and looks to her left and right, then shrugs and joins the fairy's side.

"You are not out of danger," he says, which immediately earns him a sour look. "I need to keep you on your toes. Even with your grandfather near."

"Marny?" Niena looks from the suddenly real hand on her shoulder to the lit path. "He's here? You're not just messing with my head, are you? Tell me!"

Oberon's chuckle is hollow, and he pulls her closer to him. "There's plenty of time for tears later. Walk a little with an old man, will you?"

Niena looks to the light behind her, sees it dwindle. There is darkness ahead, but Oberon's otherworldly glow does provide some measure of sight. Enough, she realises, to see that the niches grow more numerous this way.

"Have you thought on what you are going to do after this? If you survive." His gentle hands guide beyond other passages. Or graves? It's hard to tell, and her mind is more fixated on the musky smell and the fairy, letting things pass by in the dark.

"I haven't had a chance," she says.

"Left or right?"

Niena looks up, beyond the gnarly beard, and into his ghostly face. His nose wiggles when he nods. "Left," following his gesture.

"You said something about me being captured if I go to Taledric's."

"West, east, south," Oberon's words trail off. "North. I see pain, no matter which direction you take." He turns, and his gaze falls gently upon her. "Whether or not you can wield iron means nothing against the multitudes of people who would do you harm. War approaches, the Empire is crumbling. And you are alone."

She stops, and Oberon glides in front of her. "Then what's the point? Why don't I just take a dive off the tallest tower I can find?"

"You could do that," the fairy says. "Or you could learn from me in the Fairhome." Niena watches him as they drift through another junction. Looks to his eyes — what she can see. The flashes of menace that she noticed in their older interactions are not there. His face is gentle. Soft.

"There are riddles in the dark that need unravelling. Secrets that lay sleeping between man and god. And from fairy, you can walk those dreams."

"Using my power, or the lyre's?" She asks from the side of her mouth. "Why do you care so much?"

They stop. The corridor spills into a small inner courtyard where piles of bones litter the ground and sarcophaguses pockmark the cavern stone. There are three exits. "Choose your path," he says, turning. His face lays its cards upon the table.

Niena tilts her head. "I want to know," she says. "I need to know. Count it."

"Straight then," she says calmly. Niena leads at his gesture, and they plunge forward.

He starts with a whisper. "It's simple, really. I've been alone for a very, very long time." Then his timbre builds, and falls like rain on the meadow. "The sun sets on Fairhome, and me. The dreams of men are not strong enough to light the way there, not anymore."

"There were four of us only a generation ago," looking at Niena. "One, I know is lost. And old Twyl Teg's song I have not heard in an age. That leaves just me, the oldest. And you, the youngest."

She covers her face. Night flows over the field in her mind's eye, and she tries to push away the smell of decay. One breath. The sun has not completely set; the last rays are faint. But reality returns when her fingers slip down.

"What do you know about your mother?" Before she can catch another breath, "Nothing, I imagine."

"She was kind," Niena says, struggling. "I remember she would sing to me…But what am I saying? She has only been dead for a couple of years, I—"

"Not the woman that raised you," he says. Their gaze meets, and Niena's face chills as the fairy towers over her. He points to the lyre with one spectral finger. "How could a manling claim ownership of that? He has no right! It never belonged to him."

One knight of the kin. Two wills. Three chords. Four humours. Five elements. Six words. Seven days in the land of men.

"Get out of my head!"

"You are my granddaughter," Oberon says. This second statement puts the nails in the coffin of Niena's composure. And his. The fairy's mouth twists in pain. "I've lived between the worlds, watching the stars of my people veil. So when that human sought you, I saw my chance."

"No." She tries to cover her ears, but his voice envelops her.

He opens up his hands, letting their glow bloom like a phantom flower. "And yet we are still in this damned castle. I am using all of my glamour to tip what comes, but I do not know if it is enough."

"You aren't doing this for me!" she says. "What is it you want?"

"To not face oblivion alone," he whispers. "I accepted Calem's contract knowing that if I should succeed or fail, it would end the same for me. This land is no longer meant for a pure fairy, but neither can the Fairhome sustain me. I am a child of one world now: death."

"I am not going to trade one owner for another," and she stands to face the fairy. "This is my life!"

At this he smiles. "No, I see that you wouldn't." Oberon temples his fingers. "I respect that, I truly do. Yet you can only make a choice when given the opportunity."

Seeing the telltale twinkle in his eye, Niena reaches out to try to catch the fairy. But he is nothing underneath a roofless night. Four gashes mar his spectral image, and he rushes forward like a gust and sinks into a thin coil that wraps around her. She lets out a cry as he snakes up and lays those tendrils upon her lyre.

Did you ever wonder why I was able to pull you and the lyre into the Fairhome? You are both of fairy. Forgive me, child, my last hope is that you will get lost in these caverns until the hour has passed. And I must save my energy, to shield an-other.

The vapours of Oberon pulse, throb around the lyre. She fights, but a powerful force pulls her arm up, and the glow from the fairy's essence cascades over the ground, against the ceiling. It crackles, she winces.

And then he, lyre, and light all at once, are gone.

Without him or the noise from the crowds, the cavern returns to what it has always been: a tomb. Devoid of colour, absent of everything but breathing and the shuffle of her own feet on pebbles and grit.

A wild thought leads her to check the hand with the salve, and she holds it up to the air. Nothing. And now, if anything, the space between expands, instead of closing in. Her shoulders sag, and her long black hair dangles over Niena's face, but it doesn't matter. She bites her lips, tasting the blood and the dry, cracked skin. For her, it feels as if miles lie between the cavern walls.

"Hello?" she yells.

The stone answers back, "hello," and leaves her feeling empty, tired. Niena slumps to the ground in a heap. "I'm just talking to myself."

My grandfather. It's nice owning her thoughts, not so fine making conversation by them. *Marny is my grandfather, not that...thing.* A long sigh hisses. Again, only hers, She scoops up a pebble and tosses it. The little stone bounces once, twice, then hits a wall. *But that doesn't mean he isn't telling the truth.*

Dirt crumbles underneath her raw palm. The pebble took two good hops. With the strength of the toss, and the angle—Niena rubs her eyes; no, maths isn't her subject. She kneels. And patience isn't one of her virtues. "Is anyone out there?"

"Silence is an answer," she mumbles. *Two ways forward from here.* One involves hoping the fairy returns. She stands, choosing the other, and gropes around in the dark in a manner that must look, if she were not alone, entirely stupid. "Hello?"

Niena pauses. *Did someone just say hello back?* Any movement, even the caress of her thighs against each other, drowns it out, but it was there, she is sure of it. "Please! If you can hear me, can you bring a torch?"

There it is again, louder, and clearer. It's coming closer. "Hello?"

She stumbles and falls onto her rump, and for the effort is rewarded with hair full of dust, and the distinct tug of her dress ripping. Niena balls her fists and tries to sit up. At once, upon her chest, there is a deep-throated thrum and the pinpoint pressure of four paws. The smelly creature butts its head against her mouth.

Purrs. Drool, and plenty of it follows while a wave of anxiety bites, then lies down. Niena unclenches her fists. The little creature, whatever its master might be, is first and foremost just a cat. But there is one thought that leans in to pick her up: a chance, and also, a risk. "You understand me, don't you? I mean, you can understand what I say?" There is a glint of intelligence behind those amber ovals that makes her question her previous assumption. "If so, could you maybe lead me out of here?"

The mouser lets out another happy "meow-rowr," and blesses her with a healthy sneeze.

She wipes both feline and blessing off, cobbles herself together, and finds the new hole in the dress's train with her thumb. All in one motion. The effort, however, is too quick. Niena totters, dizzy, while the little bag of fur and bones weaves between unsteady legs.

"Lead on, then."

Good to its 'word' she hears the mouser pit-pat away. Niena pursues, but finds that her own steps rumble over his. She stops and listens, and as if hearing the girl's thoughts, the cat lets out another yowl.

"Keep meowin— Ouch, chords!" A rock wall greets her toes, bluntly. She leans. A chin of unworked stone supplies a decent grip while tending to her foot, but the ground is uneven and Niena almost falls again, only securing herself at the last moment on the corner of a grave.

What's this? she thinks with a wiggle of her thumb. Metal. Niena lets down her foot and explores the hole, this time with both hands. Polished steel, leather, then a fine, unblemished edge.

"Meorw?"

"I'm coming," as she tosses the knife into her satchel. *If that man, this Calem, can't be reasoned with*—another cry from ahead snaps her back. "I'm coming, I said. Chords, I am going like my great auntie, having a bleeding conversation with a cat."

The hour in silence seems much longer than the time she spent with the fairy. Ahead, flames wick. The cat lies stretched out on the cavern floor, cleaning its paw. She moves cautiously. No sound comes from the frame of light, or the darkness behind. Still, Niena expects that to change. *Where is your master?* she wonders as she looks down at the feline's belly. Three steps bring her to the threshold, and the warmth of the stone underneath the torch welcomes her hand. She looks down the stairs but doesn't recognise the path. Up, neither. The cat rolls as she steps over it, and emerges from underneath her dress as if it had been caged there.

"Thank you," she says to the mouser's yawn. It dashes ahead, surprisingly fast for such an old creature. Yet her gaze drifts down the stairs — the other way. Back into the city isn't an option.

Shouts peal down the stairs without clear speakers, and she quickens her pace past junctions, holes, alcoves. Up, with the cat's tail just in view, and the air warming from freezing to only frigid. The voices become distinct. She can make out some of the words, mostly those of one man.

Her shoulder brushes the raised portions of a mural. The top of the stairs ends in a wide single door, open to a main hall. One man stands in the middle. He is a boulder in a river, where drab tapestries and grey walls are the banks that force the water, these refugees, onwards. Their destination? Behind the man.

Laughter can come with tears. Relief can make you quake. Niena's voice is strangled as she whispers, "Grandpa?"

But there is something wrong. Daylight breaks in. This intrusion is not abnormal in a ruin, yet this arrives with a sound as of an enormous clay jar being slowly broken, crushed. Niena's toes spread out on the granite floor. She feels the groan of the castle, and the rumble climbs.

"Marny!"

Tall and rigid. Thin, yet commanding, the captain remains at the centre. His attention is on the soldiers that flank him until she calls a second time. He looks about, unsure. Niena emerges from the threshold and into the light.

Marny stares at her, through her, as if haunted. "Squirrel?"

Cracks appear in the walls. Those men at his sides pull him back and away just as the chapel's boarded-up windows rupture inwards and shower those too close to the main door with glass and wood. More sun is carried in, sliding along serpentine talons that rend the stone.

The torchlight shies, and shadows spin around her. Niena hesitates, then takes a step forward. The dress snags. She tugs-

"And where do you think you are going?"

The dress is not snagged. Someone is holding the train.

Out of panic, she launches into the figure, fists, elbows and nails doing little more than scuffing the shine on his jerkin. He snatches her hair with a dirty hand and spins her around again. In the brief turn, she sees flashes of stone falling to the chapel floor like hard rain. The wall itself begins to buckle, and collapse, first backwards as if being pulled by a great weight, then inwards.

Another hand cups her mouth and she reacts instinctually by sinking her teeth into the web at the base of his thumb. He doesn't scream, but she can feel the hallway twist. His weight forces her into the wall, head first.

The last thing she sees of the room and her grandfather is the body of the beast, great and awful, ruin the double doors and land in the chapel. The light of the torch drains away quickly, like water from a pulled plug.

Chapter 28
A Trail of Goosebumps

Dust chokes the air and obscures Marny's vision. *Roof fell*, he remembers groggily. A sharp pain in his left side draws more grumbles, and a stale odour saturates his clothes. There isn't much he can make out at his feet, but a pinhole of light near his head offers hope. His elbows bump fragments equally hard and jagged. His chin cuts itself on rock. Stone, timber, glass; together, *makes a coffin.*

An effort to clear the hole brings a ring of the outside into his world, revealing layers of blue and white. Marny thrusts his hand through, but dirt crumbles and the opening begins to collapse. His frustration brings more down and he is left again with a small window. Enough for him to hear the tragedy, but not see the actors. Resigned, he wheezes into an angry stillness.

Warmth holds his hand. "It all fell apart anyways." The taste of his own blood is on his tongue. "Deliah. I couldn't save them, any more than I could you."

"You are too hard on yourself, pipes."

He laughs at that, but it is strained. Weak.

"What about the Harbins? They are safe in the chapel's cellars. Or the Haymens with Old Mister Sharpe? The Tanglefeet? Bobbins? And little Greya from Tablewood?" That warmth slides between his fingers. "Do I need to go on?"

Marny peeks through the hole and regrets it. The same face that has hung above their mantle since they were newlywed shines through, but her smile and cheeks are as alive as the day it was painted. He turns, and silently mouths a prayer.

"Then I will: the Canewoods, the Winterstones, the Mindles —" She breaks into an exasperated sigh. "Pipes, all these people who would have died to bandits, disease, or starvation would be hurt if they knew you thought they don't count."

"They don't!" he shouts. The quiet sneaks in with the cold, leaving a trail of goosebumps. "I failed the only people who matter to me."

"No, you didn't," she says. A breathy pause stews. "Your granddaughter still needs you, can't you hear her?"

There is something. Marny holds his breath and listens. It's faint, but is someone shouting his name? His throat rattles with a dry cough, and he pounds the dirt with his fist. *Or maybe it's just a memory.*

"She's dead." He laughs hoarsely. "Just like you, come back to haunt me."

The cries become desperate. Marny cringes. "Figments of an addled, deranged mind."

"And if we are? Would it matter? Wouldn't you go back to Maidenhill right now just to save me, even if it was only for a dream?"

Marny looks to confront her. But there is no one there. *Real, or not,* her voice hiding in his head, w*hat else matters to you more than knowing out there, somewhere, your granddaughter needs you, and you are the only one who can help her?*

"Squirrel." Even in death, Deliah is right. A spike of hot anger shoots through fingers that then tear at dirt and debris. And quickly fades. The hole is still barely the size of his fist, and Marny shivers against the ground, exhausted.

She needs you.

Five fingers stab into the gap. Four pull back, dragging in more dirt, opening the hole just a little wider. Again. Three inches more open up on either side. Again. Two feet worth of sky. Again. *One more time.* Marny thrusts his fist into the open, and pulls himself out and into the sun. Alive, and free.

Not everyone was so lucky. Bodies lay between layers of rubble, more at the entrance to the tunnels; as Marny holds his head, he can see that some even tried to run out into the courtyard, and though they escaped death in the crumbling ruins, the wyrm made their ends far more violent. He looks left, searching for his soldiers. *Bip*, kneeling. *Dead.*

Marny climbs over a broken statue. *Griff.* Warm breath hits the back of his hand as he crouches over the man. He slumps, choosing a goddess' stone face as his seat. There are other signs of life, mostly shouts and cries, but Marny is lost to the stink of blood and sulphur.

"Bugger all this." He dabs his forehead with a dirty handkerchief. Mired thoughts and heavy doubts wipe away the strength in his old, chiselled features, allowing him the peace of apathy as he stares into the horizon and spreads his finger over the statue's eyes. There is no sight of the dragon, but he suspects she is near.

Marny!

Shapes move over the courtyard. There is a high-pitched screech that rattles the fillings in his teeth. His hand moves reflexively to the pommel of his sword. The way forward lies around a tree — burning — and between the buildings and battlements that guard the outer ring. Just beyond there is a fallen tower. The living have all but abandoned the field, except two.

He recognises a tall figure from before the chaos, and the one being cuffed by the wrists. "Squirrel," he whispers. Marny's feet slide on broken tile until he comes to the middle garden. The grass is now gone, shrivelled to ash, and the lone tree has been reduced to kindling. The flagstones that fence it are blackened. He walks carefully, but even so, his boots crush and pop on glass shards forged from the dragon's fire.

His eyes shift to his right, startled by a sound. The swish of giant wings, the snap of a tail punishing air, four deep thuds and the crack of tile and stone. *Thomb.* Marny's hand flies to his sword. *Ca-rack.* The whistle of steel is answered: *thomb, thomb, thomb.*

Stone gargoyles teeter and fall as the dragon adjusts its perch. Marny takes a tentative step backwards. The monster preens, the scales and spikes around its jowls shimmying. Twenty yards or more of beast stretch out over the keep, and it regards him with a menacing tilt of the head.

His grip tightens around the hilt. Knuckles crack and pop. The dragon watches him intently, matching posture for posture, long neck stretching and head arching downwards at the threat. Marny raises his sword and the wyrm rises, wings outstretched.

"Come get me, you son of a bitch."

Wind, stench, and roar swoop down upon him, and the dragon launches into the sky. Round, round, picking up speed, building a deadly arch. It rings the keep's tower, talons raking at copper wire and scaffolding as if they were awful harp strings. Marny remains still. A final arc nears completion. The monster's tail writhes and the mouth pulls back, baring several swords to match the captain's, but it is the quick intake of air that has the captain, out in the open, wise to the idea he made a mistake. A terrible gale staggers Marny, forcing him to the ground.

"Blee—" Flames issue from its maw down, and down, sweeping over the captain. Wood explodes behind him like thunder and the air crackles. Yet Marny is safe. He stands and stares at his untouched skin and clothing as the dragon disappears behind, then turns and watches the beast arc around. The tree nearby is re-kindled.

"I must be blessed." And then he squints. "Or cursed."

The wyrm hovers, slowly gaining altitude. There is a shout. A twang. And a black streak flies from the battlements and slices its neck. The monster screeches in rage, and dragon fire streams every which way. Marny rushes to his feet, profanity his only ally. Ahead, the ballista is being readied for another shot. Above, the dragon circles, building momentum.

He runs for the ramparts. There are two there: a girl, tied to the firing mechanism of the ballista, and her kidnapper. Below the noon sun, the rest of the sky is blue, happy, and free of winged beasts. At ten yards, Squirrel's captor sees him, and their gazes lock, soldier to druid. What passes from Marny to the other can only be answered by the draw of a weapon. So the man does.

"I remember you from the city." The kidnapper's stance is practiced.

"Give me back my granddaughter."

"Granddaughter?" He scoffs. "This is getting intimate, and I've no tongue for it." Behind him, Niena fights her binding, chokes on a gag. "Leave, I warn you. You approach your death, old man."

Marny's arm twitches. "I'm not here to listen to poetry or nance around your pole."

The ground he stands upon rests only a yard below the wall itself, though behind the ballista there is a sheer drop of thirty. He paces, slowly manoeuvring into a better, closer position. The response to his approach is a sword to the girl's neck.

"Let her go."

Calem shakes his head. "I have plans for her."

"Then the coroner is going to have a busy day with you."

Their eyes knife one another in the brief still, until stirred by sounds of the dragon thrashing somewhere above. Calem removes the sword from Niena's neck and readies.

The whirl of wings comes closer, and so do the two, to each other. Marny's trusty longsword is poised high and to the side, while Calem's curved blade points directly at the captain.

An edge of the wall is a short jump away. Calem backpedals against the reach of the longsword, Marny advances. Two quick moves from him spur a counter. Metal rings on the last contact.

"You fight like you're whoring," Marny growls. "That's a sword, not your bleeding dick." His slash forces the druid to the right. Calem lunges, but stabs only air. The captain then pushes the druid back with a series of lunges and swipes, all deflected. But each swing closes the distance, until the last, which locks.

"Fascinated with whores, eh?" Calem laughs. "No wonder you want her back."

Marny growls through the roar of the wind. Both push off.

He advances again, but Calem darts back, and ducks. From the south, the dragon comes, diving down with a swing of its talons. It misses both men, but the impact of stone and sudden air sends the captain down. His longsword disappears over the edge.

Seizing the opportunity, the druid recovers, and charges at him with the curved edge upheld. Marny rolls right, and Calem's downswing follows into a back-handed slash that steals a button. Forward, forward against the disarmed captain, who is pushed closer and closer to Niena.

"What the bleeding chords do you want with her?"

Marny catches Calem's wrist as he tries to bring the blade around. Hand clasps hand: his, the old man's. He snarls an answer at the captain: "Time. She needs to take on a curse meant for another."

But it's Marny response, as he steps into the druid's centre and grips his elbow with his right, that flips the scene. He pitches the druid over his shoulder without the sword.

And Marny sees that evolve into a tumble, the tumble a roll, and that into a crouch. The captain braces the stolen sword, lining up for a quick lunge should the druid rush him. Instead, he hears muttering. Incoherent grunts smooth into dangerous words, and those words string together enough menace that Marny backs away guardedly.

The chant stops, but Calem's growls and groans continue. Behind them, the tell-tale thrash of giant wings heralds the start of another pass by the dragon. They pace: the druid, low to the ground, the captain, cautiously high. Neither makes a move towards the other.

This Calem, Marny notes. *Fighting me like an animal, like a...*the thought escapes. He pulls back the sword and lowers his stance as if to face a beast. The druid's eyes glow yellow, and his teeth drip with threat.

"You are a gods-be-damned devil!"

The skin around Calem's eyes tightens, stretches. Claws, teeth and jaw sharpen. By the end of Marny's shout, he may not be a devil, but whatever the druid is rapidly transforming into is inhuman.

Calem ducks under Marny's slash. The half-wolf closes the distance. Marny tries for his dagger, but is too slow; the monstrosity leaps forward and sinks his teeth into the captain's jerkin.

Mail-bound fingers find hair. Then fur. And Calem's teeth file in from jagged, to dangerously sharp. Marny falls on his back. As he cries out in shock, the jaw of the wolf snaps into his hand. Bones pop, crack. Behind, the screech as the dragon dives.

"Shoot it! Shoot the wyrm!" the captain yells to Niena.

Marny rolls and uses his weight to break the wolf's teeth. Free, he kicks out, and the druid yelps as he crashes into a pile of rotten wood. "Here it comes!"

Talons crash and buckle the ground as it makes an explosive landing. Loose stones shatter, fly wide, or are ploughed like so much scree before an avalanche. Marny is thrown right, landing almost at his granddaughter's feet, while the immense girth of the wyrm skates by. The ballista lurches to the side in its wake.

"Bugger it, hide!" the captain screams and cuts Niena's binds with an overhead chop. The wyrm struggles to gain its footing and to keep from falling over the palisade.

Marny watches his granddaughter slip underneath the weapon's base from the corner of his right eye. He looks between her, the sky, the dragon leaning overhead, and backs away, putting as much distance between them as he safely can.

Where is the chords-be-damned wolf? he asks, having taken his eye off Calem.

"Grandpa!"

Too late. The dragon's tail slashes at the captain. The impact tosses him into the air and onto the grass to land still, in a heap. Niena looks on, helpless, from underneath the ballista.

But words build in the air around. From a whisper, into a ringing timbre. From a chant to a story. Not hers. Niena reaches into the satchel. Her fingers first touch steel, then leather. They wrap around the hilt of the knife.

The dragon roars — but it isn't the same cry as before. She rises, her stomach falls. Shoots, vines, and a snarl of creepers sprout from the ground and through the stone. They grasp at wings, talons, and maw. From behind a drift of rubble, Calem emerges and spreads his arms to the sky.

A monstrous thud shakes the ground. *The knife.* The story stops. She drops low, dismay finding her on the floor, a jungle now. Fingers slick over the pommel and hilt.

"We don't have a lot of time," Calem says. "Nothing I can do will hold that thing for long, even wounded and without its flame."

"What do you want with me?"

"Much," he answers. "I've paid the price for my part in this crime. You thought to aid that fairy, so you must as well."

The dragon writhes, only a stone's throw away. Fires burn, and people scream in the distance. But it's Calem's footsteps that thunder for Niena. He passes through the forest of weeds unmolested, and staggers first towards her, then collapses to his knees near the siege weapon. There are two more thumps as the wyrm's fight to stay upright ends.

"You!" He reaches out and claws the air, as if here, before him, is his worst enemy. But there is nothing there. Vines snap, and Calem faces the dragon. He raises his chin and stares forward blankly.

"No, no more fighting. You've won. But you and your games hold no sway over me. Not anymore."

The wyrm rages. Buildings, the keep itself, begin to topple to the flames. Stones hit the ground like rain. Yet Calem seems preoccupied with a conversation with himself. Niena squints. Something burns within that man. A fire? No. Anger? Yes.

"I am going to set things right," he says calmly. "Oh, I would kill you if I could, fey." He wipes his face as if to pull off a part of his beard. "But my wants must oblige to another's need."

"Oberon," she whispers.

Calem's lips contort into something only close to a smile. "You have given me Niena?" His laugh rips the air. "There is my wife. Look at her, you monster!"

One foot. Niena takes a step back. He doesn't seem to notice. A second, third.

The druid freezes, listening. "No, I don't believe you! This girl?" Each word bounces off stone, to return, one by one. "That's ridiculous…That's…"

Calem turns and looks up at her. His head tilts, and he blinks. "He's right. You *are* her," he says. "But just a girl, still. That damn fairy bastard. What has he done?"

Niena shakes her head, unable to find an answer.

"What have I done? I…I am ruined." His gaze drifts momentarily away, then finds her once more. "And if you die because of my chasing this dream, I will have nothing left.

"Get off the trigger," he says and stands. From a patch of briars, he retrieves the curved sword Marny dropped before and looks through the wooden arm of the great ballista, then at her. "Leave us, now."

"No," she says with a shake of her head. He takes a step forwards, and she backwards. She secretes the knife behind. "I'm tired of men thinking I need saving. Stop being so stupid! Let's all just get out of here while it's stuck."

Calem pushes away her comment. "You don't know what you are talking about." The wyrm fights against the straining foliage holding it at the edge of the wall, its great head only yards away from the ballista, and feet from him. "I got what I bargained for. You will be free of your curse…But you can never know me."

"Are you even listening to me? Don't be so melodramatic!"

With every exhale of the dragon's breath more foul air is pushed towards them. Both Calem and Niena are forced to cover their faces. Vines groan and snap. His eyes spark.

Calem's face reflects the fear in hers, and he raises the sword to her as if saying goodbye. Behind him the last threads of the spell break, the wyrm rises to its full height.

The druid turns as the dragon coils up and up. He raises his sword and cries out. But the monster strikes with terrible speed, and he is taken whole by the maw. One shake, a scream. Niena flinches. Two shakes, one final twitch. The beast then lifts its head to the sky, and his body is a man-sized bulge sliding down a scaled throat.

Claws rake teeth. Bits of gore drop. Niena covers her mouth and withdraws silently behind a pile of debris.

"What the bloody chords do I do now?" She takes a quick glance down. And down. And down. *Oh, there's snow*, the thought merrily pokes out of a door in her mind.

A buzz in one ear answers. A squeak in the other seems to jaw with the first. She sighs, relieved as one can be, when the two merge into the familiar voice of the fairy.

Sing!

That isn't the advice she hoped for. "That's it? Do you know how close I was to having 'oh snow' as my last words? And I don't have the stupid lyre!"

Doesn't matter, just do it!

Leaves crunch, and crackle. "I don't need it? Did I ever need it?"

No. Yes! But this is not that. Just distract the bloody thing will you?

And then the wyrm turns to where Niena was. It snaps the air, and a sword falls soundlessly to the foliage. Her knees knock. Above roll eyes the size of a man's head. Niena's hands slide over an oak barrel as the monster towers, blocking the view of the castle behind.

"Oh…"

A piece of the broken stone wall and the weeds from Calem's spell hide her. It won't last long, even in the most optimistic of appraisals. The wyrm moves.

Think of something!

"Snow?"

The ground shudders and Niena peeks over her shoulder. Smoke issues from the gaps between the beast's teeth.

Chapter 29
Beg for Release

Every spring morning should begin with the chirping of birds and the smell of wildflowers in a meadow. Or at least in Marny's mind, though he concedes that a farmer or fieldworker may have a different opinion on idyllic scenery. Still, between the scent of grass on a warm wind and the odour of manure, it is hard for him to believe familiarity with the former would create a desire for the latter. So here he is, on holiday in the countryside with Deliah. Long grass waves as the couple passes. Somewhere in a clutch of trees cicadas string their welcome.

Marny looks from the cherries in her basket and up to her smile. Romantic notions jump around, but the sudden movement elicits a sharp pain in his side. Or that is what he blames.

"You are the most beautiful flower in the meadow," is what he tries to say. The words that come out are completely different. Although sandwiched amidst groans and grunts, she does seem to be able to make out "beautiful" and "meadow."

"There's a tree," she says, still smiling. "Think you can make it?"

He nods, dumbly watching the green of Deliah's dress meld in with the grass. She mistakes his attention, laughing and moving the basket to her other side.

"Should I help lay out the blanket?"

"You, Pipes," her head tilts ever so slightly as she sings his nickname, "should lean against the tree. What you *may* do is keep me company while I prepare your plate."

Where did she get that look from? She has been using it ever since they saw that street show.

A quick breeze waves its hand over the meadow. Marny stretches out against the rough bark while the wind ruffles the cloth. "We should do this more often," he says. That look again. "Only without me pulling a muscle trying—"

"To be gallant," she says. And doing so, a peculiar look visits her face.

But he mistakes concern for something else and asks Deliah if she is feeling alright. She shakes her head, handing over a plate of blueberry pie. The warm buttery crust causes him to miss her words.

"Men and food, huh," she laughs.

"Look, I..." stuttering. Marny composes himself and tries to look her in the eye. Only a moment of seriousness crosses between them, before they both start laughing uncontrollably.

"It's just," he says quietly, "this morning I was thinking to myself that every day should start with the sound of birds and the fresh smell of lavender in the meadow.

"Now," fast adding, "I've already changed one; blueberry pie is so much nicer." And green eyes and a green dress. No emerald could ever be cut so beautifully.

"And?"

The button of his jacket doesn't want to come open. Somewhere Marny can hear his tailor laughing. "I was also thinking, just now, that birds are sweet, but it would be more beautiful to hear you tell me you love me every morning."

Deliah's hands wrap around his, and the ring hidden there. Her smile, warm and sweet as any spring day, embraces his heart. He finishes, "And you saying yes."

"Marny," she says, and her smile swerves into a confused purse. But it's her rare use of his given name that has him even more nervous. "Do you hear that? It sounds like singing?"

"Singing?" *Now that is odd.* Shouldn't be anyone out this way, save them. Yet there it is.

"It sounds like a lullaby."

They can hear it from where they just walked. The tune is a strange one, and nothing local.

"Lay with me, my dear sweet friend. Neath the sky on a forest bed."

The flow crests with 'me,' and 'friend,' and he is taken with the beauty of the melody.

"Below the stars, below the moon! Heaven's smile lights down on us."

"The girl, though, there is..." And he shakes that thought out of his head. *It isn't right for other women to intrude on my attention, which should be Deliah's alone.* "My parents are making me attend a dinner with them and the Duke's man tomorrow."

She is quiet, but admirably calm over the admission. "So they are really for it, then."

"Yes," he says. "My father knows him from his youth, though I hazard a guess they were both friends with the liquor, and only acquaintances of each other.. Thinks he can wine him into a commission for me, and finally get that promotion he never could gain for himself." Words escape Marny, and he falls back on an old friend, profanity. "It's bleeding ridiculous..."

He sees her frown and corrects himself. "It's not that I don't appreciate his efforts. It's just that it is all unnecessary. I have a letter of remit from Taledric's, and a full grant. Full! The Emperor's own son cannot boast that, and yet my father would hang our family's progress on me becoming an officer."

She smiles at him, but he knows it is forced. Deliah's family is a soldiering one, and she, like her father and his own, have a different view on the importance of one of their kind being raised from the ranks. His family though, outside of his father, comes from a long line of clerks. The sharpest weapon they've traditionally pushed is the quill.

"Maybe they will put me in in the quartermaster's camp," he sighs. "I'm not against a rough bed, mind. It's just a soldier's life isn't the sort I wanted to inflict on my family."

Hand over hand. A smile. Fingers twined into one. "I worry for you," she says. "I only hope that it will be short, so you can come home to me."

Her words lift him. "Home to you? Does this mean?"

"Shh," with one finger. The song from before roars in with the wind where it left off, as if it waited for them to stop talking. "Just remember, don't hesitate! Pull the trigger!"

Despite the words, Marny finds this new beginning cold. He shivers. Worse. His mind can't let go of Deliah's last phrase.

"Pull the trigger?" Why would she say something like that? "Pull the trigger, pull—"

The present staggers into the room, and Marny's head reels in its drunken blur. But no alcohol has touched his lips. Everything hurts. Everything, but mostly his left side. The world is dim, yet thinly veiled, like he is looking at it through a fogged eyeglass. He tries to reach out with his left hand and finds his fingers clutching to the end of a rope with a dead man's grip.

He raises his head, weakly. Smoke, or fog? There is a large smudge in the middle of his sight. Marny sucks his teeth. It moves, and when it moves the ground trembles.

"How did I get here?" he tries to say, but the question falls away, and Marny can see his way to utter three words: "Pull the trigger."

"Together," the singer stutters, breaking the song. "We…chords…" A chorus of coughs ends it.

That voice. Marny tries to pull himself up further, but his grip is slick and frail. The strength to call out rattles and dies in his throat.

The ground shakes to a heavy drumbeat. Two steps, in quick succession, almost throw Marny to the ground. There is a growl with them. A low, monstrous thing that rings in his ears, but the pain there gives focus. *Dragon,* he remembers. And he knows it nears the singer.

"I can't do this!" A girl, no a young woman cries. "Oberon?"

"Niena," he wheezes and grabs his sides. Marny collapses against the wooden platform behind him and holds his hand up to his face. Blood, that he can barely see even this close, mats his gauntlet. There is nothing he can do to save his granddaughter now.

Pull the trigger.

Deliah? No, that's not her. He is on the ground now, left hand still wrapped tightly around the cord.

That voice, neither her, nor his own, vibrates his bones. *Pull the trigger,* it says. He looks down at his clenched fist, confused.

Pull the trigger. Pull the trigger. Pull the trigger. Pull the trigger.

And then over his shoulder, at the dragon. In this one second, this tick of a slow clock, he can see the scene for what it is. The old wyrm, the same that terrorised his youth, now threatens his granddaughter. Its serpentine neck writhes in interest, while she, braver than most, stands under its hungry gaze. Marny looks to her, then to the ballista aimed right at the beast's neck. Finally, he understands.

"I will…I will be strong," Niena says, coughing. Her voice stretches across the way, touches the air like a bell on a winter morning. "Together we find our passions bold, and our embrace full of warmth. Close in heart 'til the evening's end, lain neath with a dear sweet friend."

Marny tugs on the cord, but it does not give. Even still, he can feel the wood yearn, the bow behind beg for release. He closes his eyes. Memories of his Deliah, of that first spring morning bloom. And then, of his young granddaughter, and the day, many years after, she came into their lives and touched his poet's heart. Marny feels under his waist to the journal secreted there. The pages flutter open as it falls to the ground.

He can still feel the wyrm's presence when the rest of his senses fade. Marny falls back against the ballista platform. The air the dragon breathes upon them is warm, even as his fingers grow numb, and his sight dark. With the image of Deliah frozen in mind, he gathers the last of his strength and pulls.

The release of the bolt crackles in the air, but it's the impact that brings the real thunder. There is a ferocious cry of pain and the mountain rolls. Marny slumps to the ground. The wyrm's twitches touch him through the chill of the stone.

After the fall he lays there, ready. The dying thumps of the creature's tail are his only companion, and they fade, almost in rhythm with the slowing of Marny's own heart. Sounds withdraw. Muffled as under heavy wool to ward off winter. But what envelops him now is chill, and lonely.

Yet he reaches out into that darkness with hope. A last breeze from the dragon's wings assails him weakly. His arm weathers it like a tattered banner, drooping, falling, held up only by the of a stricken soldier. Just as the last of that too disappears, a hand grasps it and holds his aloft.

"Deliah?" he whispers, as warmth twines between his fingers. "Is she safe? Our granddaughter? I tried, I—"

"Yes," comes a reply that is faint, distant, but full of love. Another hand blankets his own. Marny smiles and reaches out to try to hold onto that feeling. But he cannot.

"That's all I ever wanted," he says. "All…"

Niena holds on, even as Marny lets go.

Chapter 30
A Bow Before Departing

At the end of a short row of cells, a soldier stops. Pikes lean against the jail wall and there are stacks and stacks of long shafts wrapped in cloth. Yet instinct tells him that the clutter might hold something more valuable, and he wraps his hands around the rough, pitted metal doors. The hinges squawk with years of rust and neglect. In the corner, a raven-haired woman regards his lantern cautiously.

The mountain man, whose beard is more dirt than hair, looks within. The girl stares at him as if she's just jerked awake. It's nearing evening, but the sun has only recently made a re-appearance, and here in the cellar of the armoury it is a rare guest.

Griff's face solidifies as the light warms him. "You must be Marny's granddaughter, Niena. They told me you'd be in here. Well, they, he. The people who found you. Him," he says, and keeps talking despite the awkward silence from her. "We all thought well of your grandfather, I—" He sees finally, and nods gently at her expression. "It is almost time."

"I'll be up soon," she says.

The man turns, but hangs at the door. "Was there someone else here? I thought I heard two people talking."

"I'm alone."

He nods again, then gives a short bow before depart-ing. The jail remains quiet until his footsteps disappear around a corner.

"So what happens now?"

Oberon emerges from the shadows of the corner op-posite, and stretches his hands across the one lonely window. "Marny killed the dragon, and then perished to the wound Calem gave him." Sunlight plays upon his hands, and he marvels at it. "Course, he too was de-voured. I don't know what it all means, but all the play-ers in the wyrm's death are gone. So too, I suspect, is the curse, for all time."

"And you won," she whispers in an accusing tone.

"Marny was doomed from the beginning," Oberon says. "In this timeline, or the other. The dragon, he, they were both fated to perish—though one more has been added to the butcher's bill. But death is easy, life is hard."

"That doesn't make this right."

"Marny once died in darkness and in doubt," Oberon explains as she stands. "Never knowing what became of you, only that failure was his legacy, and now, that is changed. He took with him the knowledge that you are safe, and his actions led to this, redeeming his hurt for the loss of his wife. He could never know how much, though."

The fairy stoops and Niena looks on, curious. He was always an old, ancient looking creature, but before there was a hint of spryness that belied his years. Like a dance before winter solstice. That is gone now. Only an old, withered man remains.

"You cannot understand this, young as you are," he says slowly. "But there will come a time when such knowledge is a greater comfort, and a softer bed, than whatever time in this world you might have left."

"I had better go," Niena says, choked. Oberon offers no resistance, letting her squeeze through the halfway open door without a word. But at the corner, just before the corner towards the stairs, the fairy does call out.

"What will you do?"

She hesitates. "I don't know," not turning. "Right now, I just want to say goodbye."

Oberon nods. "Will you come see me after?"

"Calem wanted to own me. What is it you really want from me?" Her tone hard as she snaps around. Yet in return, he just smiles, regarding his granddaughter with soft and patient features that only time can give.

"As I said before, and only the same as Marny, I suppose," Oberon says quietly. "Before I, too, leave."

The fairy smiles once more, before returning to the door of the cell. And she lingers at the cusp, watching him dodder. Niena sighs, and ascends. The stairs circle, and open onto the greater building. There are people here. Families. Many more lived than those few who perished up top. Several wainsmen and their womenfolk alike are among these, making an account of the stores. She passes them. Everyone's seems reserved and sombre. Yet is there a hint of relief, and hope.

An evening sun greets her in the courtyard. The bodies and lighter debris from the earlier fight have been cleared away, replaced by the sweet smell of smoke. Several pyres line the front of the fallen chapel. Some still smoulder. Most are silent. People drift in with the wind, tween them and the rubble.

She sees Griff near the place where Marny fell, standing, not unlike a boulder in a trickling stream of mourners. Another is with him, but this man she does not recognise. Alone on a bed made of stone taken from the broken tower and timber from the chapel rests her grandfather.

The mountain man sees her and waves. She takes her time, weaving through the few onlookers at what will probably be the last fire before nightfall. A few recognise her. Most don't, and Niena is happy for that. The sun is setting in the west, and there is a stiff wind facing the pyre. She approaches Griff, still bandaged from earlier, his beard caked with grime and blood. In his hand is the same torch from before, and here, the loss of her grandfather becomes real.

"Are we waiting on anyone?" she asks, eyes dancing from the flame to his face.

He smiles faintly. "Just you." Griff gestures at the man beside him, who removes his cap. "We're all that's come tonight; you, me, and Brother here. The priest said he'd be here, but—" And he shrugs.

"Your brother?"

"Pardon, lady," Brother says. "Just a name."

"Well." Niena looks between the two and they both repeat the 'well.' Almost as one, they turn to the pyre. Wood stacks upon wood, nearly a man in height. Each of them, in turn, is drawn to the thin layer of straw on top. There lays Marny. His sword and armour have been removed, and someone has taken the care to clear most of the ash from his face.

"We saved the wood for him," Brother says. "So's he won't have to share."

"At least that," Griff adds. "At most, too, sadly. Would you like to say anything?"

Niena shakes her head. She watches as Brother produces another faggot, tips it to Graham's torch, and the two circle the platform to put the flames to either side. The torches bite. Fire blooms. The three step back and the two brands are added to the growing blaze.

"Shame this," Graham spits. "All these people, and only three."

"Did you know him?" asks Niena, distracted by distant thunder.

"Not me," he answers. Brother also shakes his head. "Not long enough, anyways." He shifts and regards her with a sideways glance. "I've got to be with my family now, miss."

She lets him leave in peace and silence. Brother remains to tend to the fire. But as the hour grows late, and the fires and sun dim, he too fades with the shadows of men and women, passing this way and that tween the monuments of the morning's tally. And finally, when there is less smoke, and more shade reaching towards the sky, and the embers have passed on from here to that canvas, only she lingers.

Niena fumbles in her sack. There is a book there. A journal; hers once. She found it near Marny's body, found, but tears and grief are the claimants here. Bound within the leather spine are all the things she wished she could have known about him. Most of all, the tenderness of the script under a piece of blue wool, used as a place-mark.

It was hers, but he added these last pages, his and Deliah's. By now, she has read them over and over again, until word and phrase have ridden into memory. She flips the pages between her fingers for comfort and closes her eyes. Her face feels pale set against a backdrop of stars.

"Are you asleep, my heart? What would you dream?"

The night hides Marny's remains, and only the shallow rise and fall of Niena's chest hints at any other life. And to her, that might only be an illusion. Someone is crying.

"Why don't you wake, my heart? And sing with me?"

The wind rushes Niena, rips the song from her lungs, and spills it to the night. She stares up, and out. Clouds draw over.

"Please do not fly, my heart."

"You are my light." Then more. The smell of ash and burnt flesh hits her in the gut.

"We belong together, my heart. Two songs of spring in winter's night."

Niena's voice cracks, breaks, as she struggles with the words. "Do you hear it, my heart? Can you not see?"

"I will not forget you, my heart," only to herself. "My love is no dream."

The journal drops from her hand and falls at the edge of the snuffed pyre. Niena hugs herself and stares out across the battlements. Wherever her grandparents are, she only hopes that they are together. For her, she thinks, the rest of the journey will be a lone one. She turns and leaves the book and her grandfather's remains, never to look back.

But a raspy purr that sounds a little too much like a drunk bumblebee — if bees were to drink — follows.

If you enjoyed this book, please consider leaving a review or a rating online.

For author news, new titles, and discount offers, subscribe to the Sulis International mailing list:
https://goo.gl/2SVDju

ABOUT THE AUTHOR

Stephen Reeves was born in Huntsville, Alabama in 1980, but grew up in a small community just on the edge; Madison. After living in the same area for over thirty years Stephen met his future wife in 2010, and in 2012 they were married. He currently resides in Switzerland with his wife, two cats, and an obsessive Pomeranian.